"No, Thalionmel, don't do it. He has a knife!" Zulhamin pleaded, but her sister ignored the warning. Suddenly the dagger shot out. Thalionmel anticipated the attack and leapt aside. While she fell, she kicked her opponent's leg so that he stumbled. Although Rupert was able to catch himself with his right hand, he lost the dagger in the process. Nonetheless, she underestimated the skinny boy's abilities, and in the last moment Rupert was able to extend his right hand toward the dagger and just grasp it with his finger tips . . .

The *Realms of Arkania®* Series

The Charlatan
by Ulrich Kiesow

The Lioness
(Book One in the Saga of Brave Thalionmel)
by Ina Kramer

The Sacrifice (forthcoming)
(Book Two in the Saga of Brave Thalionmel)
by Ina Kramer

REALMS OF ARKANIA®
The Lioness

A Novel

INA KRAMER

Translated by Amy Katherine Kile

PRIMA PUBLISHING

Proteus™ and the distinctive Proteus logo are trademarks of
Prima Publishing, a division of Prima Communications, Inc.

P™ is a trademark of Prima Publishing, a division of
Prima Communications, Inc.

Prima Publishing™ is a trademark of Prima Communications, Inc.

Die Löwin von Neetha copyright © 1995 by Wilhelm Heyne Verlag
GmbH & Co. KG, München und Schmidt Spiele + Freizeit GmbH,
Eching.

Translation copyright © 1996 by Prima Publishing. All rights reserved.

Realms of Arkania is a registered trademark of Sirtech Software, Inc.

No part of this book may be reproduced or transmitted in any form
or by any means, electronic or mechanical, including photocopying,
recording, or by any information storage or retrieval system without
written permission from Prima Publishing, except for the inclusion
of quotations in a review. All products and characters mentioned in
this book are trademarks of their respective companies.

Cover art by Oliver Frey

ISBN: 0-7615-0477-X
Library of Congress Catalog Card Number: 96-067257
Printed in the United States of America
96 97 98 EE 10 9 8 7 6 5 4 3 2 1

*To my friends who supported
and encouraged me.*

The Song of the Lioness of Neetha

Thalionmel the warrior saved us,
Her defense of our bridge was most courageous.
Now she rests with a crown of glory,
She is part of our hearts and this is her story.

Thalionmel was a farmer's daughter fair,
With eyes of blue and golden hair.
Lovely of form and kind of manner,
N'er a better maid fought under our banner.

At Neetha's Temple to the Goddess of War,
The brave virgin kneeled on the floor.
She asked the Goddess to grant her grace,
So that she could take up her noble place.

Rastullah, the Desert Demon, was hate laden,
He begrudged Lady Rondra the courageous maiden.
"Kill that uppity wench and burn the city!"
Beni Novad's men were scornful and took no pity.

The dastardly bunch from the sandy dunes,
Came in droves for Neetha to leave it in ruins.
They spread fire and death across the land,
Ever true to their evil idol's command.

When the people of Neetha asked in despair,
"Is there anyone who will face their dare?"
Thalionmel cried out, "With Rondra's grace,
I will stop the enemy and put them in their place!"

She held our bridge, brave as a she-lion,
with her flashing sword cutting and flying.
She fought with courage 'til day came,
And enemy blood made the Chabab flow red as flame.

Though mortally wounded the Goddess assured,
She could continue the fight true to her word.
"Help, Goddess Rondra, be my guide!"
The villagers heard her cry from the other side.

Rondra set out on revenge divine,
And made the Chabab's waters climb.
The rage washed the enemy army away,
Not one man or woman escaped the fray.

That is how Neetha was saved with Rondra's aid,
And the young warrior's life was taken in trade.
The blooming flower, warrior of laurel,
Our praise unto you, holy Thalionmel.

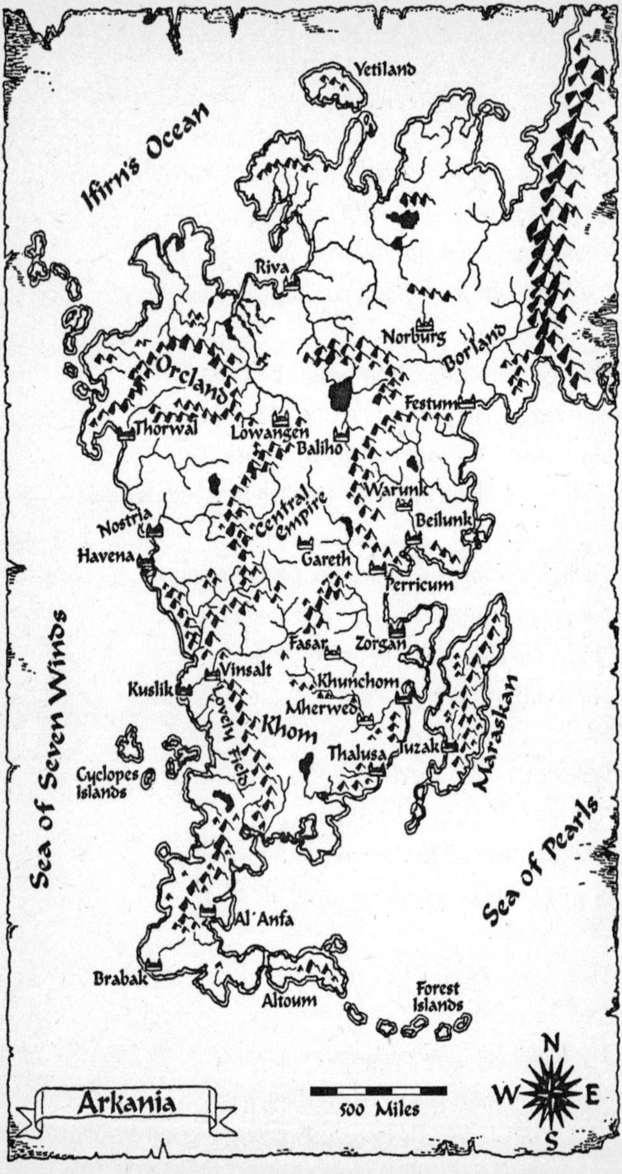
Yetiland
Ifirn's Ocean
Riva
Norburg
Borland
Orcland
Festum
Thorwal
Lowangen
Baliho
Warunk
Central Empire
Nostria
Beilunk
Havena
Gareth
Perricum
Sea of Seven Winds
Fasar
Zorgan
Vinsalt
Kuslik
Khunchom
Mherwed
Lovely Field
Khom
Maraskan
Thalusa
Tuzak
Cyclopes Islands
Sea of Pearls
Al'Anfa
Brabak
Altoum
Forest Islands
N
W
E
S
Arkania
500 Miles

The Lovely Field

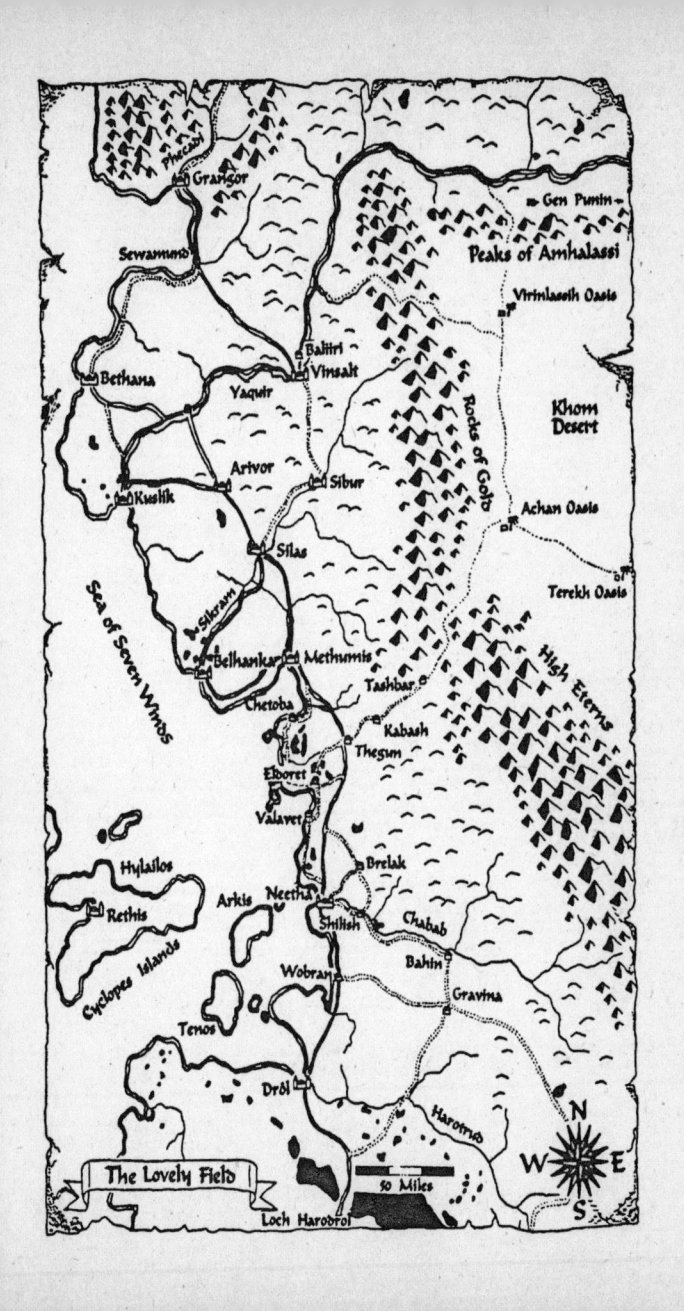

Prologue

I HAVE OFTEN ASKED myself what I really meant to her. I don't think she ever saw me as her soul mate or confidant. In her eyes I was only a stupid boy to whom she could open her heart without risking a show of weakness or expecting advice, as if she was sharing her worries and problems with a loyal dog. Yet to this day, I treasure her every word in my heart, for I loved her. And the first time I saw her—I was ten and she was eleven—I knew that my love would remain unrequited.

Of course, she was not as beautiful as the legends and ballads would like us to believe, nor was she always as brave. Her nose was a bit too pointy and her eyes were a bit too close together. Oh, those wonderful eyes! Pale blue like the dawn sky on a cold autumn day with golden streaks. And when she looked at you, it was so attentively and intently as if she wanted to look at the bottom of your soul. It was probably just a habit and meant nothing. She certainly would not have wanted to fathom the mysteries of my soul.

Yes, the legends and the ballad, "The Song of the Lioness of Neetha"—that despicable rhyme! Why don't songs ever tell the truth? She was neither the child of peasants nor a virgin. She was a woman, even by the time of our second meeting. But what does that have to do with anything? Does it diminish her deed? Does it make her sacrifice any less? Nor was she a "blooming flower" as that shoddy poem claims. When she gave her life to save Neetha she was an experienced warrior of twenty-one.

And who am I, you ask? I am a 92-year-old nobody without a name, a wayward student of Praios, a scribe, an unimportant calligrapher who can feel that his end is nearing. But perhaps I, too, am part of the divine plan and godly order. Perhaps she confided in me so I would someday share with the rest of the world her true story. And perhaps the sole reason I became a scribe was to be able to write down what I witnessed in my fevered youth. It will be difficult to call up those memories, for mine is the soul of a tired old man desiring peace in Boron's presence.

Let me begin my task, for I do not have much time to complete it. I met her for the first time at the hour of Praios in the moon of Tsa at Neetha's harbor. The second time I met her in a foul alley in Eldort. She had seen thirteen cycles of the Twelve and six moons. But it began on a stormy night in Firun on a manor near Neetha: the life of holy Thalionmel.

1

FIRUN WAS PARTICULARLY cruel that year. The Beleman had raged incessantly for weeks out of Efferd, tearing off roof shingles, uprooting trees, and mussing the winter coats of the peaceful Brelak goats. The storm drove icy spray down the harbor alleys in Neetha and hid Praios's countenance from view behind an endless train of gray clouds that passed from the Sea of Seven Winds to the Etern Mountains. "They're flirting again," the locals commented with a worried look, immediately following their remark with the gesture against blaspheme—a wave of the right hand in front of the mouth as if to fan off the words so the Twelve would not know who uttered them. It was a well-practiced gesture and done almost unconsciously, just as one doffs one's hat for a lady or a nobleman while mumbling "Praios be with you!" After all, every schoolchild knows that Lord Efferd was trying to win over proud Lady Rondra again by stirring up the oceans and sending out storms over land and sea; and everyone secretly wished that the bold lioness would finally yield to her godly suitor so that his love sickness would not wreak havoc.

※ ※ ※

"A bad omen," growled Hilgert, squinting his eyes as if it enabled him to look through the gray mass which obscured the nearby mountain tops to the east.

"You should be ashamed of yourself, old man. How could you say such a thing?" Damilla replied genuinely upset. "The lady is in the midst of birth-throes and you're blathering on about bad omens." The stout young maid had been sent out for firewood for the delivery room and met the stable master in the yard where he stood with his legs spread and his arms at his side to brace himself against the storm. The gale winds tugged at his heavy coat and blew strands of his ruffled, long gray hair in his face so that he continually had to shake his head to maintain a clear line of sight. He stared with concern, even though it appeared to Damilla that there was nothing but the clouds and wind that surrounded them. The young woman had difficulty gathering the wood stacked under the stable porch because the wind kept trying to blow away the empty basket. She was also careful to keep her skirts tucked between her legs so that no gust would embarrass her. She quickly gathered up the wood in anger as the wind played with her long braid and tried to loosen it. "Why are you staring into the eastern sky?" she called. "There's nothing to see. You should look to the west and pray that Efferd takes pity on the poor fishermen and seafarers."

"It's a bad omen," insisted Hilgert. "As long as I've lived, the Beleman has never raged for twenty-seven cycles of Praios in a row. That's not the Beleman nor is it Efferd's passion . . ." He tossed back his head again and furrowed his bushy brows.

"What else would it be?" Damilla replied in a cheeky tone. "The Baltrir, or the Horoban, or the . . ." She wondered if the names of the rest of the seven winds would come to her. "Anyway, the Beleman always blows in Firun, even if it's a bit strong this year."

"You're an ignorant child." Hilgert continued to stare off into the distance. At sixty-seven years he was the oldest of the baron's hands, but if it weren't for his gray hair no one would have ever given him credit for his age. The stable master was a tall man with a serious, strict manner. He avoided company, drink, and dice, spoke little, and laughed even less. His dark brows, large hooked nose, and black eyes gave the impression that he was of Tulamidian origin, and that his gray hair may once have been black. "It's going to happen over there, far beyond the Eterns," he said more to himself than to the girl. "Evil and change are brewing..."

"Change? What do you mean by that?"

"I don't know, girl, I don't know. But it will come from the desert whence the ghosts fled and the elements gathered to stop it... Yet, it's too late, too late..."

"Are you drunk? Or is it the storm that is getting to you?" Damilla watched the old stable master with worry. "Why don't you go back to your room, warm yourself, and pray to Tsa to make things easier for you. And pray for the child so that it will be a handsome, healthy baby boy." She picked up the basket, felt for the leather straps, and threw it over her shoulder. Just then a strong gust caused her skirt to free itself from between her legs and fly up around her head. The cold, sharp wind painfully cut into her naked body. "By Efferd, what foul weather. And look, it's starting to rain!" she called out angrily as she unsuccessfully tried to regain control of her skirt. She quickly glanced over at Hilgert to see if he had noticed her mishap, but the old man was oblivious. "I have to get going," said Damilla, "and you should too, old man. Forget about your crazy ideas." She stomped off to the manor, her head pulled in and her eyes half shut. "That isn't rain, it's snow," she heard Hilgert say behind her.

"Snow?!" Damilla almost dropped the basket. Skeptically she opened her eyes. Indeed, in the light of the lanterns she saw the dancing white crystals. The storm drove clouds of white powder from the west. "Snow! Look, old man, it's snowing! I'll have to tell Lady Kusmine." Damilla was so excited that she forgot the wind and the cold. She was intrigued by the rare phenomenon.

"Yes, snow—ghosts and elements are coming together in the desert. Pray to the Twelve that it's not too late. There's no danger to the girl, yet. At least I hope not."

"What girl?" Damilla wanted to ask, but by the time she opened the kitchen door and hurriedly put down her burden, she had already forgotten the question. "It's snowing, it's snowing!" she yelled to the maids and hands around the fire.

※ ※ ※

Baron Durenald of Brelak had been pacing through the rooms of his manor for hours. Wherever he turned, his servants greeted him with sympathetic friendliness. They inquired with understanding smiles about their master's wishes, as if the baron were chronically ill, although he was the picture of health.

Durenald of Brelak was a stocky man in his early thirties. His brown eyes beneath chestnut curls often glowed with a roguish smile. These eyes, his smoothly shaven, round cheeks, and the beginning of a small belly gave him the appearance of a man in harmony with his surroundings. His even temperament, his kindness and truthfulness, and his earnestness in all religious matters made him a well-liked and respected lord. Although he, like every nobleman's son, had attended the garrison school in Neetha (where he learned the art of fencing while studying the cult of Rondra and singing the holy songs during the Sword Ceremony in the Temple of Victory), his true love was the kind Lady Peraine. When he inspected his fields, felt the topsoil between his fingers, and observed the fresh young plants with pride and concern, the only difference between him and his peasants was the quality of his clothes.

The baron's lands were well-protected from the rough sea winds by large forests, and open to the grace of the hot desert winds of the Northeast. The fields brought forth not only turnips, flax, and wheat, but also rare Golden Land vegetables, such as the red-cheeked tomato and the long, ribbed sweet paprika, for the few nights of frost each year were limited to Firun and sowing usually started at the end of Tsa.

Brelak Manor had not been in the family long. Durenald's grandfather received the lands when he was forty-eight, in appreciation for his bravery and courage while discovering a plot against the margrave. That allowed old Robak to make the jump from a landless noble to a baron. Durenald's mother inherited the property from her father and maintained the fief carefully, though her heart was not truly in it. She married, gave birth to Durenald, built the manor in the Arivor style, and eventually died as quietly as she had lived.

That was twelve years ago, and since then Durenald had been the Lord of Brelak. Now his restless wanderings through the house brought the baron to the warm, cozy library, which was actually a room for gaming, talking, and drinking tea. It was only called "the library" because of a rather insignificant book cabinet with a few religious books, travel logs, and novels; some select books about the arts of war, politics, and law; and a considerable number of books on agriculture. Without thinking he took a book from the shelf and began to flip through it while the wind whipped at the closed shutters. It was a colorfully illuminated breviary of the Twelve Commandments. Durenald, however, could not concentrate on the text, nor could he truly focus his attention on the delicate illustrations, as he usually did with great appreciation. No, he was definitely not in the mood for a pious lesson. What he needed at that moment was the solace of the Twelve. He would have preferred to go for a ride or chop some wood, but the servants had already done that. "Oh, Kusmine, dear heart, if I could only be with you and help you," he thought, but naturally he was not permitted in the delivery room.

Two days ago after the midday meal, his wife whispered to him, "Durenald, dearest, I think it's time," and since then he had found no rest. Not that Kusmine was not well prepared, oh no, she was a prudent, planning woman. Weeks ago she met with the midwife from the village and gained knowledge in womanly secrets, but Durenald had not been included. A doctor from Neetha had already been called. At the birth of a noble child, it was more seemly to have both the midwife, good old Danja—who like her mother before her, ushered the peasant children of Brelak into the world—and a university-educated man. The young man—Durenald forgot his name, but he was sure Kusmine had selected the most competent doctor—had spent five days in one of the guest rooms waiting to be called upon. The delivery room had been ready for weeks as well. There really was no reason to worry; Kusmine was a healthy woman and much stronger than one would guess judging by her slight build. Her pregnancy had also gone smoothly. He loved her rosy cheeks and her swollen stomach, even though he did not understand them completely. "Just like an eighteen-year-old," Danja told him with a smile, for the lady was already thirty, one year younger than him and four fingers taller.

He was concerned about this unusually fierce storm, but he was also worried about Kusmine. They had avoided mentioning their concerns, as well as the pains she would have to suffer, preferring instead to speak about the weather. . . . That morning, he saw his wife for the last time, as she ceremoniously said good-bye in front of the delivery room. "Farewell, my dear husband, we will see each other when you are a father. Pray for our child and for me," she said, and then at a quarter past twelve, as the dark day grew even darker, he heard her first cry. Now the cries were following in closer proximity. It seemed absurd to him that proud Kusmine had to suffer more in something as common as labor than she ever did during her fencing lessons or her only duel. Durenald almost hated the child for causing her pain.

He rose from the chair where he had briefly rested and replaced the book. No, he couldn't read now, and he couldn't pray either, although he constantly murmured, "Boron, look kindly on her" and "Tsa, have mercy." Pacing restlessly across the room and forcing himself to wait for the next cry without horror, he tried to visualize his wife's face.

He met Kusmine when she had just turned twenty. Yet, he wished he had known the wild, blonde girl and the graduate of the Vinsalt Academy earlier. If Durenald secretly wanted a daughter, unlike his wife who wanted a son and often prayed for one, it was because he desired to see a little Kusmine grow up at Brelak Manor.

Kusmine's family came from an old noble house of the domain of Malur. Because their daughter's gifts in the arts of Rondra were recognized early on, the girl went to the Vinsalt Academy at the age of nine, where she grew up as a proud, young woman, known as the best swordswoman in her class. She passed her final exams at seventeen with honors not only in fencing, but also in etiquette and Rondrian poetry. Her long noble lineage, her substantial expected inheritance, her fine education, and, last but not least, her beauty made the young woman attractive to suitors throughout the empire. Along with the number of men interested in her she quickly had a collection of portraits and love letters in her desk drawer. Even though she knew that a marriage of love was unlikely, she had decided to carefully look over all the suitors to find one who was a good match for her position, character, and physique. Unfortunately, before Kusmine could make her choice, the family was struck with two terrible events. Four moons after Kusmine's graduation, her cherished older brother Roderick, a captain in the Kuslik Marines, fell victim to the Zorgan Pox. Barely half a year later the family stood at the brink of financial ruin. The old baron, half mad with grief for the loss of his son, had put almost his entire fortune into a project to build a paved road through the Desert Khom. It promised substantial returns, but turned out to be a scam and was never built. Marriage was now out of the question, for that was below Kusmine's honor. So, the young woman went to live with her aunt Melsine, a captain at the margrave's garrison in Neetha. Her excellent grades, her standing, and her self-assured manner quickly earned Kusmine the position of sergeant and, because she was so attentive and disciplined, she certainly would have made it to colonel, had she not met Durenald.

Durenald always enjoyed the memory of their first encounter. It happened in a harbor alleyway in Neetha. As he was walking home from a large meal with friends, he saw the young soldier. She was leading a small troop of armed men in the uniform of the margrave's guards. Her shiny coat of mail and the plumes on her helmet told Durenald that she was a sergeant. Although the young baron was not inexperienced in dealings with the opposite sex, he had never experienced such a sudden wave of passion—which he called a love cramp—

as he did when he saw this lady. Was it her tall stature, her fair skin, her slender shape enhanced by the line of her uniform? Or was it the serene look of her blue eyes beneath her slightly furrowed brow that woke that feeling in him? Durenald could not say. He only knew that he absolutely had to meet the sergeant, and there was not much time to act. Nothing better occurred to him than to bow deeply, doff his hat, and say with a mischievous smile, "Fair maiden, may I offer you my protection and accompany you?" To Durenald's surprise the guardswoman did not ignore him, but replied with a suppressed smile, "If I'm in need of your protection or wish you to accompany me, I will let you know, kind gentleman."

On the following day, the baron sent a letter of apology to the garrison along with a cake from the best confectioner in town. He had hastily ordered a creation of icing and marzipan with a roaring lioness bearing long claws. It was the beginning of the romance between Kusmine and Durenald.

"I won your heart with the cake," Durenald liked to say when the couple recalled the beginning of their love.

"No, it was your brown curls," Kusmine replied every time. "Brown, curly hair leaves me weak. I also immediately noticed that you are half a span shorter than I."

"Four fingers, dear heart, four fingers," was his standard reply.

Kusmine asked to be discharged as soon as it was clear to her that she wanted to spend the rest of her life at Durenald's side. It was not easy for her to give up her soldier's life, but the prospect of mustering a citizen's militia in Brelak made it easier for her to leave Neetha, the garrison, and her aunt. She also hoped to give Durenald many children, whom she would personally instruct in the arts of Rondra before sending them on to school in Neetha. In her mind's eye she could already picture the little, curly-headed soldier boys and girls, and how they would fence with their wooden swords and ride wild jousts on their ponies. But Tsa had other plans for them. The couple lived together for five years before little Tsafried saw Praios's light, and he remained without siblings for the four years that he was granted.

Little Tsafried, with his father's brown curly hair and his mother's bright blue eyes, was his parents' pride and joy. Everybody agreed there never was a child more beautiful, neither in Brelak nor the rest of the margrave's lands. He inherited the love of all living things from his father and he stared in equal wonder at spring's first green sprouts and newborn kittens. Yet, he was not weak, as Kusmine noted with satisfaction. He tested his strength against the children from the village at an early age, and even when injured he seldom cried. He also enjoyed riding. At the tender age of three he was already at home in his pony's saddle. When Kusmine watched him spur on his little mount to a fast trot by madly squeezing the animal with his little thighs and loud calls, there was both motherly concern and pride for his daring nature which surely pleased Rondra.

It happened while he was riding. No one knew why the pony shied and lost the little rider, but villagers found the unconscious boy and the peacefully grazing animal in a meadow near the forest and brought both home with heavy hearts. It took three days for Boron to put an end to little Tsafried's suffering and call the boy to him, and neither the doctor nor his parents' desperate prayers could save him.

After the loss of her child Kusmine was a different woman. She did not pull out her hair or claw at her breast, she did not scream or shed any tears, she did not even rail against the Twelve—at least not in front of anyone's eyes or ears. No, her heart seemed to die. Although Durenald also mourned the loss of his son and shed many a tear for him, the extent of her grief was strange and almost eerie to him. Fifteen miserable moons came and went during which Kusmine did not smile or crack a single joke with her husband. She lived with him without pleasure or joy, so that the baron eventually began to doubt their love. Then Tsa blessed her body again, and with the new life blossoming within her, courage, power, and confidence came back to her.

Yes, the last nine months had been beautiful, thought Durenald. Only a gentle mist of worry had come with last weeks' endless storm. Why did unpredictable Efferd and proud Rondra refuse to grant his poor wife any peace? The baron balled his fist and angrily pounded on the desk by the window. Then his eyes fell on a letter that had been laying there unopened since the courier had brought it that morning. It was from Zordan Foxfell, Kusmine's half brother. What did he want? Durenald had only met him twice and did not particularly care for him, but that did not mean much. He just did not like dandyish clothes and waxed mustaches. "The letter will distract me," he thought as he broke the seal. "Foxfell can write as smoothly as he talks, and it will be a difficult task to find out his purpose among the droning of the pretty words." But he was wrong. The letter was brief and after the usual greeting it read, "... *it will be my pleasure as soon as the weather permits to pay my courtesies to you, dear brother-in-law and you, beautiful sister, as well as the new prince or princess.*" Now that was nice, thought Durenald, and it will please Kusmine, too.

The door flew open, and Danja stormed in the room—red, sweating, and smiling wide. "Your

Highness, praise be to Tsa, it's over! And I congratulate you from the bottom of my heart on the birth of your beautiful daughter!" It took Durenald a moment to digest what the midwife had said. Suddenly he felt tears come to his eyes and blinking them away he embraced the large woman in his arms and gave her a kiss on the cheek. "How's my wife?" he whispered.

"Excellent, my lord, she's just a bit tired. Come, you can visit the new mother, and she wants to show you the baby."

Half dazed, he followed Danja to the delivery room. There lay his wife in a large bed with fresh, white linen sheets, greeting him with a happy and tired smile. In the candlelight she did not seem as pale as he expected, and only her mussed, damp hair gave any indication of the exertion. A small, well-tied bundle rested in her arms. As soon as Durenald saw Kusmine he was struck with a wave of love. He rushed to her and buried his head on her shoulder so she would not see his tears. "I thank you, my dearest heart," he stuttered in a whisper, "I thank you for this beautiful daughter."

"Then look and see if she really is beautiful." Kusmine smiled and handed Durenald the bundle. He tentatively peeked at the little face, which was red and slightly swollen from birth. "No, she's not beautiful," he thought, "but with the Twelves' blessing she shall be." He felt that he already loved the child. He listened to her thin cry, then raised his head, aware of a change. He could clearly hear the baby and the crackling of the fire, but nothing else. It was still outside, the storm was over!

The others had noticed it, too, but Kusmine was the first to say anything. "It has finally stopped storming, thank Rondra," she said with a sigh of relief. "I think it's a good omen. Damilla, please open the window and let in a bit of fresh air. It will do me good." The maid obeyed and opened the window, then the shutter. Then she cried out, "Look, everything is white!" Danja, who had quietly disapproved of the lady's request because she did not think that a winter's draft belonged in a delivery room, went to the window and looked out. "By Firun, what glory!" she mumbled and was moved. "I have never seen so much snow in all my days."

The entire landscape was mystical. All the clouds were gone, and in the silver shine of the waxing Madamal, the delicate crystals shone where they formed a softly rounded, white blanket over the fields, houses, and trees. There was a profound peace in this sight, almost as if you could hear the silence. "What is that?" Danja asked suddenly. "There is an animal over there, but I can't tell what it is. Is it a stag?"

"Where?" asked Damilla, and the midwife pointed in the distance. "That's a lion!" said the servant girl. "No, a lioness, she has no mane!" With eyes wide with fear, she shrank back from the window.

Durenald, who desired to see the rare sight of snow but could not seem to tear himself away from his wife and daughter, looked questioningly at Kusmine. "Well, go already, dear husband, and look at the snow," she said with a smile. "Just give me our daughter back, the cold air may be bad for her. And tell me what strange animal whiles in our gardens."

Durenald stepped up to the window and looked out. He was silent for a long time, rapt in the beauty of the scene. Yet there was no animal to be seen. "There's nothing," he said, "but Firun's glory. There are no lions in Brelak," he turned toward Damilla. "You must have seen a jackal that lost its way in the mountains. Tomorrow we will find its tracks and, if it's Firun's will, we will hunt it down so that it does not take any of our goats. Now I want to be left alone with my wife and daughter for a moment."

When everyone left the room, Durenald sat down on a stool next to the bed and reached for his wife's hand. "I'm so proud of you, my brave little soldier." He looked lovingly in her eyes. "Have you already selected a name for her? Tsaiane perhaps?"

"Tsaiane is a beautiful name," replied Kusmine, "and since I know that you had wished for a daughter all along, I have often thought about her name.

I think we should name her after my aunt, Melsine, and your father, Thalion. Melsine and Thalion—Thalionmel."

2

THE GRANDSTAND AT the racetrack outside the gates of Methumis was splendidly ornamented with pennants, garlands, bouquets of Firunbells, and the first Ilmengreens. The duke and the archduke from Arivor had announced their intentions to attend the grand Phex Race. Even the Twelve seemed to look kindly upon this year's race. Lord Praios let his face shine brightly for days, and generous Lady Peraine wrapped the fields in a cloth of fresh green dotted with colorful jewels. Lord Efferd granted the fishermen a bountiful catch and the air was heavy with the smell of fried sea perch, pearl mouths, and silver eels for sale at little booths along the track. Lord Phex, in whose honor the race was held, let the merchants, thieves, and beggars rejoice in past and pending exploits. Even the pleasuring spirit of Lady Rahja led many enchanted couples to stroll into the nearby woods . . .

To honor Phex as the ninth month, every year there were nine races—three royal races and six for the citizenry. The citizen's races customarily began at the tenth hour and ended, if all went well and if there weren't too many accidents, at the second hour after midday. It was a spectacular jumble with few decent mounts, let alone true race horses. There were shaggy ponies, bony cart nags, and cold-blooded horses whose true calling was pulling a plow, but all were groomed and bearing their finery, just as their riders. Anyone with a mount vaguely resembling a horse and who was at the starting gate in time was allowed to participate.

Most participants were not particularly serious about winning. Only the owners of the better horses—such as coachmen, couriers, or horse traders—tried to win the grand prize, which was either a keg of beer, donated by the brethren of the Temple of Phex, or a barrel of wine donated by the priestesses of Rahja. No one needed to go without, not the losers and certainly not the crowd of spectators, for the duke's free beer flowed from every tap.

Of course, the royal boxes remained empty while the rabble had their fun. Members of the finer society preferred to delay their appearance until around the third hour after noon, when the racetrack was cleared of drunken cobbler apprentices and scruffy mounts. Watching the noble lords and ladies parade in their fabulous finery was almost a greater event for the commoners to watch than the preceding races. The crowd eagerly awaited the appearance of the archduke and his young wife, a former Rahja priestess from Belhanka, whom he had married at the ripe age of sixty.

As the crowd pressed as closely to the grandstand as the guards would allow, the track was prepared for the last three races. The royal races were the true event of the day. After scooping up the manure, the liveried servants pulled out the brightly colored wooden scaffolds, which they assembled into jumps of different heights. Elsewhere they removed heavy oaken planks from the ground to reveal water hazards. The most beautiful obstacles were the hedges made from bound evergreen branches and decorated with red silk ribbons, so that they looked like blooming rose bushes. The competitors had a total of nine obstacles to clear: three hurdles, three water hazards, two hedges, and the final obstacle— a hedge with a water hazard hidden from the horse's view. Of course, the water hazard was shallow enough for a horse to be able to jump in and wade through, for it was no one's intention to injure any of the precious animals.

The first race was scheduled to begin at the fourth hour and the grandstand was already crowded. Only the royal box remained empty awaiting the entrance of the duke and the archduke. Meanwhile, the crowd enjoyed the procession of fabulously clad ladies and gentlemen who arrived, according to their rank, wealth, and taste, in golden carriages or on magificently decorated horses. When the delicate Tulamidian head priestess of the Temple of Rahja climbed up the rostrum at the foot of the grandstand where the winners of the next three races would be honored, a murmur ran through the crowd and their interest in the archduke's wife took second stage. Reverend Ludilla—the title was ill-suited to her gestures and clothing—was certainly more beautiful than the archduke's wife, according to most. The black-haired priestess wore a short robe of translucent red silk, as was customary in the cult. Her long hair was down, but part of it was finely braided and bound with a golden bow. Golden sandals cradled her dainty feet. Her belt was also of gold and its clasp was in the form of a grapevine, as were the bracelets and anklets she wore. Ludilla first greeted the guest on the rostrum with a smile. Then she turned to the riders who had just taken up their starting positions, and finally she acknowledged the cheering crowd. Next, she poured red wine into one of the four richly embellished silver goblets standing on a table next to her. It was Tharf from the temple, but it was not blessed, for holy wine can only be drunk by a priestess within the confines of the temple's walls.

"In honor of Lord Phex, the wily, and in celebration of Lady Rahja, the beautiful, let the races begin!" Ludilla called in a dark, carrying voice. "May the Twelve watch over the animals and the riders, and may the best three win. Hereby . . .," and with these words she raised the goblet to the sky and then emptied it in one draught, "I declare the race open. Riders, take your places!"

The crowd had listened in silence to the short speech, but now they went wild. The stands reverberated with calls, whistles, and screams. Hats and scarves flew through the air, so much so that the horses on the starting line grew uneasy. Despite the cheers there was hardly anyone among the spectators who truly wished the race to be completed without incident, for the whole reason they came was to see a little prince take a mudbath and limp off discretely rubbing his painful behind. But there was rarely a Phex Race without jostling, shying horses, or astounding falls, so they were fairly certain that they would not be cheated this time either.

※ ※ ※

Zordan Foxfell patted his black mare, "Easy there, Meriban," he said calmly, "we'll show them, right my beauty?"

Foxfell's mare was indeed the most beautiful and noble animal on the track. She was a true Shadif bred by a hairan from Achan. Foxfell was unhappy that he drew to be in the first race, for the victor of the final race was always more celebrated.

Foxfell was a rather slender man in his mid-twenties. His medium-sized frame gave clear indication of his Tulamidian heritage. His raven-black hair was worn in a braid, and his eyes were of the same shade. His eyelids were heavy, which made him look either tired or bored. His black eyebrows were arched and complemented his carefully twisted mustache. He also inherited his olive-colored skin from his mother. Only his short, round nose could be traced to his father. He wore his best riding clothes for today's Phex Race. Tight red leggings encased his thighs and a dark green doublet with fur trim emphasized his thin but muscular appearance. A black, wide-brimmed hat with a feather and carefully polished black riding boots completed the picture.

Only due to his father's influence was it possible for him, a bastard child, to participate in today's race. Ridiculous, he thought, especially since his father had acknowledged him as his own years ago. Foxfell never doubted for a moment that he would be the winner. Meriban was a well-trained race horse and, as the old hairan told him, she had never lost any of the numerous Tulamidian competitions she had been in. Also, he was an exceptional rider, something he inherited from his Tulamidian mother. "Riding is in our blood," he thought proudly.

This pride was something that Foxfell had felt all day—pride in his riding skills and his noble, sensitive Meriban—but he was angry at his second-class birth. His competitors let him know that he was not one of them, one of those pale, self-confident lords of tomorrow, and they treated him with condescension. But Meriban had impressed them. None of his opponents had been able to look at the black beauty without showing some sign of appreciation. Jealousy flashed in their eyes as he turned down the tempting offers they made to purchase her. No, he would not sell Meriban, not for all the ducats in the world, and certainly not now, not at the peak of her career. "We are an unbeatable team, my dear," he whispered to the mare, and as if the animal understood, she turned to look at him with her wonderful, dark, shiny eyes.

There really was only one serious competitor in the field and the Nameless One or whoever set it up so they were both in the first race together. Sindar was a muscular, fiery, gray stallion. His rider, young Brinna of Efferdas, was a cool, competitive woman. He stole a glance at the baroness, but she was looking straight ahead, almost as if she were asleep or in a dream. "Perhaps I should concentrate more on the race," thought Foxfell. "Meriban is always a bit slow in the start and we will fall behind by a few strides, but after the second jump we will lead the pack, except for Sindar. I should have looked at that stallion more closely in order to size him up, but who could have known that we would draw the same race? Well, the jumps and the water hazards won't be a problem for Meriban. The hedges are trickier. Obstacles that she can't see over always make her nervous. That's my job, to take away her fear. She must listen to me and trust me . . ."

At that moment, the head Phex priest took up his traditional place next to the starting line. He held a bag made of the finest paper in his right hand which he raised to his mouth and inflated. When the bag was completely full, he extended his left hand. "On your mark, get set," his voice rang out across the breathless silence that descended on the racetrack. The following "Go!" was drowned out by the loud bang as the priest brought his hands together on the bag.

Six horses thundered off with Praios Flower in the lead. She was a dun-colored mare from Onjaro. Meriban was taken aback by the loud noise and let out a quiet whinny, so it took her a moment to collect herself enough to let her rider direct her. Now she was running thirty paces behind the field and

Foxfell dug his heels angrily into her flanks. "Faster, girl, don't embarrass me!" he yelled. As if she understood his words, the mare flared her nostrils, raised her proud head, and began to run faster and faster, until her hooves barely seemed to touch the ground. "That's a good girl," Foxfell yelled with excitement, "show them what you've got!" As the mare caught his feverish excitement, he nearly forgot about their poor start. The rider and his animal became one and that always made him feel good.

Foxfell was closing in on the field and could soon differentiate all the animals and their riders. He passed Aldara before they reached the first obstacle, but she was the weakest of the competition. Sindar, Nightbird, and Praios Flower were still in the lead and reached the first jump at almost the same instant. Sindar and Praios Flower cleared the fence without any trouble, but Nightbird hesitated and Foxfell saw how the rider cruelly pulled his horse around to make a second attempt. "Two less," he thought happily, because even the strong half-bred Shadif would not be able to make up for that much time lost.

Meriban had found her stride. She flew forward, taking the hurdle effortlessly and continued running as if she had not even been interrupted by the jump. "That's the spirit, Meriban! Run, beauty, run!" He now only gently urged his animal on, because with the elegant jump he had gained so much ground that he was almost abreast of Beleman, a somewhat stocky chestnut gelding. "But Beleman is not fast and does not have the endurance to profit from his good start," thought Foxfell, and just as Beleman began the next jump, Meriban caught up with him. Again she flew gracefully over the obstacle, without any prodding from her rider. As she continued her fast pace after a gentle landing, Foxfell heard a splash. He looked over his shoulder to see Baroness Firisia of Marudret crawling out of the water and Beleman desperately trying to scramble out of the pit. "Good, only two left, and the race is far from over," Foxfell thought as his lips formed a smile.

The racetrack was designed so that one fence, one water hazard, and one hedge were built on a flat, round track. The riders had to go around the track two and a half times so that the riders cleared eight obstacles, and then when they directed their horse towards the finish line down the three-hundred-stride straightaway, they had to clear the final and most difficult obstacle—the hedge with the hidden water hazard behind it.

The next hedge grew closer and Sindar was now clearly in the lead. He was ahead of Praios Flower by approximately one length, but the distance between Meriban and Sindar decreased dramatically.

"Oh, Meriban, my beauty, my gem, I love you!" Foxfell called excitedly. For a moment he felt a rush of elation, and again it was as if the animal understood each and every of his words. A shiver ran through the mare and she shook her head as if to say, "I love you too, my dear master, and this is only a game—a beautiful, wild game that we are going to win."

Sindar cleared the hedge, followed closely by Praios Flower. Foxfell saw that both horses brushed against the top branches. That can't happen to Meriban. The sudden lash of pain on her sensitive pasterns could throw the mare out of stride. "Don't be afraid, my beauty, you'll make it," he whispered to her as he prodded her on to jump with a short pull of the reins. But Meriban was alert and expected her rider's command and jumped so high that the apex of her jump was almost a span above the hedge.

As the second lap began Foxfell was certain that he would win the race. The distance between Praios Flower was so short that Meriban would pass him before they reached the water basin. Although she was breathing hard and her neck was wet with sweat, Foxfell knew her endurance. No, she would not give up before the finish, but first she had to clear the hurdle. Sindar took it without trouble. Then Praios Flower jumped, but what was that? Either the horse or the rider miscalculated the jump and started too early. Praios Flower struck the top of the obstacle so powerfully that he fell, and the Baron of Onjet flew off and landed in the middle of the racetrack where he lay motionless. The baron's head lay exactly where Meriban's delicate hoof would land in a few seconds. It was too late, for Meriban had already begun her jump, as Foxfell had subconsciously instructed her. Too late, too late, he thought, for now she was in the air. Foxfell closed his eyes, and moved his body to one side, changing the direction of the jump in midair. They landed a few spans from the baron.

"Oh, Meriban, my gem!" praised Foxfell. "Not only are you smart and beautiful, you're also considerate!" As he looked back he saw how the baron staggered to his feet, but his injuries seemed minor.

"Now we only have one more opponent," Foxfell thought with joy. Indeed, Sindar was not able to gain distance even though Meriban lost a bit of time avoiding the baron. The stallion only barely cleared the basin, but Meriban had no trouble. Then on the straightaway, between the basin and the hedge, she passed Sindar. Foxfell looked over at his opponent, but Brinna of Efferdas was staring straight ahead, her brow furrowed and her lips pressed tightly together.

As Foxfell prepared his mare for the next jump, he realized that her strength had its limits. She jumped over the hedge fearlessly, but he felt her shudder and realized that she must have brushed against the top branches. "Hang on, hang on, my beauty, only three more obstacles!" he instructed her, but Meriban did not respond. Her entire body was covered with sweat, and her mouth foamed.

Before they reached the hurdle Foxfell looked around. Sindar was three lengths behind. His coat was shiny with sweat, his breath fast and his mouth foamed. The tension of approaching victory engulfed his thoughts and he felt closer than ever to his horse.

Meriban took the hurdles, but brushed them. Yet she landed without complaint. Foxfell knew that the delicate mare was in pain, but he avoided thinking of it. Then Meriban cleared the water basin, but just barely. Now they were in the straightaway with only one more hurdle between them and victory.

A new feeling of triumph rushed through Foxfell. He looked around and saw that Sindar had fallen thirty paces behind. "Oh, Meriban, you can do it!" he called, as he guided her to the hedge. Yet, her racing breath seemed to say, "I can't, I can't." But Foxfell did not hear her pleas. One last hurdle was all that was left. One last high, wide jump remained. She had to collect all her powers and show everyone what she was made of. Yes, she would make it in perfect form. He would attend the victory ceremony and Meriban would get sweets, as many as she wanted . . .

The hedge was just a few strides ahead. Foxfell judged the distance and squeezed his thighs at the right moment and pulled up on the reins. Good Meriban obeyed: She leapt up and flew over the hedge like a bird and then . . .

Foxfell felt a dull pain in his shoulder. He needed a moment to comprehend what had happened. Meriban had fallen and he was on the ground. Lost! The race is lost! That was his first thought. As he stood up he realized he was uninjured. His arm was only bruised, not broken. But what about Meriban? "Perhaps we can still do it," he had a flash of hope. But when he saw the mare, he knew that all was lost.

Meriban lay on the edge of the basin. Her beautiful, muscular body heaved with exertion and pain. Her hooves struggled to gain purchase, but she could not stand up. Her left front leg had an odd bend to it where there was no joint. Foxfell's heart wrenched as he saw it. Meriban would not finish this race, nor any other. And when she turned her head toward him and looked at him with her wonderful black eyes, they almost seemed to be full of tears.

As if through a fog Foxfell saw Sindar leap over the hedge. In midair Brinna of Efferdas yelled something that sounded like "Bastard!" and then she was gone. Beleman and Aldara followed later. The others had given up.

Foxfell knew what he had to do. He looked for the spot between her ribs, drew his rapier, aimed, covered his eyes with his left hand, and drove it in. Meriban flinched and her hooves twitched one last time. She let out a strange, raw painful sound and it was over.

Blind with tears, Zordan Foxfell left the track.

※ ※ ※

A warm, sunny week had passed since the grand Phex Race. During that week seven people died in the city of Methumis—two at the gallows, one of cholera, and four of old age. Nine new inhabitants of ethra, four boys and five girls, saw Praios's light. The people pursued their daily work, some with satisfaction and others less so, some with jokes and others with curses, each according to their temperament and the place that had been assigned to them by the Twelve. All the almond, cherry, and pear trees unfolded their buds, while the tender, yellow Tsacups in the forests slowly faded away. Down by the water, master builders and masons had begun work on a dramatic, large Temple of Efferd to replace the smaller place of worship.

Zordan Foxfell was oblivious to everything. The

first true stroke of destiny's hand in his life made him blind and deaf to everything around him. He was also dull from wine that he had drunk in copious quantities since the unfortunate day. He had to deaden himself. He had to silence the voices in his head that kept saying, "It was your fault, and your fault alone."

He wandered aimlessly through the city as he had done on the days before. He let his feet decide were he was going. He could not even remember how many taverns he had visited. He didn't want to be reminded of that, nor of the fact that his money was running out.

The sinking praiosdisc transformed the sea into an endless carpet of blue and green with a shiny gold pattern. Just above the horizon violet clouds formed streaks across the sky and faded on their edges to a dark purple. Tomorrow would also be a mild day for the fishermen and merchant ships. "Thank Efferd," many thought as they checked the sky.

As Foxfell's feet turned into an alley toward the harbor, the golden sky had faded. Evening had already fallen upon Methumis, with its scents of coal, bacon, and fish wafting out of the kitchens and restaurants as the first beauties of the night took up their places. Foxfell was immune to these temptations. Only a tavern sign that waved in the wind caught his limited attention. Its pale wooden planks were decorated with a poorly drawn fish that had an odd, long horn coming out of its mouth. *Drill Fish Tavern* was written beneath. The name seemed familiar to Foxfell, but he could not say if it was a pleasant memory or not. "Why not? Any dive here is as good as the next," he thought with irritation as he opened the door to the beer hall.

Despite the early hour, the Drill Fish was crowded. Sailors, longshoremen, and fisher folk were milling around the bar and most of the tables in the dark, low-ceiling room were full. Among the people who could be identified by their dress and speech as seafarers, there were figures with adventurous appearances and unidentifiable occupations. As Foxfell moved toward an empty table in the back of the hall, where a stout pillar would hide him from curious glances, he was invited to join a red-headed amazon in a game of Boltan. "Excuse me, lovely lady," Foxfell heard himself say, "but Phex is not on my side this evening, so I will have to decline your tempting offer." He gave the sailing woman a smile and a curt bow, then he continued toward his table. A drone of laughter followed him from the table of Boltan players, and Foxfell was certain that they were amused at his words, clothing, and gestures. He secretly felt for the handle of his rapier. Even with the trembling in his hands and the lack of recent practice, he was ready for any parry.

The barmaid, a wane, bony figure with stringy blond hair, took Foxfell's request for a large carafe of warm, sweet wine. "It was all my fault," rang through his head. "If I hadn't driven her so hard, she would still be alive..." He greedily emptied his first glass. "I could have won." With trembling fingers he refilled his glass.

"Well, Foxfell, you old horse killer," sounded a cheerful, and somehow familiar voice from behind.

For a week Zordan Foxfell had been waiting to hear these words. All week long he had imagined what he would do if someone made light of his misfortune. Now he cringed under the weight of the words. Without even thinking his right hand shot out behind him and the bejeweled ring on his middle finger struck the jokester on the chin.

An iron grip closed around Foxfell's wrist. "Tisk, tisk!" The voice remained as friendly as before. "Is that the way to treat an old friend who is here to help you? Perhaps you should drink less, if you can't handle it." The clamping hand around his wrist grew tighter as his arm was twisted to his back. "Will you be good when I let go?" asked the stranger and Foxfell nodded glumly.

As Foxfell rubbed his wrist, the stranger sat down on a stool next to him. The man was in his late twenties, wearing well-worn leather garb with a broad lace collar displayed on top of his doublet. While he carefully watched Foxfell he drew an intricately bejeweled Tulamidian dagger and began to clean his fingernails. Although his face was hidden behind a wide-brimmed, feathered hat, Foxfell knew with whom he shared his table. It was Ratzo Nattel, known as "the Rat." He was a childhood friend, whom Foxfell had no desire to ever meet again. Ratzo finished up his manicure and signaled to the barmaid to bring another glass. Then he removed his hat, blew an invisible speck of dust from its brim, and tossed it without looking toward the wall where it landed on a hook. The girl brought the glass and Ratzo poured himself some wine without waiting for Foxfell to speak. His broad smile exposed large, yellow incisors, which, together with his tiny black eyes and pointy nose, lent him a distinct resemblance to a rodent.

"I can't recall extending an invitation for you to join me, Rat," growled Foxfell. "Finish up and be off!"

At the mention of his nickname, Ratzo's smile flashed with hate for a split second, but he quickly had his expression under control again. "Why are you so unfriendly?" he queried. "Who would scare off an old friend and future business associate so abruptly? It seems that your noble father neglected to introduce you to the subtleties of etiquette. But let me get to the point. Aischa, bring us another carafe." He tossed the maid a silver coin, which quickly disappeared down her bodice.

"Friend? Business associate?" Foxfell shook with laughter, which quickly turned to a coughing attack. "To the point, then," he said gasping for air. As he wiped the tears from his cheeks and held back the last of his coughing, he looked in disgust across the table. "The years have hardly changed you, and here you are making a business proposal. I can hardly wait to hear what that is about."

"I heard you rode your horse to death," Ratzo feigned a look of concern. "Since your incomparable black mare recently died in a tragic accident you'll need a new horse sooner or later. You wouldn't want to appear as a wage-earner at your beautiful, well-to-do sister's castle, would you?"

"How do you know all that?" Foxfell took a big swallow and looked at Ratzo through half-closed eyes. "I mean my plans to visit my sister?"

"I have eyes." Ratzo pointed to his black, beady eyes and opened them wide to emphasize his point. "I have ears." He touched his surprisingly small ears, which seemed red in the candlelight. "And I have a good nose." He tapped the tip of his nose. "And I know that you're running out of powers." The Rat let out a high-pitched squeal. "Yes, my little baron, you do have problems."

Foxfell started to get up, "What do you mean by running out of powers?"

"Sit back down!" A sympathetic smile crept across Ratzo's lips as he stared across the table. "Well, you should remember: our childhood, our close friendship, and the game of Boltan, when your dice fell so curiously and my little dagger . . ." He looked at his dagger with an almost adoring expression, ". . . almost changed owners. Almost . . ." He grew silent and flashed his ugly teeth. "But I was faster." Suddenly the dagger shot forth and dug into the table top between Foxfell's right index and middle fingers. "And I still am. Nice ring, by the way," he continued, still smiling as he pulled the blade from the wood. "But why are you trembling? Is the wine disagreeing with you, you old horse killer? It's taking the last of your strength, isn't it?"

"Get to the point . . ." Foxfell looked at his hand and saw that there was not a scratch, only the old silvery scar on his hand. But it was trembling more than before. Angrily he made a fist to conceal the shaking. ". . . Rat!" he ended his sentence and looked at the ground. The Rat stuck his dagger back into his belt, inspected his nails one more time, and pursed his lips. Then he took a leisurely look around the tavern. "You're impolite, Foxfell," he finally said, "You curse the people who try to help you. I think I should offer my beautiful Fatima to someone else . . ."

"What kind of a horse is she?" interrupted Foxfell. "And how did you get her? Is she stolen?"

"Stolen? What an ugly word!" Ratzo raised his eyebrows again and shook his head in disapproval. "Besides, you know that horse thieves hang, and I am completely alive. No, really, I think that my Fatima is too good for you. She's an Appaloosa mare, as beautiful as Madamal. Her sire was an Elenviner and her mother was a Shadif. Her nostrils are softer than velvet and her soul is more loyal than gold. Good old Khalid had tears in his eyes when he had to give her to me . . ."

"She's probably a hundred years old and too weak to even walk to the slaughter house." Foxfell laughed an ugly laugh and quickly took a sip of wine when he noticed that he was about to cough again. "But tell me how you came upon her, I have time for a good story."

"Impolite, distrusting, insulting . . . Foxfell, Foxfell, how you have changed. I'm truly concerned for your soul. Perhaps you should go to the temple more often." This time it was Ratzo's ugly laugh that cut through the air. "But back to Fatima. She's seven years old, well fed, healthy, and obedient. And I won her. Not at Boltan, that is your specialty— or rather, was your specialty." Ratzo gestured toward the red-headed woman's table. "The children of the desert prefer a game of Camel, as you know, and I just happen to know a bit about Camel. It's a game of tactics and strategy, if you can tell the difference. And if you are fast enough and don't let the smoke get into your lungs, it becomes a game of skill."

"So you pinched it cheating, and now she has to get out of Methumis as soon as possible," summarized Foxfell. "How much do you want for her? I don't have much money." As if to prove his point he reached into his right pocket and jingled a few coins.

"Who mentioned money?" The Rat opened his eyes wide. "Do you think that I would give up my little treasure for mere gold?" He watched Foxfell carefully then added, "I like your ring."

"My ring is not for sale." Foxfell pounded the table with his right hand in a fist. "It's an heirloom."

"I know, you got it from your mother Suleibeth Foxfell, may Boron keep her. By the way, Foxfell is an odd name for a Tulamidian. But I didn't want to buy it, I wanted to trade for it. The ring for the second-best horse in the world, complete with saddle, tack, and . . ."

"You seem to be in a big hurry, Rat. Are they already after you?" Foxfell laughed and reached for his glass, but it was empty and so was the second carafe. "What's that bony girl's name? Aischa, hey, Aischa, another carafe please!" He waved the empty carafe to get her attention. She brought the wine and then carefully counted the six copper bits. "Back to my ring." Foxfell looked at it briefly and then reached for the carafe. But before he could grasp the handle, Ratzo's hand closed around his wrist. "You drink too much, my friend. It steals your—"

"Powers, I know, as meager as they are," Foxfell interrupted. "That's what you wanted to say, right?"

Ratzo nodded without changing his expression. "Yes, I did want to mention that."

"Then take heed," Foxfell continued, "my powers should interest you as much as a load of demon's shit. They're so stunted anyway it would hardly matter if they were shrinking." Lost in thought he reached for the carafe again, and this time Ratzo let him. "That was my mother's contention early on . . . and my teacher's, and later it was documented by the priests of Tsa. But what are you getting at?" He watched Ratzo suspiciously.

"That a game of Boltan is always good for a few silver crowns. Why so flustered? I saw you entering the Drill Fish—after all, I've been waiting for you since the twelfth hour." Ratzo laughed out loud and to Foxfell he looked more like a rat than ever. "Here's the deal," Ratzo continued seriously. "Your ring for the horse, complete with saddle and a bit of power that will be yours forever, if you're careful."

"What magician would give you or me any of his power?"

"A charlatan. And I know more about him than he would like. But don't you worry about the details of this deal." Ratzo's eyes looked deeply into Foxfell's. "You just have to decide, and make it fast. Yes or no."

"How do I know that you're not lying?" Foxfell suddenly felt very uncomfortable. "I shouldn't drink so much," he thought.

"You can't," interrupted Ratzo's voice, "just as I can't know if you're going to stab me between the ribs as soon as you see the horse. You desire power, but you're only a puny flame." Ratzo's voice was clear, but soft. "Well, you will always be you. My man can't make a strapping warrior out of you, but he could improve things a bit. And you need a horse and have no money. That's the way it is." He laughed. "And I have to disappear for a while and want your ring. I've always wanted it. So decide and hurry up. I have other prospective customers for Fatima."

"How much power?" asked Foxfell.

"You were usually successful at modest displays of magic in the past. Well, in the future you could be better at them. Perhaps my man could show you something from his bag of tricks, colorful flames and the like, you know."

"Fine," agreed Foxfell after a moment. "You've got a deal. Take me to the horse first. Then we will call on your charlatan."

Ratzo stood up and took his hat from the hook. "Come on," he said, "and keep a good grip on your blade so that no robber has a chance." He laughed as he cleared the way to the door.

The night was cold and clear above Methumis. Laughter and song filtered out of the taverns, but otherwise it was quiet. A gong sounded at the distant Temple of Hesinde.

As Zordan Foxfell followed Ratzo Nattel through the dark, deserted alleys, his right hand held his rapier tight. That night, however, his life was not in danger.

3

LITTLE THALIONMEL CRIED fiercely. She did not at all like having her diaper changed. She much preferred restlessly thrashing her pudgy legs in the bright sunshine that beamed in through the nursery window and onto the changing table, but the nanny took no pity, and with a steady hand she held on to the rosy feet, holding the infant's legs where she needed them. "You're a strong little person," she said smiling, "but there is nothing you can do, I'm still stronger. So stop crying. What will the lady think of us when she sees your tear-streaked cheeks and runny nose?" Widow Westfahr carefully wiped the child's face clean. The exertions of cleaning and caring for the baby loosened her hair and a large strand dangled within reach of the infant's tiny hands. "Ouch!" the nanny cried as the little fingers wrapped around her hair and gave a strong tug. "You're as strong as a bear, my darling, let go now!" But the child would not. She pulled harder and harder until her tears dried up and her little face shone with glee.

The door burst open and Kusmine strode into the room. She was slightly out of breath because she had just come from her fencing lessons. Once every moon since she was married, she had a teacher come in from Neetha and stay for several days as a guest, instructor, and practice partner. Early in their marriage Durenald eagerly participated, but the good food prepared by Titina, their cook, reduced his agility and he participated more and more as an observer. He never missed a chance to mention to Kusmine after the session that the teacher should actually be paying her, rather than the other way around. This morning, however, he rode out early to find the wild boar he promised his wife for the roast next Praiosday's table.

"Thalionmel, little warrior, let me have a look at you!" exclaimed Kusmine as she reached for her daughter. The nanny handed her the child who lit up as soon as she saw her mother. "What's that, Susa?" asked Kusmine pointing to the child's little fist.

"Oh, Your Highness, the child grabbed my hair while I was changing her and actually pulled some of it out."

"She's that strong already?" Kusmine murmured not without pride. "I hope she didn't hurt you too badly."

Kusmine held her daughter in her outstretched arms. The child laughed and circled her arms. Even her little legs ran through the air as much as her swaddling clothes would allow. Suddenly Kusmine tossed the infant into the air.

"What are you doing, my lady?" the nanny cried out in panic. "By the Twelve, no!" But the baroness caught her daughter again and the gurgles of pleasure reassured her that the baby had enjoyed the flight.

"See, Susa, she's not afraid," determined Kusmine with satisfaction, "Irineius of Malur's granddaughter is not afraid of flying." She granted the child the pleasure three more tosses and each time Thalionmel seemed to say, "More, more!" Then Kusmine impetuously pulled the child to her light leather armor and kissed the delicate blond hair energetically. "And now let's go see how your father is doing with that roast," she said, opening the window to give the stable hands in the yard the order to saddle up her horse. "Susa, get me a blanket and the baby's bonnet."

Widow Westfahr looked at her in surprise, "Why?" she asked.

"So she won't get chilled, of course. A young child shouldn't be out in the forest in the middle of Peraine without proper clothing." Kusmine gestured with her index finger in jest at the woman.

"As a nanny you should know that."

"You don't want to take her with you, my lady! For Praios's sake, no!" Susa desperately grasped to take her charge from Kusmine, but the baroness held her daughter tight and began to spin her around. *"Out we ride into the darkest wood, where the wolf and nightwinds dwell . . ."* she sang part of the old song.

"Ride?" Susa interrupted the song. "Oh, Your Highness, don't do that to me. How are you going to do that? Do you want to tie her to your back? Oh, my poor little darling!"

"Tie her to my back, that's not a bad idea," Kusmine laughed, ignoring Susa's worried looks. "I've heard that the Moha women carry their children on their backs, as do the Nivese mothers and even some of the peasant women in these parts. But I have another idea, which seems more appropriate. Listen . . ." And then she carefully explained the shape and features of the saddle bassinet old Hilgert had woven according to her instructions. It had leather straps to prevent the child from falling out and to keep the bassinet securely attached to the saddle. "I think she should get used to riding now that she is almost three moons old," she concluded her description, "what do you think, my little warrior?" As if in confirmation Thalionmel let out a high-pitched laugh.

As Kusmine rode out with her daughter, Susa looked on and shook her head. Her look suggested that she was concerned about the wild lady's sanity.

The ninth hour was almost half gone as Kusmine left the village. She had traded her leather armor for a riding dress of light green, a short jacket, and tight leggings. It was one of Durenald's favorite outfits. Because she hoped to meet up with him for lunch, she packed a little food as well as a skin of wine. She was happy knowing that she carried the food for her daughter inside her. She turned around to look at the child, but Thalionmel did not notice. Her wide eyes were fixed on the surroundings she could see from her well-upholstered position: the sky, delicate clouds rolling in from the west, trees, and birds busy building nests.

Kusmine rode to the northwest on a path that lead to the Imperial Road. It was not much more than a well-used cart path and when she reached the forest after almost an hour's ride, it could not even be called that. "They really should do something about this road," she thought as the branches closed in around her. The dark path was home to all sorts of riffraff, but as long as the local nobility and the count remained unconcerned nothing would happen. She continued down the narrow way enjoying the cool air, the songs of the birds, and the pleasant play of light and shadow created by the sun and leaves. "Durenald will be displeased that I came alone," she thought and chuckled to herself. When it came to her safety, he often forgot that she was an experienced warrior and not some dainty lady from Vinsalt. Besides, since she organized the citizen's militia things were much quieter here in the "Wild South"—at least around Brelak. The number of attacks by footpads and waylayers had markedly decreased.

In high spirits and full of trust in Rondra, Kusmine continued on her way. Durenald would be pleasantly surprised to see not only her, but also their sweet daughter. Just then the child began to cry. "What's the matter, little warrior, are you hungry again already?" She turned and smiled at the infant as the cries grew louder and more intense. "You'll have to wait just a little longer so we can find a good place to rest," she continued. "You know, I can't wait to relieve my breasts of the weight of the milk, either." Again, it was as if the child understood what she said, and after a few heavy final sighs the tears ebbed. "That's a brave little warrior girl," praised Kusmine. "Overcome your hunger and fight back the anger. Soon you will be rewarded by Lady Peraine. Do you see the meadow up ahead? That's where we will rest."

A few moments later they reached the clearing. Kusmine dismounted and spread a blanket on the ground, then she carefully lifted the child out of the bassinet. Even though the praiosdisc had not quite reached its apex, she also felt the slight tug of hunger. After she had tied the horse's reins to the branches of a tree, she got the bread and wine out of the saddle bags to refresh herself after nursing. "Do you think we should wait here for your father?" She turned to the infant as she undid her corset, but Thalionmel was absorbed in anticipation of her mother's breast as she waved her little arms. When she felt the firm nipple on her gums she began to suck greedily.

Kusmine enjoyed nursing, especially here in the forest surrounded by the scents of the earth and the plants, and the lively quiet and the cool warmth of the semishadows. She closed her eyes halfway, leaned against a tree trunk in their camp, and let her thoughts wander. Before her eyes passed colorful images of last night's passion, her daughter's growing strength and beauty, the morning's fencing lesson, and the armored glove she was having made in Neetha. She then gave the infant her right breast after she had half satisfied herself with the left one.

Suddenly the child rejected the breast. Kusmine was immediately awakened from her half slumber and returned to reality. "What is it, Thalionmel?" She looked at the child in surprise. Thalionmel had raised her delicate eyebrows and turned her head to listen in the direction of the road. Kusmine followed suit, but before she could see anything she heard it, too: a brief whinny and then the sound of galloping hooves on soft ground. "Is that your father?" she said to herself, but the child's expression showed surprise, almost consternation, not the usual joy she expressed at the mention of her father. Kusmine strained to look through the branches. She saw an unfamiliar-looking horse, a dapple gray mount. "There must have been an accident," she mumbled as she stood up. She put the child down on the blanket, fastened her corset, and in a few blinks of the eye she was mounted and riding off. "Lady Rondra, watch over my little one!" she said as she galloped to the road. "And if you take this one from me, too," she thought angrily, "I will never grace your hall again."

As soon as Kusmine reached the road she realized what had happened. About fifty strides away she saw three figures rolling on the ground. Instantly, Kusmine knew how the attack must have happened. Two waylayers must have waited for their victim after following him from the Imperial Road, which meant they were mounted as well. They must have pulled the poor man from his horse and were now trying to overpower and rob him. His attackers were a husband-and-wife team with Northern features, probably from Albernia. The fight was unfair, because, as Kusmine could see as she approached, the young, well-dressed victim had fallen such that he could not get at his rapier. The robbers were poorly armed, but they were much stronger than their victim. The woman perched over the young man and pounded him with her large, bony fists as he balled up and whimpered. Her accomplice kicked him again and again with his heavy boots.

When Kusmine saw the flash of a knife, she was almost in striking range with her sword drawn. But the robbers had caught sight of her and froze. After exchanging a quick glance, the woman fled into the forest to the right of the street. Her companion, however, knew he had a chance, so trusting in himself, and in the fact that the unconscious victim lay between him and the dangerous horse hooves, he cracked an ugly smile at Kusmine with his horribly disfigured face. Then, in one swift motion, he cut loose and grabbed the purse on the young man's belt and was off into the undergrowth in no time. "Dregs! Don't you try that again," called out Kusmine, then she leapt from the saddle to hurry to the aid of the wounded man.

The young man didn't seem seriously injured, although he moaned and rolled over in the dirt with his right hand clenched to his stomach and the left pressed between his legs. Kusmine bent over him and carefully touched his shoulder. "My dear Sir," she began, "how are you? Can you speak? Or get up?" At the sound of the voice the man cautiously lifted his head and looked at her with a swollen eye. "Zordan! For Praios's sake!" cried out Kusmine. "What are you doing here? What have they done to you?" Then, without waiting for his reply, she began to examine her half brother's wounds with her expert fingers. "Thank Rondra, it doesn't look as if anything is broken," she murmured. "Try to get up," she continued, "I will help you." Instead of answering, Foxfell let out a loud sigh as Kusmine grabbed him under the arms and tried to put him on his feet. "Grit your teeth, little brother," she said tenderly, but firmly. "You can do it."

Zordan Foxfell was the picture of suffering as he finally got to his feet. He stood on wobbly knees, his back bent and his hands still clenched to his stomach. With Kusmine's help he took a few cautious steps. "Can you ride?" she asked compassionately.

Foxfell shook his head. "Not ride," he moaned.

"Well," she thought aloud, "If you can't ride then you will have to walk. It will be difficult, but we will make it."

Zordan Foxfell shook his head again. "Not walk," he whimpered. "Get a wagon."

"Be reasonable, Zordan," replied his sister. "I can't leave you here alone. They could come back. . . ."

A violent wave passed through her, it was like the swath cut by a sword. An ice-cold hand grabbed Kusmine's heart and for a moment it seemed to stop beating. "My daughter!" she cried out. "My child!" She raced to her horse and urged it back to the clearing. If the bandits had taken her child—she did not dare complete the thought. She only knew one thing, that she would follow the culprits to the end of the world if she had to and she would punish them by skinning them alive . . .

Kusmine reached the clearing and saw little Thalionmel lying there, happy and content, smiling in the sunshine and reaching for a butterfly with her little fingers.

Jumping from the horse, scooping up the child in the blanket, and mounting up was done in a flash.

Kusmine returned to her half brother, who was leaning on a tree, her child pressed to her chest when she heard the distant sound of hooves. She glanced around to secure the perimeter, then she tried to hand the infant to Zordan, who wouldn't take her. "What's the matter?" she asked sharper than intended. "Won't you hold your niece while I face off against your attackers?" But Foxfell did not seem to hear her. "Get a wagon, a doctor. Don't leave me here alone," he whimpered apparently unaware of the contradiction in his demands.

"By Rondra, I don't understand," hissed Kusmine with wild anger in her eyes. "Pull yourself together, sissy, you're fine."

"Sississis," repeated Thalionmel and little bits of spit flew from her mouth. The rough ride in her mother's arms had pleased her and she repeatedly made loud joyous cries. Now she looked at Zordan with her alert blue eyes. "Sississis," she said.

As if struck by lightening Kusmine looked on in surprise. "You can speak?!" she finally managed to say.

"Sississis, rererer," the infant replied laughing, reaching for her mothers hair. Kusmine regained her composure and took stock of her duties. She put the resisting bundle in the bassinet and quickly tied the straps. "Well, let's go see who is coming," she whispered to her daughter. Sitting perfectly upright in the saddle, she drew her sword, waiting for the bandits to arrive.

There were two riders and three men on foot approaching as they rounded the distant curve in the road. They did not seem to be in a hurry, nor were they trying to remain out of sight. It even looked as if they were talking or joking with each other.

"Durenald!" cried Kusmine. "Durenald!" She waved her left hand, then slid her sword back into the sheath and raced towards her husband. Durenald also recognized her and sped up his pace.

"Kusmine, dear heart, what a pleasure to see you," he said when he reached her. "What's wrong?" he added as he noticed the strange look on her face, which was full of anger and relief. "And what is hiding in that strange basket behind your saddle?"

"Our daughter," replied Kusmine curtly. "She likes to ride." Durenald pushed the blanket to one side and smiled warmly when he saw the delicate face of his child. Thalionmel grew excited at seeing him.

"Don't you think she's still a little too young to be riding?" he turned to his wife. "Well, you know best," he added after a brief pause. "But tell me, what is bothering you?" Before Kusmine could reply, Durenald saw the wounded Foxfell, who was still leaning against the tree where his sister had left him. "By good Lady Peraine, who's that? What happened?"

Quietly and determined to control the shaking in her voice, Kusmine relayed the events. Instead of replying, Durenald took her hand and squeezed it tight. There was no reprimand for her as she had expected. "My poor heart," he whispered, then he turned to his companions, a huntsman and three peasants from the village. "Your lady's brother was attacked by waylayers. He's in bad shape. It seems he is too weak to ride. Cut down some saplings and build a pannier so that we can take him back to the manner in good shape." He dismounted, rushed to Foxfell's side, and exchanged a few quiet words with him. "Kusmine," he said, "don't worry. Go on ahead. I'll take care of your brother. The villains won't return, and if they do . . ." He smiled and patted the sword at his side and gestured at his companions who were armed with bows, spears, and daggers.

"I will send a wagon as soon as I reach Brelak," she said loudly so that her brother could hear her for she felt badly for being so harsh with him. "The maids will prepare a sickroom, and I will call Danja, the midwife. She knows all the healing herbs. Farewell!" She smiled intensely at Durenald and nodded at his companions. "See you later."

🌿 🌿 🌿

Danja had just left the sickroom. Quiet on her feet and with one finger on her lips she approached the Baron of Brelak, who awaited her with a serious face. "He's asleep," she whispered, "and that's the best thing for him."

"But how is he?" Durenald wanted to know.

"Oh, Your Highness," Danja smiled, as she always did when the Twelve and her arts had prevented disaster, "we have to thank our good Lady Peraine.

She had her hand on your brother-in-law's shoulder so that no serious damage was done. No, there is not a broken bone, and he has no internal wounds. Because he is young and healthy and his wounds are well tended, by tomorrow," she was silent and thought for a moment, "no, by the day after tomorrow, he'll be able to dance, fence, ride . . . and love again." She winked at Durenald in conspiracy. "In a nutshell, the Lord of Foxfell—"

"Just Foxfell," interrupted Durenald.

"What do you mean, Your Honor?" Danja was confused.

"His name is Foxfell, without the 'Lord of.'"

"Fine. Sir Foxfell will be himself again by the day after tomorrow. Except for a few bruises, of course, but they will go away."

"Thank you, Danja." Durenald patted her on the shoulder and put a small purse in her hand.

"Don't thank me, my lord, thank Lady Peraine, who lets the good herbs grow," she replied, but she gladly took the purse and began to feel for the contents with her trained fingers as she put it in her pocket.

Shortly after Danja, Kusmine left the sickroom. As an experienced warrior, she knew almost as much about wounds and their treatment as the herbalist. She smiled at her husband. "Everything's fine for having begun so terribly," she said taking

Durenald's hands. "We gave him a sleeping potion, because sleep is the best medicine. It will make him forget the fear, anger, and shock."

"Oh, Kusmine, dear heart," laughed Durenald, "you are such a good sister! But your little brother seems to be, if you will forgive me, a real weakling." He looked into his wife's eyes to make sure his words had not hurt her, but she smiled understandingly. "Anyway," he continued, "why did he fall victim to two half-starved and unarmed footpads? You did say they were unarmed, didn't you?"

She nodded. "One had a knife," she said.

"Either way, your brother had a rapier. Does he wear it for show?"

Kusmine shrugged. "I don't know, dear husband," she said. "But don't be too tough on him. Zordan is not a warrior. He never liked fencing and he didn't learn it well. Perhaps he really does wear his weapon more for show or to scare off the riffraff."

"Scare off the riffraff? Well, that seems to be working. They were so afraid they didn't take his life, only his ducats! He's an honor to the man who made his weapon!"

"Durenald, you're not yourself," Kusmine laughed. "It's cruel, but I can't say I disagree. We will know tomorrow what happened. Don't worry too much about Zordan's ducats. I'm sure that he didn't carry all his money on his belt. No one is that stupid, not even Zordan. He probably had a few copper bits or silver crowns . . . or tobacco . . ." She shrugged again. "But . . .," she concentrated, "I didn't find any money in his boots and there was nothing sewn into his belt. Maybe he keeps it in his saddle bags, but that's not particularly sensible . . ." Suddenly she cut herself short. "Saddle bags? Did they find his horse?"

"They found a dappled gray mare. She's pretty but skittish. Hilgert is taking good care of her in our stable," Durenald reassured his wife, "and your brother's luggage is safe. If you want I will have it brought to his room."

"That can wait until morning. I don't want to wake him." Kusmine paused for a moment, reflecting, "I'm very happy that Zordan found his way to us. That just goes to show he belongs with us and the child . . . Who wouldn't love our little treasure . . ." She took her husband by the arm and led him to the nursery. "I used to be under the impression that he resented me," she continued, "even though I was never unfriendly to him or treated him with arrogance or condescension. It must have been the jealousy of a bastard, I think. Jealousy of my birth, of my standing, of my good education . . ."

"Of your beauty," interrupted Durenald as he wrapped his arms around her waist.

"Of my good marriage," continued Kusmine with a laugh as she put her arm on Durenald's shoulder and pulled him tight. "Of my luck . . ."

"You weren't always lucky, nor were you always happy," contradicted Durenald. He immediately regretted his words as he felt how Kusmine tensed up.

"No, not always," she admitted quietly, "but I still think the Twelve have blessed me." She grew silent and looked at her husband with a loving, but serious expression. "Should I tell you what I think? I think Boron took our little Tsafried to show us that we are not in charge of our luck, but subject to it. And every day and every hour we must thank them for their gifts and blessings . . . Wasn't it Lady Rahja who brought us together in Neetha? And isn't it Lady Peraine who blesses the fields year after year? Or Lady Tsa who we thank for our beautiful daughter?"

"You're right, as usual," Durenald said tenderly. "And now that you mention her, I would like to see her."

"Yes, let's see our darling. She grows more beautiful and stronger each day. I want to feed her as well."

In a moment of thoughtful silence, the pair continued toward the nursery. Suddenly Kusmine laughed. "And isn't it Lord Firun who gave us the tasty roast?" she asked. "Or did he not favor you?

You know that you promised me a young sow for Praiosday."

"Anyway, I keep my promises, dear heart." Durenald pulled Kusmine to him and kissed her. "On Praiosday you will enjoy the most tender, juiciest game to ever cross your lips."

The couple stood for a long time at their daughter's crib. They played and played with her, caught up in their admiration of her fine build, bright blue eyes, and curly blond hair, which was abundant for her age. "And now please leave us alone," said Kusmine, "You know that I prefer to nurse alone." Durenald feigned disappointment and turned to go. "Can I hope for you to call on me this evening?" he asked.

"Of course, darling."

"I can hardly wait, love." With an elegant bow Durenald left his wife.

⚜ ⚜ ⚜

Two days later, Zordan Foxfell had almost completely recovered. His swollen and bruised eye was concealed under a colorful silk scarf, which gave him the look of a terribly daring pirate according to Damilla. The young maid was very impressed by the house guest. Her heart quickened even though she had only seen him three times since his arrival in Brelak. The first time was two days ago. He was pale and suffering, yet still wonderfully elegant, lying in the open coach as he arrived at the manor. The second time was yesterday when she had to sweep out his room, and the third time was this morning when she was allowed to bring his breakfast to him.

"Keep away from that young sir," Hilgert warned her when she told him with blushed cheeks about his exceptionally beautiful and manly hands, the deep look in his one eye, the warm sound of his voice, and his extremely delicate choice of words.

"Why?" the girl asked in surprise. The cold look of the stable master was so intense that it seemed he was looking through her, and a feeling of uneasiness went through her and took her joy with it. "Tell me! Why?" she repeated stubbornly.

"He will bring you trouble and misfortune if you get too close to him."

"You're always talking like that, old man." Damilla lowered her eyes and twisted her braid around her finger. "Can't you let anyone be happy, or can you look into the future and see only bad things?" She did not mean to ask a question, and continued as she angrily played with her hair. "When the little lady came, you also spoke of ill omens, but the child is in good health, and she has all her fingers and toes. Even the baroness got up after three days. The child is growing well, and the lord and lady are living happily together, and now . . . and now that I tell you what an exceptional and friendly man the lady's half brother is and how well he speaks you say that he will bring me misfortune. Why? Do you want to upset me? I haven't done any wrong."

"I don't want to upset you, child," Hilgert replied gently, but he looked at the girl so seriously that she unconsciously took a step back, "and I cannot look into the future, but I often can tell when misfortune is brewing. It might not be tomorrow, or the day after tomorrow, or even in a moon . . ."

"In a moon Sir Foxfell will be long gone. I overheard him saying that he had important business in Kabash." Damilla continued to fuss with her braid and jutted her lower lip forward.

"Then why didn't he go there straight from Methumis? It's on the way."

"I don't know where Methumis and Kabash are, but he probably wanted to visit his niece first. You see, that's what I mean. You are so suspicious and make such a bad Firun's face that you make me get one, too." Damilla grew quiet and the old man didn't seem to have heard her words.

"I'm not glad that I have this gift. It's really more of a burden," he said, "because I don't know what the future will bring, nor how I can prevent the disaster. You won't follow my advice either . . ."

"He's not even interested in me," Damilla interrupted. "He probably knows the finest ladies in Methumis and Kabash, so how could I please him? I'm too fat and stupid for him . . ."

"You are fresh and young. He likes you," Hilgert stated, "but now I must get back to work and I'm sure that they need you in the kitchen." The old man turned abruptly away and strode off to the stable.

※ ※ ※

"And when may I finally see the little princess?" Foxfell asked as he raised his eyebrows and the eyelid of his good eye in expectation. He had just joined Durenald and Kusmine for supper. It was their first meal together.

"May you?" Kusmine laughed as she cut herself a big slice of juicy wild boar roast. It was another of Titina's masterpieces, smothered with a sauce of fresh spring herbs, Tulamidian spices, and dried forest mushrooms. "No one is keeping her from you, and this is the first time that you have asked about her. But I'm happy that you did and you also seem to be feeling better." She paused for a moment to put a bite into her mouth and enjoy it. "Well," she said with a slight furrow to her brow looking at the pale blue of the sky through the Arivorian leaded windows, "it must be about an hour after noon. If it coincides with your plans, then both warriors will expect you in the nursery at the third hour."

Zordan Foxfell took a slight bow toward his half sister. "It would be a pleasure and an honor to pay my courtesies to the beauties of the house."

Then he smiled and turned to Durenald to pass him a steaming bowl of delicious-smelling millet dumplings. "But won't you also join me, dear brother? The whole family should be there." His smile grew wider. "And if my recollection serves me correctly, I have a present for the delightful warriors as well as a little something for you."

Two hours later when Zordan Foxfell entered the nursery, what he saw could not have pleased Travia more. Kusmine reigned from a red chair with a happy infant on her lap. Her husband sat at her side on a low stool and tried to make the child laugh by making strange sounds. Kusmine smiled and shook her head as she watched Durenald's antics, but she joined in and laughed heartily.

Susa ushered in the newcomer and with a brief curtsey. "Do you still require me, Your Highness?" she asked.

"No, go ahead, Susa," replied Kusmine, "let Titina make you some refreshment, and tell Damilla to bring us tea."

Foxfell paused when he saw the family, and in

feigned awe he pressed his left hand to his chest. "What a moving sight. Someone should capture it on canvas," he gasped. Then he approached his niece with graceful steps and took a low bow, "Delightful maiden, take my heart. I lay it at your feet."

The child no longer looked at her father, who had regained his composure with Foxfell's entrance. Instead she looked at her guest with wide eyes. Foxfell stood up and smiled at his niece. Thalionmel looked back at his one black eye. She was serious, but not afraid. "Indeed, she is a beautiful child, dear sister," Foxfell said turning to Kusmine. "What's her name again?"

"Thalionmel."

"An unusual name, but it will grow on you, right little Thalionmel? In a few years you won't only be breaking every man's heart, you will also be making your opponents fear you. Yes, you have a brilliant career ahead of you, my dearest. I would be jealous of you if I weren't your uncle and a loyal servant. May I now place a kiss on your forehead as a sign of my affection?"

As Foxfell approached the blond head with his pursed lips, the child shrunk back and tried to hide her face between her mother's breasts.

"Oh, you are being coy?" Foxfell could not suppress a slight hint of anger in his voice and expression.

"It must be your eye patch that frightens her, dear brother," Durenald said with a laugh. "She has not yet seen anyone with one eye."

"Well, if I don't please her, perhaps my gifts will." Foxfell took a bundle from his bag, which rattled as he carefully opened it. It contained brightly painted wooden figures: horses, riders, and soldiers.

Thalionmel lifted her head up at the sound of the toys and watched intensely as Foxfell pulled a tiny soldier girl (who, judging by the lavish silver and gold paint on her helmet, must have been a colonel) and carefully handed it to her. With a cry of glee she reached for it. Her hand closed tightly around the flashy toy and she began to wiggle and bounce wildly.

"Yes, that toy is to your liking, little warrior!" laughed Kusmine. "When you are bigger you will really be able to play with it. Thank you, Zordan." She turned to her brother, "You can see how much she likes your gift." As if to emphasize her mother's words, the child reached out with her empty left hand for something more.

"Well, let me see if I have something for the other hand," said Foxfell, searching his bag. "How about this daring mercenary?" He handed Thalionmel the colorful figure. She reached for it, but suddenly she threw both toys across the room, barely missing her uncle. "How can you be so impolite and ungrateful?"

Foxfell asked quietly. For a wink of the eye there was anger in his face. Then he bent down to pick up the figures. "That's enough for today," he said putting them back into the sack.

"Don't take it too seriously, she doesn't know what she's doing." Durenald smiled. "Show those darling dolls to me." Foxfell carefully emptied the bag onto the changing table and set up the contents. There was an entire army of little warriors and she-warriors, complete with chargers, knaves, and foot soldiers armed with bows and axes. There were even opponents: an ogre, two trolls, a handful of orcs, and a group of armed robbers including the mercenary.

"Absolutely fabulous," said Kusmine watching her husband. "That will certainly be her favorite toy when she is old enough for it. Until then I will take good care of all the toys, and perhaps play with them myself now and again," she added with a chuckle. "Now it occurs to me," she continued, looking first at the wooden robbers and then at her half brother, "I didn't tell you that my best hands looked through that bit of wood where you were attacked. I always say 'where there are two there could be more,' but we didn't see any trace of a camp. It was probably only the two of them and they took off as fast as they could. I think they might have been following you from the Imperial Road. You certainly . . ." Suddenly she paused. "Where is you ring?" she asked in surprise. "Why aren't you wearing your mother's ring anymore?"

"My ring, uh . . ." Foxfell flinched slightly at the mention of it. Now he looked at his hand and kneaded his ringless finger. "My mother's ring—"

"Did the robbers get it, too?" interrupted Kusmine.

"Yes, they must have," replied Foxfell with relief. Then he pulled himself together and put as much anger and outrage in his voice as seemed appropriate. "While we're on the subject, dear sister," he continued, "I must also mention that not only was I robbed of my dearest remembrance of my beloved mother, may she rest in peace, but the thieves also took my entire fortune from my belt, so that I now stand before you naked." He let out a deep sigh.

"Your entire fortune?!" exclaimed Durenald.

"So it is. The footpads in your forest took my last copper bit."

"Not so fast, Brother!" Kusmine raised her eyebrows and her cheeks blushed. "You're making it sound as if we were responsible for every ruffian who prowls in the local forests. Let me tell you something. The forest where you were attacked does not belong to us. It belongs to the count. Durenald only leases the hunting rights." Her voice grew a bit harsher, "For ten years I've kept Durenald's fief virtually free of riffraff and robbers with my citizen's militia. Anyway, I can't believe that you kept all your money on your belt. I saw the pooch, and no more than fifty ducats would have fit in it."

"Thirty-four ducats, two silver crowns, and five copper bits," Foxfell corrected sharply, "in addition to—"

"Is that all?" cried out Kusmine in anger. "What did you do with our father's money?"

"Don't interrupt me, Sister!" Foxfell raised his voice. "There were also three promissory notes for thirty, ninety, and one hundred ducats, so that my stolen fortune totaled two hundred and forty-four ducats, two silver crowns, and five copper bits, which is forty ducats more than father gave me."

"Promissory notes?" asked Durenald. "How did you obtain promissory notes of that magnitude? Are you loaning money for interest?"

"No, dear brother, but perhaps you know that I am good at Boltan, and that is a game in which one cannot only lose a fortune, but also win one."

"Gambling . . .," growled Durenald, but Kusmine interrupted.

"Zordan, Brother," she said in a serious tone, "you don't expect me to believe that you wore your entire fortune of two hundred and forty ducats on your belt. You're saying this in jest, aren't you?"

"I'm afraid not, beautiful sister. Unfortunately it is the sad truth." Foxfell nodded pathetically. "Please don't chastise me. I've been punished enough. I thought my money was safest there on my belt. Who expects gold there? I was wrong. Very wrong, as I now know." He was silent for a moment, his brow furrowed. "In addition," he continued, "I didn't at all expect to be attacked and robbed in your forest."

"There you go again about our forests!" An angry groove formed in Durenald's forehead and he pounded his right hand on the changing table so firmly that the wooden figures tumbled. "Those are not our forests, they belong to the count! Instead of thanking the Twelve and your sister for coming to your aid so quickly and possibly sparing you from greater harm, you are babbling on as if you expect us to replace your money." He continued in a more reconciliatory tone, "Don't think that I don't feel for your loss. It's harsh to lose two hundred and forty ducats because of your own stupidity, but what do you want from us?"

"You'll certainly need money," Kusmine added, "and I think," she looked at Durenald and he nodded, "that we can do something. So don't despair."

Just then there was a knock at the door and Damilla brought in the requested refreshments. As she poured the tea in the little earthenware cups she fawned over Foxfell. Even though her breasts were well-formed and her behind was round and womanly, he did not think she was more than fifteen, because her features were soft and childish, and her large brown eyes were shy and enchantingly naïve.

"Excuse me, dear sister and brother-in-law, for angering you. The princess seems to be bothered as well, since her serious, blue eyes keep following me and she won't even smile at me. What can I do to please you . . .?" He paused thoughtfully to make certain that Damilla heard him, "How about a little magic trick I recently learned?" He searched their eyes for an answer.

Durenald and Kusmine exchanged looks of surprise. "A trick? Well if you think so," said Kusmine.

Zordan Foxfell went to the center of the room and looked deeply into each of them, pausing a bit longer at Damilla who had crossed her arms under her breasts and was anxiously waiting. Then he placed his palms together and closed his eyes. He stood there a long time, deep in concentration. Suddenly he opened his eyes and mumbled, "Selemsalamander, mutoborinanother, hylailomander," while extending his right hand, palm up. He had barely mumbled the phrase when a green flame appeared in his palm. It stood there motionlessly, only flickering slightly with a draft through the window. Now Foxfell raised his left hand, entranced the flame with his slender fingers, and mumbled another phrase. The flame began to change color—first it was blue, then violet, and finally bright purple. It twisted and turned in his hand, twitched and grew, until finally it leapt from one finger to another of his open hand. It was the highlight of the show and then the flame shrank, and Foxfell quickly closed his hand. He was breathing heavily and there were fine beads of sweat on his forehead and cheeks.

"You're a magician!" exclaimed Kusmine, "I didn't know that." But Foxfell did not reply, he was busy wiping his fingers and forehead with a handkerchief.

Durenald looked at his brother-in-law with his head cocked in question, and Damilla had let her arms fall and stood in the middle of the room with her mouth wide open and her eyes fixed on Foxfell. Only Thalionmel was uncontrollably impressed by the demonstration. She squealed and squirmed powerfully as if to ask for an encore.

"Yes, Sister, I know a bit about it," Foxfell said finally. "It's a gift I inherited from my mother."

"Zordan, for Hesinde's sake, why didn't you go to the academy?" asked Kusmine. "You could have been a respected magus."

"My dear sister, how was my poor mother going to get the money for an expensive education? I'm only a little bastard, as you know."

"Zordan!" Kusmine's voice grew louder and anger blushed her cheeks again. "You know as well as I do that our father did everything in his power to support you and your mother. He wanted to send you to Vinsalt, only you didn't want to go. He certainly would have been proud to have a magus in the family, and he would have financed your education. Why did you keep your gift a secret?"

"Would have, could have, it's too late, as you correctly stated, dear Kusmine. Let's not talk of what could have been. I'm happy to perform here with dear friends and family . . . but please allow me to excuse myself." He took a bow. "My injuries are beginning to bother me again and I think it would be best if I could rest a bit."

Damilla also turned to leave. She curtseyed and slipped through the door. Foxfell had to take a few long strides to catch up with her in the hall. "Wait, beautiful child," he whispered and pulled gently on her braid. Damilla froze. "Did you like my display?" he asked quietly. The girl nodded without turning around. "Well, if you want to see more come by my room tonight." Damilla nodded again and raced off.

※ ※ ※

"What do you think of all that?" Durenald turned to his wife after Damilla and Foxfell left the nursery. He ran his hand through his curls thoughtfully.

"Do you mean the story with the ring and the money, or his secret magical powers?" asked Kusmine.

"All of it, dear heart," replied Durenald, "the story with the ring and the money, and his secret magical powers." He paused briefly then continued, "Don't ask me what I think of brother . . ."

"Tell me, dear husband!"

"Oh no, I'd rather not. You would say that I can't stand him."

Kusmine laughed, "Now you have to tell me your theory. I'm sure it will help me with mine." She smiled at him, "Come on!" She patted him on the shoulder. "Why don't you tell me?"

"Fine," began Durenald, "if you insist, I will tell you my opinion of your brother and his story. I think that good Zordan gambled and wasted his fortune, or rather your father's fortune. Further, I'm convinced that he is in debt up to his neck and only visited us to come up with a few ducats—and it seems to be working. And the ring, I don't recall it, but it seems to be a valuable heirloom, and I think he lost it gambling, too. As far as the robbers are concerned, they definitely attacked him, but it could not have happened at a better time, because his purse was certainly empty. If I weren't such a trusting soul, I would think that Zordan set up the robbers or that they were in it with him. No, seriously, Kusmine, I don't think that he's had his magical gift for long. Not that Zordan's demonstration didn't impress me. A magician's tricks are always fascinating, but he's not cut out to be a magus. Which makes me wonder . . ."

"You are wondering about something," interrupted Kusmine a bit sharper than she intended. "I was under the impression you knew everything about my brother."

"See, dear heart," replied Durenald sadly, "now you're angry. I shouldn't have shared my thoughts about your brother with you. We could easily get into an argument, and I want nothing more than to live in peace with you. Let's end this talk."

"First I want to know what you are wondering about," insisted Kusmine.

"I wonder," said Durenald in a firm voice, "why your brother is riding a dapple gray mare. Didn't your father tell us about a black Shadif he gave your brother?"

"Some people have more than one horse." Kusmine tried to sound calm. She opened her mouth to continue, but she saw her husband's worried look and paused. Her gestures lost their harshness and the fire in her eyes died down. "Oh, Durenald, dear husband," she said quietly, "forgive me for being so angry. You're right. We should stop arguing about Zordan. You're probably so hard on him because I'm so soft, and the truth lies somewhere in-between. Certainly he is foolish and has debts, but—"

"But he is not a bad person, right? That's what you were going to say?" Kusmine nodded and smiled.

"And he's a fine guest," continued Durenald, "attentive and charming. Did you see how he stared at Damilla?"

Kusmine laughed. "No, I didn't notice."

※ ※ ※

On the twenty-seventh of Peraine, ten cycles of Praios after his arrival, Zordan Foxfell left Brelak Manor in good spirits and fifty ducats richer. Damilla waved good-bye with a red silk handkerchief which he had given her, until her arm hurt. Because her eyes were full of tears, she could not see that he never looked back.

4

EIGHT MOONS AND nine cycles of Praios had come and gone since Zordan Foxfell left Brelak. Damilla knew these details because she had been counting the days, even the hours, but who could she tell? Who cared to know?

She lumbered along the dusty path to the manor. It had not rained for a long time, just like twelve moons ago around this time. Back then the little princess floated happily in the lady's stomach, and now she was taking her first tentative steps. The last eight moons were not very good to Damilla. She reflected on them as she looked down at her straw shoes kicking up the cold dust. She recalled Ingerimm and how it had rained excessively, too much according to the lord of the manor. "If Rahja is rainy, too," he said, "I fear for our harvest." Then, at the end of Ingerimm, on a lovely, warm day around noon, the lord had gathered all the servants in the yard. Everyone prayed to good Peraine, thanking her for all her gracious gifts and asking for her blessings for the coming harvest. It was also the first day Damilla felt ill from the fumes in the kitchen. She remembered how she had to excuse herself while the others sang, *"Peraine, blessed provider, mother incomparable. I follow you with my heart and soul and will not stray from you."* Damilla hummed the tune as she watched how the pale brown dust slowly coated her straw shoes and bare feet.

When Rahja came, it was as sunny as the end of Ingerimm, proof that their prayers had been heard. The wheat stood tall and the tomatoes were already bigger than chestnuts, although still green. And in mid-Rahja Hilgert discovered her behind the stable, unable to keep her breakfast down. She had tried to hide her condition from everyone, but he looked at her sharply and said, "Poor child, you should go to Danja, perhaps she can help you."

She followed Hilgert's advice, because she needed to talk to someone about the strange changes in her body. After all, she could not go to the lady, she was too strict and unapproachable. What would she have told her, anyway? That her stomach was often upset in the morning? That she skipped last time? No, one doesn't talk to the lady about these things! And Titina? No, she's too impatient and her hand flies out so easily if someone does something not to her liking. And Widow Westfahr is too busy with the little lady and does not have any time for stupid questions. And it was too far to Shilish to go visit her mother. . . . So she took her seven copper bits and went to Danja and told her everything. Danja laughed and explained to her that she need not worry, that what she had was the result of love, which made Damilla very happy. Yes, back on the eighteenth of Rahja she was truly happy. Danja was very kind to her and gave her a piece of sugar cake and two sachets with herbs. "You can pay me a silver crown when you have it," she said.

Some of the herbs were for the morning sickness and some others would help force the embryo out of her stomach. She did not want to take them all, but Danja insisted. "Think about it, child," she said, "you are very young and you don't have any money. Who's going to take care of the little thing? You still have time. You can think about it for ten cycles of Praios, but after that it is too late. Do you hear me, child? After ten cycles it's too late! If you drink the tea after that, you can get very sick and maybe even bleed to death!" And then she took the herbs back and told Damilla she could stop by anytime within the next ten cycles of Praios. If she decided not to, she would not owe her any more money. The seven copper bits paid for the advice, the morning tea, and the sugar cake.

Damilla had to smile when she thought of all the bandying about the herbs. There was no question in her mind, no decision to be made. What would Lady Tsa say if she killed the child in her stomach? And what would Master Foxfell say if he learned she murdered his child, no *their* child? He would certainly cast her off and never want to see her again, and all she wanted to do was to see him again, to listen to him speak. Of course she had not seen him since the twenty-seventh of Peraine, nor had she even heard from him.

In the beginning she was ecstatic; not even Hilgert's Firun face could take away her joy. "I can see you've made up your mind," he remarked when she returned from the village, "but what are you going to do now, child?" She was glad he asked, because that was exactly what she had been thinking about on the long dusty road back from Danja's cottage to the manor.

"I will write Master Foxfell a letter," she said immediately. "Will you help me with that, old man? I'll pay you a copper bit."

"So, you want to write to him. Then follow me to my room and let's sit down and do it. You can keep your money," the stable master said.

In his room, Hilgert pulled a thin sheet of parchment out of his drawer. Damilla remembered how embarrassed she was to dictate the letter that was already finished in her mind to the old man, the words sounded so foolish when she pronounced them aloud. Hilgert grimly smiled at her first line—"Honored Master Foxfell"—and Damilla knew that she was not following the proper etiquette, so she asked him to improve upon her wording.

"It's fine, child, continue."

She told him the words she had arranged on her walk home. "By your love and the blessing of Lady Tsa, I have conceived a child. I am very happy. Certainly you are happy to learn this as well. I request that you return soon, for I miss you dearly. Your Damilla."

"Don't forget to tell Lady Kusmine about your condition," Hilgert said after he folded the letter, addressed it, sealed it with wax, and handed it to her. Danja had told her to go to the lady as well, so with her heart pounding, she went to the library where Lady Kusmine was studying the newly arrived folios of warring arts from Neetha. Damilla really could not say why she was so fearful of her. The lady was strict and exacting, but also fair. All the servants agreed on that. Perhaps it was because of her cold blue eyes. They seldom looked friendly and if they did, they seemed sarcastic. This time, it was worse than she had expected.

Damilla had expected that the lady would be slightly happy for her, but that was not at all the case. "So, you are pregnant," she said, "and my half brother is the father, hm . . . now what?" But Damilla didn't know how to respond to the baroness's question. Instead, she looked at her shoes and shrugged. "Do you really think that he will marry you? Do you expect that? Do you require that? Look at me when I talk to you!" Then she angrily slammed the folios closed and paced up and down the room with her hands behind her back. Damilla secretly hoped that the lady would comfort her on the way past. Instead the baroness put her hand on Damilla's lowered head and pulled up her face to look into her harsh blue eyes. "Is my half brother Zordan Foxfell the father of your child? Tell the truth, girl!" she demanded, and when Damilla nodded, she silently continued her pacing. "That figures," she mumbled. Then she stopped in front of the bookcase and pulled out a blue, leather-bound book with gold-foil stamping, which she studied as she walked. "Well," she said after a moment, "you're free, but you still can't force him to marry you. Did he promise to marry you?" Damilla just lowered her head again and shrugged, because she did not understand what the lady was talking about. Master Foxfell had spoken of love, and she loved him, too, but she couldn't tell the lady that, and she didn't know what that had to do with the lady's question. "Well," the baroness continued, "here it says . . ." She flipped through the book until she found the right passage. "Here it says that there is no right to compensation if there was no promise of marriage and no marriage contract was signed. Regarding the child . . . can you prove that Sir Foxfell is really the father of the child?" Damilla shrugged in silence. Prove? What was there to prove? Who else would be the father? She grew confused. "But you are over twelve, aren't you?"

"I will be fifteen day after tomorrow," she whispered.

"Well, that's good, not for you, girl, but for the honorable Sir Foxfell. It doesn't look good at all for you and the child, as far as I can tell right now. But I will look into it further. Well, what shall we do now? Don't worry, I won't run you off . . ."

"Run me off?" That thought had not even crossed Damilla's mind, but she had heard of such a thing and suddenly she grew cold around her heart and so fearful that she could no longer even listen.

"If the lady runs me off then I will search the countryside until I find Master Foxfell. Yes, that's what I will do . . .," she thought as she returned to the servants' quarters. Damilla began to shiver and pulled the woolen shawl tighter around her shoulders. Then she stopped to catch her breath. The child was moving inside her, and she gently stroked the pleats in her coarse skirt, making her swollen stomach seem even bigger than it was. She leaned against one of the apple trees lining the path to the manor. Well, it's not much further, thank Peraine. She could already count the chimneys on the red tile roofs and the tiny windows in the front of the house. In the pale light of the winter afternoon, the whitewashed building seemed to glow. "Almost more than in the summer when the praiosdisc is high in the sky," she thought.

Yes, in the summer, in Rahja she was better off than now and more mobile, even though she was never one of the nimble. At least no one noticed during the hay harvest, and she could easily keep up with the other knaves and maids. She certainly had Danja's morning tea to thank for curing her of her sickness. Damilla loved mowing hay—the slow, even steps, the same motion of the arms, the hiss of the sickle as it cut the grass—and when one looked around the meadow and saw the even rows of cut grass, then one knew what one had done. It felt good. The wheat harvest in Praios wasn't as easy for her, but compared to today she was as nimble as an elf. It was even hard for her to walk now. But Danja had told her that it would not be much longer before the delivery, only one or two more weeks. Damilla was glad that she did not have to do any more hard labor. She helped Titina in the kitchen, polished the silver spoons and knives and mended the other servants' clothes, all of which could be done sitting down.

The lady had spoken about that in the library, too, "... and if hard work is no longer possible for you in a few moons, then you will be given easier tasks," she said. Damilla did not understand at first what the lady had meant. She could not think ahead that many moons, nor was she consciously aware that she would ever be as shapeless and stiff as she was now, even though she knew it. Then the lady said that she would write to her half brother, tell him what had happened, and ask him for an explanation. Then Damilla remembered Hilgert's letter and pulled it from her apron pocket. "I also wrote him," she said softly, as she reluctantly handed the baroness her letter. She looked at it with an odd smile and checked the wax seal, then she said, "Tomorrow I will send a courier with both letters to Methumis, and now get back to work, girl!" With these words it was clear to Damilla for the first time that a courier cost money, much more than she had. So she took a deep bow before the baroness and reached for her hand to kiss it, but the lady shook her off and said, "Forget that nonsense! Now get back to work!"

There was no reply from Methumis in Rahja, Praios, or Rondra. In Efferd, the lady wrote again, and a third time in the beginning of Boron. But when the couriers returned they always reported that Sir Foxfell could not be found, or that he was on a business trip. Eventually Damilla began to worry. "Perhaps," she thought, "that's why the past moons have seemed so sad, because they were full of waiting, pining, and worry." She had closed her heart to the beauty around her. Not knowing his whereabouts was the worst part. Anything could happen on such a long trip. Master Foxfell did not return to his residence in Methumis from his trip to Kabash, she thought. Otherwise it was clear to her that he would have found the letters the couriers left there and answered. Images and names of terrible diseases danced in Damilla's head: the blue cough, battlefield fever, Zorgan pox, Duglum plague . . . She had to stop worrying, otherwise the child would come early or be born with two heads as Danja said. Two heads, sure, a child can only be born with two heads if a demon takes human form and lies with a woman . . .

When Damilla reached the manor, the building shimmered red in the light of the setting sun. The maid was glad that the clear shape of the manor house was not spoiled by the other buildings. The stables, the smiths, the kitchen, the wash house, the servant's quarters—they all had been built around the large yard to the east, on the side towards the hill. With heavy steps she walked along the gravel path lined with trees pruned in round shapes leading to the buildings. She had to hurry, the dinner gong would sound in two hours and Titina certainly had a lot left for her to do. Damilla looked forward to the warm kitchen—she had gotten chilled on the long walk, and hungry. She hoped for her favorite dish—carrots with bacon and groats. As she turned into the yard she saw Widow Westfahr approaching. She had a large empty basket on her arm. She had just taken the little lady's laundry to the wash house.

"Damilla, where are you coming from, child?" Widow Westfahr called to the girl.

"From the village," replied the maid.

"I thought so, you are awfully dusty. What did Danja say? How much longer?"

"Seven to fourteen cycles of Praios."

"That's reason to be happy. Soon, it will be behind you, even though pregnancy suits you. You have become very pretty, with rosy cheeks. If you didn't have that big stomach I would almost think you look more slender than before." Damilla smiled widely. Since Master Foxfell left no one had paid her a compliment. Just as she thought of her beloved, Susa turned around again to say, "While you were gone, a courier came. I think I heard the lady tell her husband that she got news from her brother. Perhaps it will all work out, child!"

A letter from Master Foxfell! Damilla's thoughts grew confused. She leaned on the kitchen wall for a moment to collect herself. She did not know if she should be happy or sad. She wanted to run to the lady, but she was afraid, not of the lady, but of learning the contents of the letter, or to learn that there was nothing in the letter, and that it was a business or family letter.... For eight moons and nine cycles of Praios she had waited for news, and now that it was here she was desperate in the face of happiness and hope.

Damilla had difficulty cleaning the carrots that night and she almost cut herself twice. When Titina tossed the bacon into the huge kettle over the fire and it began to sizzle and smell good, the girl did not even want to get up and watch how the pieces shriveled and melted as she usually did. In silence, she handed the cook the bowl with the cleaned carrots and sat back down on her stool.

"What's wrong, Damilla, don't you want any bacon today?" asked Titina. "You must be hungry though." The maid only shook her head. No, she really was not hungry. She had lost her appetite, and her desire to sleep. She knew she would not sleep a wink tonight.

※ ※ ※

"Well," Kusmine turned to her husband, who had just finished reading the letter, "What do you think of that?" Durenald carefully folded the letter and handed it back. He watched her for a moment in silence, then he smiled.

"Dear heart," he began, "you know exactly what I think, but if I tell you, you will say that I don't like your brother. Why should we ruin a beautiful evening with a disagreement?"

Kusmine put the letter aside on a small table, then she grasped her husband's right hand with both her hands. "Durenald, darling, I think the same thing you do this time. I don't believe a single word that shady man says. Well, that may be too harsh . . ." She feigned intense concentration. "I don't believe three fourths of what he says. The rest is clear, there is nothing to interpret. She shouldn't have gotten involved with him. But what now? Soon the baby will be born and if he won't help pay for it, who will?"

"I've already thought about that," replied Durenald, "because, if you will excuse me, I didn't expect anything different of your brother. I recently had a long talk about the situation with Lechdan, the young widower with the little farm at the edge of the village. He needs an able-bodied woman to take care of his two children and the animals, and he is prepared to marry Damilla and recognize her child as his own. He even refused my offer of some money. Look, Zordan's bastard is still technically your niece or nephew, and I think we should help steer his or her destiny, if the father won't."

"If he is the father," added Kusmine.

"Do you doubt it, dear heart? Then you believe the shady man more than a fourth. At least half, I would say." Durenald could not keep from shaking his head slightly. "Of course Zordan is the father! Who else? He seduced the naïve girl, and it couldn't have been too difficult. It's only too bad that she still seems to be crazy about him after all these moons, if you can believe what the servants say, and that worries me. Lechdan is a good fellow and Damilla is a sweet girl, and I'm certain that they could come to love each other if they spent a little time together under Travia's eye. But what if the girl refuses to take Lechdan? Perhaps she wants to remain true to her love? That happens . . ." He squeezed his wife's hand.

"I don't know what to do, dear husband," said Kusmine as she thoughtfully brushed some hair from her forehead. "If she doesn't want to, then she doesn't want to—we can't force them to marry. Even if she were a serf, we couldn't legally force her, but since she is free . . ."

"Wife! Darling! Stop the legalities. The girl will have to forget Zordan and learn to love Lechdan. That's all there is to it. If she knew what your brother wrote about her, she would spit on him, I'm sure. I almost want to myself . . ."

"But Durenald, that makes it simple." She smiled at her husband. "Have her come up, and then read her the letter. It will be harsh, but often the harshest treatment is the most effective."

⚜ ⚜ ⚜

When Damilla walked into the royal library a few moments later, her heart was beating wildly. She was sure she would faint before she counted to one hundred, she was so afraid and queasy. If Master Foxfell had written that he loved her and would soon come to get her and the little one, she would certainly loose her composure in the face of such joy, but if he had written that he no longer loved her and that another woman was now with him, then she would loose her composure in the face of such a shock, that was certain, too. If the news was that he was on his death bed, then she no longer wanted to live herself . . ."

"Sit down, child," said Durenald in a friendly tone gesturing to an upholstered chair. Damilla obeyed, but didn't dare to take up more than half a span of the seat. She stared at her lord with wide eyes. "Well," he said smiling, "it's almost over, isn't it?"

The maid nodded.

"Are you afraid?"

She shook her head.

"There's no need to be," she heard her lord say, "because you are young and healthy and Danja and Susa will help you." Durenald paused and looked at his wife.

If she had counted, she would have reached fifty by now, and she was far from being unconscious.

"You know Lechdan the farmer, don't you?" Durenald asked suddenly, and even though the girl mechanically nodded, he added, "The one with the little farm on the edge of the village, whose wife died six moons ago."

"What did Lechdan the farmer have to do with the letter?" Damilla thought. "I think I'm about to loose my mind."

"Lechdan wants to take you as his wife."

"What?!" blurted Damilla.

"He wants to marry you, child," she heard her lord say, "Join with you in the bond of Travia, isn't that lovely?" And because she did not reply, he continued, "Look, Lechdan needs a woman, his children need a mother, and your little one will soon need a father. You don't have to decide right now, take your time to think about the proposal. If you are afraid of Lechdan because he so seldom speaks and furrows his brow like Hilgert does, I can assure you, he's a good, honest man. He only drinks moderately, and he promised me that he would never beat you."

"But . . . I . . .," stuttered Damilla, "but I can't marry him," she said quietly. The maid felt two pairs of eyes come to rest on her.

"Why not, child?" the lady spoke for the first time. "Are you related to him or is there some other reason?" Damilla shook her head. How could she tell the lord and lady of her love for Master Foxfell? "Do you still love Zordan Foxfell?" she heard her lord say.

Zordan Foxfell! Finally his name was mentioned and the horrible game of cat and mouse with Lechdan was over. Damilla never thought that her heart could beat so fast as it did when her beloved man's name was mentioned. She thought it would soon burst, but at the same time she felt relief. She nodded with her head low.

"Well . . .," Durenald hesitated. He did not know how to tell the silly girl the truth about Foxfell. "That's woman's talk, about men and love," he thought and looked to his wife for help, but Kusmine sat in a chair with her legs crossed, and carefully watched the young maid with her blue eyes. Just then she began to tap out the rhythm of a tune that Durenald did not recognize on the arm rest. "A letter came from Zordan Foxfell today," said Durenald in a loud voice. "My wife's half brother denies being the father of your child." Durenald sighed audibly. He watched the girl carefully and expected her to break out in tears or contradict him, but neither occurred. Instead she sat on the edge of her chair with her head lowered and her lower lip trembling as if she were murmuring a prayer. "Did you hear me, child? Sir Foxfell contests his paternity, and he . . . doesn't have the same feelings for you as you do for him. It would be best if you forget about him, and seriously consider Lechdan's offer," the baron said. Damilla shook her head.

"What do you have to say about that, girl?" The baroness's voice sounded a bit irritated. "Open your mouth, will you? Do you reject Lechdan?" Damilla nodded. "What does that mean? Yes or no? Speak up, I said!"

"No," replied the maid softly.

"You are still hoping after all these moons that Sir Foxfell will come back to you?" Durenald looked questioningly at Damilla, who nodded and then whispered, "Yes."

He reached for the letter his wife handed him. "Then perhaps you should hear what he thinks of you. I tell you, child, he doesn't love you and he never did. Should I read to you what he wrote?" Durenald hoped that the girl would spare him from reading Foxfell's harsh words, but after a moment she nodded again with fear and expectation in her face.

The baron let out a heavy sigh. "Damilla," he said

hesitantly, "you are still young and don't have much experience with people. You probably think that Sir Foxfell is an honorable man. Well, it's not my place to tell you otherwise. The letter, how should I put it . . . ?"

"Please," interrupted the maid, "I want to know what Sir Foxfell writes about me."

Durenald unhappily unfolded the letter, scanning the beginning until he found the discriminating section, "Here . . . it says *'After I succumbed to the seductive ways of the young prostitute, I determined that she was not a virgin. At my question she admitted that I was neither the first nor the only one, and then she asked for two silver crowns for her services. Because I was robbed of all my money as you know, I gave her a silk handkerchief that cost me almost four silver crowns. I did not admit her to my chamber a second time, despite her persistence, because I do not associate with those who give their bodies for money. I do not know your thoughts in this matter, but I am certain that half of Brelak could be the bastard's father. I am certainly not responsible, because I know how to be careful . . .'* Should I continue?" asked Durenald, but the girl remained silent. Without saying a word she stood up and left the library without excusing herself. "Consider Lechdan's proposal," Durenald reminded her again, "Lechdan is a good man."

"She seems to have taken it well," Kusmine

turned to her husband. "What do you think?"

"Oh, dear heart, I don't know. I think it was a harsh blow. I'm just glad she didn't break out in tears. I can't stand to see women cry."

Kusmine smiled, "My dear husband, if all pregnant maids had lords as thoughtful as you, then . . ."

"What then?"

Kusmine got up and looked thoughtfully at her husband. Then she grasped his hands and pulled him up out of his chair.

"Well," she said wrapping her strong arms around his body and lifting him up so that they were eye to eye, "then the world would be a better place."

※ ※ ※

Damilla expected to feel Titina's powerful hand on her shoulder any moment. "Wake up, child! What do you think you're doing sleeping on the job?" the cook said, then she woke up and found herself in the warm kitchen again. She wanted this horrible nightmare to end.

As she mechanically placed one foot in front of the other she wondered if one could think about dreaming while dreaming. She decided that it was probably not possible, at least she had never done it herself. Her dreams would be different if she could. When she was younger, just after her parents sent her off to find work, she would sometimes dream of home. As a child she often dreamed of food, but these dreams were rare now that she lived at Brelak Manor. She had also dreamed of dragons, fairies, beautiful clothes, and skull owls, after which she awoke with a pounding heart. Just like after the dream she had had a few times over the last weeks. She had dreamed that her baby was healthy and beautiful, but as soon as it was born it had run off. It made her so sad the feeling remained with her when she got up, even though she was relieved it was only a dream. She was also sad when she dreamed of Master Foxfell . . .

"In my dream Master Foxfell wrote terrible things about me," she thought. "He said that I was a whore and that I seduced him and that I couple with everyone . . . It must have been a dream, because the real Master Foxfell told me that I'm beautiful and that he loves me and that it makes him happy that I love him, too. . . . I had best go back to the maids' quarters and lie down. And when I wake up and the sun is shining, I will know that it was all a bad dream."

The young woman reached the back door. She was dizzy and she leaned on the wall for a moment before she set out to cross the ward. "I could go to Master Hilgert," she thought. "That is closer and he will be able to tell me whether I'm dreaming."

Since the old stable master had helped Damilla

with her letter the two had grown closer. Some evenings the maid visited the old man in his quarters and brought him a piece of cake or a bowl of compote. The stable master made herbal tea and then they sat together in silence and watched the fire. Damilla began to call him Master Hilgert.

With unsure steps the maid crossed the yard. She was happy when she finally reached the horse stable. She was also happy that she did not run into anyone who would ask her about what the letter said. When she opened the door the warm air seemed alive with the scent of horses. A few animals snorted as she entered and turned their heads to look at her, but this time Damilla did not go over and pet the dumb, friendly animals' velvety nostrils. She caught sight of the fresh straw in an empty stall. "I have to lie down," she thought, "before I fall down."

The stable floor swayed and the odd motion did not even stop when Damilla laid down on the straw. She looked around and saw in the pale, smoky light of the lanterns that the ceiling and the walls no longer appeared to be solid. They were bent and shook under the influence of unknown forces. "What a terrible dream . . .," thought the girl. "It's getting worse and worse. I should close my eyes. Perhaps it will stop." But it didn't. She thought that this is what it must be like on a rocking boat on the high seas. To see the ocean, to circumnavigate the world on a proud schivone, that was always her greatest wish. She told Master Foxfell and he promised to take her on such a voyage and show her the whole world: proud, cold Festum, the poisonous swamps of Selem, mysterious Khunchom, terribly beautiful Al'Anfa . . . Suddenly he stood next to her, his one eye glaring at her. "Why did you betray me, Zordan?" she asked. "Why did you betray our love, our child?" But Zordan did not reply. Instead, he tore the bandage from his eye, and what Damilla saw was not a human eye—it was yellow like a toad's and the pupil was a slit, like a goat's. Damilla did not want to look, she was so disgusted, but she was unable to close her eyes. "Help me, Zordan. Help me get up!" she shouted, "I dearly want to see the ocean, but I can only see the red sky."

Instead of replying, Zordan laughed and kicked her in the stomach. The maid noticed he was wearing riding boots with spurs. A hot, shooting pain raced through her. It was so strong that it woke the child. As soon as it was awake it tried to get out. "Stay inside, little Zulhamin, it's too early!" pleaded Damilla, but the baby forced its way out of her body and the maid began to push, just as Danja had instructed her. "Stay with me, little Zulhamin, don't leave me!" she begged again, but she knew there was no hope. Waves of pain filled her and wrapped around her, meeting up with the swells of the ocean. Then she finally saw it. It was red, just as crimson as the sky. Black snow fell from the sky, fine flakes at first, then heavier and heavier.

※ ※ ※

When Hilgert repeatedly kicked the back door with his heavy boots late that night, the noise awoke the entire manor. A servant opened it and froze when he caught sight of the stable master and his burden. Hilgert's hair seemed grayer than ever and it was disheveled so that the torchlight made it look like flames around his old face. The look in his black eyes was that of a crazed man and raw anger licked in them. In his arms Hilgert carried a bundle wrapped in a heavy blanket. A brown braid hung out of one end. On the other side were the limp, pale legs of a young woman. There was blood on her legs and it also dripped out of the blanket. A whimper came from the bundle.

"What are you doing standing there and staring?!" the old man yelled at the servant as he rushed towards the sickroom without hesitation. "Wake the lord! Get help! And tell them to send for Danja. Something happened to Damilla."

※ ※ ※

In the gray dawn Danja and Susa left the sickroom worried. Durenald rushed towards the women. "How does it look, Danja? Will she live?"

The midwife shook her head sadly. "My lord, the poor thing . . ." Two tears ran down her wrinkled cheeks. "She lost so much blood. I don't understand. It was a normal birth, but we can't stop the bleeding. It seems to me that something inside is torn . . . and the child is a bit small, but healthy and of good form . . ."

"Is she still alive?" Kusmine asked with a strangely foreign voice. "Or is she already resting in Boron's arms?"

"Oh, Your Highness, she is still breathing, but there is so little life in her that by noon . . ." Sobbing, Danja turned away.

"I'm going to her side," decided Kusmine. "Alone, dear husband," she added when she noticed Durenald wanted to follow her.

Kusmine stood silently at the dying girl's bedside for a long time. The maid seemed to be asleep. She could see the black fuzz on the newborn's head where it lay in her arm. Kusmine kneeled next to the bed and took Damilla's hand. "Your short life will soon be over, my child," she said finally, "and I'm sorry that it was not more pleasant. If I have wronged you, please forgive me . . ." She was silent for a moment. "I will pray to Boron and

Peraine for you . . . Don't worry about your baby. I give you my word that your little one will be well cared for. I will adopt your child as my own, and it will grow up as Thalionmel's sibling . . ." Kusmine did not know what else to say, so she sat on a stool, looking at the childish, pale face and the red infant's head. The sky was growing brighter through the window. Suddenly she noticed that the hand she was holding grew noticeably colder.

Kusmine carefully took the child from the dead maid's arm. She took the tiny bundle and turned to leave. "Sleep well, little Damilla. Farewell and may Boron have mercy," she said before leaving the room.

Durenald, Danja, Susa, and Hilgert were waiting outside the sickroom for the Baroness of Brelak. In silence Kusmine placed the infant in Danja's arms. "It's over," she said, and the women burst into tears. "Take the child to a good wet nurse in the village. The little one should stay there until it is weaned from breast milk, then," she looked into Durenald's eyes, "the child will come stay with us as Thalionmel's brother or . . ."

"It's a girl," sobbed Danja.

"She'll be Thalionmel's sister. Do you agree, dear husband?"

Durenald squeezed her hand and said nothing. He looked at her with moist brown eyes which seemed to say, "Thank you, darling." Aloud he said, "What shall we name her?

"Zulhamin!" In surprise everyone turned to Hilgert. It was the first word that the stable master had spoken since he told the servant about the unconscious, bleeding woman and the child he found in the stall. "She always said that if it was a boy it should be Zordan, and if it was a girl, it should be Zulhamin. So Zulhamin it is."

Hilgert bowed, and then strode out of the house.

5

"THERE YOU ARE!" Zulhamin panted as she collapsed into the tall grass beside her adopted sister. "I looked everywhere for you, but no one knew where you went. I knew you couldn't be far off, because your horse was in the stable. Why did you leave without telling me, and what are you doing here anyway?"

"Just thinking," replied Thalionmel, without moving. She lay on her back with one hand behind her head and the other resting in the grass. Her foot was propped on her bent knee, and she chewed on a long piece of grass while she spoke. "I didn't tell you where I was going because you would have wanted to come along, and would have pleaded until I conceded. I really just wanted to be alone."

Zulhamin's lower lip jutted forward in a pout. "You promised me we would go riding and then you left without me. That wasn't nice. A promise is a promise!" Suddenly the black-haired girl bent over her sister and began to pound on Thalionmel's stomach with her little fists. "Stop that!" Thalionmel's hands closed firmly, but not painfully, around Zulhamin's delicate wrists. "I don't want to fight! Fighting makes little sissy cry and I don't like that."

"I'm not a sissy, my name is Zulhamin!" The girl tried to free herself, but Thalionmel would not let go of her.

"Promise me that you won't hit me, then I'll let you go."

"Fine, I won't hit you. Promise. Now let go of me."

Thalionmel opened her hands and returned to her relaxed pose. She looked at her younger sister and seemed to smile, but with the praiosdisc high in the cloudless sky, her blue eyes were squinted shut and her nose wrinkled. No one could say for certain what her expression meant. "Look up at the praiosdisc," she told her friend, "and tell me what time it is."

The delicate nine-year-old leaned back and mimicked the expression of the older girl. "Maybe eleven?" she estimated after a while, then she sneezed.

"Oh, Zulhamin, what would you do without me?" Thalionmel shook her head in disapproval and wrinkled her brow. "How often have I told you that you have to divide the path of the praiosdisc by the number of hours in a day, and that it is noon when it is at the highest point? Now look!" She pointed to the sun with her right hand and Zulhamin's eyes followed her arm. "It's past the highest point by almost a twelfth, which means that the first hour after noon is not yet over. I promised to go riding with you between the second and third hour. As you can see, I kept my word and always will. Always."

"It's that late already!" said Zulhamin in shock. "We have to get moving if we're going to make it to lunch on time." She got up, expecting her friend to do the same, but Thalionmel stayed where she was.

"I'm not going to eat today. Go ahead on your own and excuse me to our parents," she said, chewing on the blade of grass.

"But Titina said she'd prepare jugged hare and white bread dumplings. That's one of your favorites," said Zulhamin. "But if you're not eating, neither am I!" She sat down next to her friend and wrapped her arms around her legs and pressed her head into her knees, so that her long black hair flowed like a cloak over her arms and shoulders. "I'm staying here with you, and I won't eat, either," she repeated.

"When you bury your face in your lap and mumble no one can understand you. Besides, you have to eat, otherwise you won't grow . . . and you don't want to stay as small as you are forever."

"First of all I'm not small, and secondly you have to grow too, because you're not nearly as big as Auntie." Zulhamin did not change her posture, but she did speak a little louder, so that her friend could hear her.

"I'm large for my age," replied Thalionmel, "and will continue to grow, and I'll eat as well, just not today . . . Look an eagle is circling up there!"

"Where?"

Zulhamin forgot that she was playing the little martyr and stood up. She shaded her eyes with her hand as she looked for the rare bird in the sky. "How do you know it's an eagle?" she asked when she finally spotted him. "It could just as well be a vulture."

"A vulture? No way!" Thalionmel shook her blond curls in revulsion. "You can tell by the shape of the wings that it's an eagle," she said with determination, even though she was not at all certain. In fact, the contours of the bird were difficult to see. "And by its path, which is truly majestic," she continued. She was silent for a moment, as she watched the circling bird. "The eagle is the king of the skies and related to the griffin," she recited, "just as the lion is the king of the steppe. The lioness is our goddess Rondra's symbol, and queen of all the animals . . . This morning a letter came from Neetha," she said suddenly, "from the school. I will start there next market day."

"Next market day?" Zulhamin counted on her fingers. "But that's only three cycles of Praios away! I didn't know you would leave so soon . . ." She looked worriedly into the distance. "I would really like to go with you. Why can't I?"

"Zulhamin!" Thalionmel sat up and took the same posture as her adopted sister, with her head on her knees. "We've already talked about this! Auntie explained it to you, Uncle explained it to you, and I've explained it to you. The school in Neetha is a garrison school. That's where warriors are trained, but you don't even want to be a soldier. It's not your calling and—"

"Uncle isn't a soldier, either," Zulhamin interrupted, "and he went to that school! He didn't become a warrior, he chose to be a baron . . ."

"One doesn't decide to be a baron or baroness like one chooses to be a baker or a smith. One is granted a title of nobility and a fief by a lord or lady, or they are passed on within families—"

"That doesn't matter," Zulhamin interrupted. "In any case, Uncle did not become a warrior, even though he went to the warrior school. And that's why I can go there and become a writer later . . . no, not a writer, a dancer . . ."

"It really does matter," Thalionmel replied forcefully, "but never mind." She was silent for a moment. "A dancer?" she asked suddenly. "Since when do you want to be a dancer? Last week you wanted to be a cook, and last moon a healer." She turned her head and looked at her sister thoughtfully, almost as if she were inspecting her thoughts. "You haven't even had a dancing lesson, not counting the steps of the Kuslikana that Mother taught us, and you've never even seen a dancer. So, how did you get that idea?"

"I have too seen a dancer before," Zulhamin replied triumphantly, "in a book. Yesterday. She had black hair like I do, and she was very beautiful. That's the kind of dancer I want to be."

"But if you want to be a dancer you wouldn't go to the garrison school." Thalionmel explained. "You would apprentice to a dancer, and that's why you can't come. Oh, don't look so sad, little sister." The girl took a blade of grass and tickled the younger one on the ear, but Zulhamin angrily swatted it away.

"Don't bother me," she said grumpily, "and you also shouldn't go away and leave me alone." Now she was on the verge of tears.

"But I'm not leaving you alone, Zulhamin. Don't cry, you know that I can't stand that! You are staying here with Mother and Father, and the servants, and the children of the village. How can you say that you will be alone? I will also come home two or three times a year to visit, as well as write. Now run so you won't be late for lunch . . . Hurry!" But Zulhamin made no attempt to go. She crouched again in a tight ball and sat quietly. Suddenly, Thalionmel noticed that her sister's delicate shoulders were shaking under her cascade of hair. She reached out to stroke her head, but in the last moment she pulled back. Then she stood up, turned away, and put her hands on her hips. "Now you are crying, even though I told you not to. I thought I wanted to give you my wooden sword and knight dolls as a farewell gift, but I think that I will keep them—it's not the right present for a girl like you."

"You," Zulhamin sniffed, trying not to cry, "you don't like me at all. You're glad that you're finally going to school, but I . . ." The girl could not keep talking, for she broke into uncontrollable sobs. Thalionmel shook her head. She pressed her lips together and looked from under her gently furrowed brow at a point on the distant horizon.

Standing there she looked so very much as her mother did as a girl, except for her father's curls. "Of course I'm glad to be going to school," she said finally, "and why shouldn't I be? But I'm also sad to be leaving you, I just don't cry as much as you do. I never cry. Crying doesn't suit a future warrior."

"I can't help it that I always have to cry when I'm sad," Zulhamin replied, interrupting herself with gasps. "It's because I was born prematurely, says Susa, and that my mother was sad when I was in her stomach. In any case, it's not my fault. And you're leaving me behind and not taking me to Neetha—that makes me sad." As if to confirm what she had said she sniffed a few times.

"That's fine, little sister. You've cried, and now everything is fine," Thalionmel replied, a little sharper than she meant to. "It's not that I don't want to take you to Neetha, it's that I can't. Where would you live? Who would take care of you? See, you don't have an answer. But perhaps you can accompany my mother and me when we go to Neetha in three days. Then you could see the school and the hall where I will sleep with the other boarding students, and the hall where we will eat, and the lecture room where we will learn about the warring arts and history and the cult of Rondra and weapons and fencing . . ." She concentrated for a moment, again looking strikingly like her mother. Then she tipped her head to one side and looked over at the blue sky out of the corner of her eye, ". . . and anatomy and healing."

"I want to see the tournament ring, too!" Zulhamin's tears were drying. The prospect of traveling with her aunt and sister to Neetha was very exciting and she jumped around in the grass on nimble feet.

"But Zulhamin, it's a garrison, not a castle, where I will be learning the ways of a warrior! There is no tournament ring—you must mean the drill arena. I will show it to you and the fencing hall as well . . . *if* you can come along, because that's not my decision."

Thalionmel turned to her adopted sister and friend. "Will you promise to run home as fast as you can if I'll talk to my parents tonight about you coming?" The younger girl nodded eagerly and reached out with her hand to shake on the agreement. "No, that's not right. You have to stand up! And I said run, not hop along on your behind."

In the end, the bargain was agreed and Zulhamin ran off faster and more gracefully than one would have expected from her delicate frame. "Tell my parents that I'm sorry I can't come. Tell them that I have to think, and that I do that best when I'm alone and the praiosdisc is shining on my head!" Thalionmel called to her sister.

"Yes, think," she mused, as she watched Zulhamin hurry to the distant manor. For the first time it occurred to her that the girl was nimble and beautiful, much more so than Thalionmel. Perhaps she did have what it takes to be a dancer.

After Zulhamin disappeared, Thalionmel laid back down in the grass again. She closed her eyes and enjoyed the warmth of the praiosdisc and the hum and buzz of countless, crawling insects all around. Although it was not particularly hot, it felt like a summer day. The first mowing was complete, and the girl was happy that her secret hiding place was spared by the sickle this year. She lay close to the pond, but far enough away from the reeds to stay dry. She had taken it upon herself to think about her past and future life. Even before her sister had come along and disturbed her, it was clear that this type of thinking was not appropriate for a warrior. Proper contemplation was done standing at a lectern, she thought, with feather and parchment at hand to note important thoughts. "But I don't like to write, and my handwriting is hard to read. Zulhamin's hand is much more beautiful than mine, even if she never spells the words correctly. And here in the grass it is much more beautiful than at the desk in my room. Yes, it's undisciplined and weak of me not to pull myself together and go to my room rather than letting the praiosdisc shine on my head. I know that I'm more likely to dream than to think. If I were in my room I would write: Be less forgiving of yourself, show no weakness, and practice discipline. As I am now, I would not want Rondra's eyes to see me."

Thalionmel imagined her first visit to the Temple of Victory. She had already reverently viewed the simple, light sandstone dome from the outside, although she had never been inside it. She knew children were not permitted to enter the building unless they passed the character examination given by a committee of three clergy, and showed enough steadfastness and maturity to step before the Goddess. She wondered if she would pass the examination before her eleventh birthday. Her mother was eleven and a half when she was first allowed to visit the temple.

Kusmine had noticed that her daughter took more after her in talent, tendencies, and build than after her husband, so she often told the child stories of the Goddess, the temple, and the basics of the cult. These woke a hot hunger in her daughter's heart. Kusmine thought that Thalionmel was more serious and thoughtful than she was at her age, and also more self-disciplined. Perhaps it was Thalionmel's calling to serve the Goddess. But Kusmine was not sure if that was her wish.

Thalionmel knew nothing of her mother's secret thoughts. She lay still in the grass and let her thoughts wander. The girl was large for her age. She had turned ten on the twenty-second of Firun, but everyone who did not know her age guessed she was twelve. Not only her size, but her features made her seem older than she was. There was little that was soft or childish about her. When the girl laughed, which did not happen very often, or made an ironic smile, which happened more often, dimples appeared on either side of her mouth, giving her strident beauty a touch of beguiling charm that would please Rahja.

Her eyes were her greatest feature, even though they were set a bit too close together to be truly beautiful, and often had blue shadows in their corners. They had dark lashes which emphasized her unusual fairness dramatically, and her blue irises had golden flecks.

Now her eyes were closed and the barely visible arches of her blond brows were relaxed as if she were asleep. Her shapely lips rested on one another but they were not open, as one often sees in sleeping or dreaming children.

Thalionmel wore her blond curls down, a habit she had picked up from her mother. Kusmine thought it was a waste of time and energy to have her hair arranged in artful braids every day, as was the style of the Empire's leading ladies. And just like her mother, the girl preferred comfortable clothes of linen, wool, or leather.

Today Thalionmel wore knee-length linen knickers and a loose-fitting top with a belt, similar to the fashions of the desert nomads. She was completely different from her sister in these matters. Zulhamin preferred beautiful clothes with embroidery, decorations, and jewelry. For Thalionmel, the best decoration was a gleaming sword and helmet...

Thalionmel's sword was to be delivered that day. For a moment the girl was tempted to run home and ask about her sword, but she fought the temptation. A secret observer would only have seen a slight twitch of her brow and her right hand squeeze into a fist. She would have to wait until evening to satisfy her curiosity, after her ride with Zulhamin. Thalionmel was sure that if her sword had arrived, Zulhamin would tell her about it. . . . As much as Thalionmel tried to order her thoughts and focus on the joys and obligations of her future life as a garrison student, she could not help but think of the sword again.

At the Neetha garrison, just as in the other academies of the empire, it was traditional that each student arrive at the school with an iron sword of the proper size. Naturally, these were practice swords to teach the students the weight and dangers of the weapon, and were not sharpened . . . but they could be. They were small swords, worn in a sheath on the belt.

Kusmine kept her three school swords in the armory. She used them from the age of nine to sixteen, and each one grew with her. During the past year she had allowed her daughter to use the smallest sword in fencing practice against her. With each lesson Kusmine realized how much talent the child had. It was a pleasure to be her teacher. She almost regretted turning Thalionmel's education over to a stranger.

"I will be better with my own sword than I was with my mother's," thought Thalionmel. "That is because it will be my own and I won't have to ask for permission to use it. I will also care for my own with more love and attention to detail. Why's that? It will not be any more elegant than my mother's. In fact, it may be simpler. The shape of the blade, handle, and hilt are all prescribed and it would be arrogant to give the sword a name and engrave words such as 'Rondra's Honor.' In fact, it would be so out of place that it would be almost blasphemous. Why is it that I can't wait to hold my own sword? Perhaps it is because it will be brand new and I will be the first to wield it. I will know the full story behind every nick in the blade . . . To be as good as mother, I will have to practice for years, but I know that I can become a skilled soldier. I have talent in fencing, and I am brave. I can see Mother's recognition of that in her eyes, even if she is reluctant with her praise. The fact that I know of my gift is perhaps not good. It could make me arrogant. They say that I'm proud, but that is something else. Pride is a virtue that pleases the Goddess, but arrogance is a vice, yet they are related and not always easy to distinguish from each other. I should make up a list of my good and bad qualities, so that I can work on the bad ones and improve on the good ones. Well, my bad side includes curiosity and wrath, although I'm not so sure they're all bad. Is not the hunger for knowledge the sister of curiosity? Is not rightful, holy anger the brother of wrath? Before I make the list I will have to define the terms explicitly so I know whether I'm possessed by rightful anger or if it is blind and evil wrath. Sincerity is not one of my good characteristics, because I harbor no such thoughts when I am full of wrath. I know this, but I am rarely able to suppress it . . . So I'm lacking self-control, but I'm trying to improve . . . Yes, Father is right: Suffering silently in physical pain and making sacrifices is one way to practice self-control. And what about courage? Am I truly courageous?"

Thalionmel thought about the beggars on the temple steps, most of whom are veterans, and how each of them made her feel oddly apprehensive when she imagined them. All of the disfigured men and women had lost limbs in battle honoring the Goddess, and now, not only could they no longer serve Her, they aren't even in a position to take care of themselves. They depend on pious warriors and clergy for alms. "If Lady Rondra wants one of my arms, legs, or eyes, rather than my life," she thought, "then . . ." She began to shiver despite the midday warmth. "Crippled or maimed, that is my greatest fear—may Rondra forgive me, but I would rather die before I am twenty-five than to live the life of a cripple, a burden to others and repulsive to boot. Yes, I'm repulsed by those pathetic figures, although it is not right. I should honor them for their bravery," thought Thalionmel. "I'm repulsed by their ugliness, by their empty eyes, their arm stumps, and their legless rumps close to the dusty ground on boards with rollers . . . I would rather die young, or kill myself, than live such a useless, horrible, disgusting life . . ." Thalionmel opened her eyes and blinked at the sky. Then she got up and with a wrinkled brow she walked in even strides back to her parents' manor.

Zulhamin was busy in front of the stable saddling her horse. Elgor, the new stable master, stood next to her and watched with a smile as she worked with a serious face. He had been instructed by the lord not to help the girls with their work on the horses, but only to make certain that their tack and saddles sat properly.

Although Elgor had worked almost five years at Brelak manor, he was still referred to as the new stable master, because Hilgert, his predecessor, had held the job for almost forty years. One morning, Hilgert disappeared without saying anything, not even good-bye, and without his pay for the last two weeks. They found his room empty and neatly swept out, and all the horses in the stable fed. Since that day no one had heard from him.

"You're late," yelled Zulhamin when she saw her sister, "and that's why I won't tell you about the surprise!" Thalionmel laughed—her sword had arrived.

"I'm not too late," she replied, "and I will have my horse saddled before the beginning of the third hour." Although she would have preferred to race back to the manor, storm in, and try out her new sword, she did not, nor did she ask her sister about it. "Curbing my curiosity is good practice in self-control," she thought, "and I will not hurry back from our ride because of it either."

It was exactly three as the girls rode out of the yard. Both were riding dappled steppe ponies—Thalionmel on a gelding and Zulhamin on a mare. "Don't you want to know about the surprise?" asked the younger.

Thalionmel tried to keep a neutral expression. "My sword must have arrived," she said.

Zulhamin seemed a bit disappointed at her friend's reaction. "Aren't you glad?" she asked. "Don't you want to know what it looks like? I saw it. It's this long." She pulled her hands apart, causing her horse to shy. "Oh, sorry, Dari, I didn't mean to scare you." Zulhamin patted the horse's neck and urged her up to her previous pace with a short, practiced motion of the thighs. "So," she turned to her adopted sister, "it's really long, maybe a stride, and it's shiny, and the hilt is made of brass, and the grip is wrapped in leather . . ."

Thalionmel's head whipped around. "Did you hold it?"

"No, I was not allowed to," the younger replied. "Auntie and Uncle thought that you should be the first to hold it, but your mother says that it is well made, and perhaps you can practice with her tonight, and the saddlemaker will bring the belt . . . The jugged hare was delicious, you really missed something. Titina put onions spiked with shadif needles into the sauce . . . Why are you so quiet?"

Thalionmel blushed at what her sister said, and her eyes were bright. Her lips hinted at a smile. "I'm happy about my sword," she said quietly, "and I'm sorry to have missed the jugged hare . . . Oh, Zulhamin, I'm so happy . . ."

"Yes, the jugged hare . . ." the younger girl said seriously. "I hope you will remember our deal—you promised to take me to Neetha if I ate my jugged hare!"

Thalionmel laughed out loud, "You will be a true intriguer. You can twist words so well already. I promised to speak for you if you ate your lunch, which does not seem to have been much of a sacrifice—of course I will ask my parents to allow you—"

"You have to!" Zulhamin interrupted excitedly. "I think that they won't let me. I asked Auntie and Uncle at lunch and they just looked at me, nodded, and thought that there would be time to think about it. But I think Auntie doesn't want me to come. I overheard her telling Uncle that she wanted me to accompany you to Neetha, but that I'm still too small and delicate for such a long ride."

"You ride well," said Thalionmel, "just as well as I do, even though you are much younger and smaller."

"I'm just slightly younger and a bit smaller," contradicted Zulhamin, glowing in her sister's praise, "and I'm not delicate—I have hard bones, and I have never broken any. Do you really think that I ride well?"

"Excellently," replied the older girl, but she could not help but add, "for your size and age."

But Zulhamin seemed not to hear the teasing. Proudly she raised her little nose in the air and her light-brown cheeks blushed.

"I can ride so well because I'm a Tulamidian," she explained. "We Tulamidians have riding in our blood."

"You're not exactly a Tulamidian," contradicted Thalionmel, "because your father, who is my uncle and my mother's half-brother, is himself only one half Tulamidian, so your Tulamidian heritage can only be—"

"Do you mean Uncle Foxfell?" Zulhamin interrupted. "He's not my father." The girl said the words with such conviction that her friend turned to her in surprise.

"Why do you think that he's not your father?" she asked.

"Your Uncle Foxfell was very mean to my mother. He broke her heart, and that's why she died. My father would never have done that. In addition, he has never given me anything and never visited." Zulhamin paused. "And he denies that I'm his daughter," she added.

"How do you know all that?" asked Thalionmel after she silently rode up next to her friend. "I always thought that your father, Uncle Foxfell, was traveling on important business all over the world; and that is why he could not take care of you himself and gave you to my parents . . . And you say that your mother died of a broken heart? I thought she bled to death at your birth . . ."

Zulhamin thought for a moment before she continued. "They say my mother was a maid," she said suddenly. "Do you believe that?"

"My uncle's fiancée, a maid? Never! Who said that? Zulhamin you are acting oddly. Who is telling you these things?"

"Uncle. I asked him yesterday after Titina scolded me for breaking a bowl. She said that I inherited all my thumbs from my mother, who was clumsy in the kitchen. So I went to Uncle and asked him why my mother had to work in the kitchen, and he told me everything. He also told me that my alleged father, Uncle Foxfell, is not a good person and that he mistreated my mother. He didn't want to tell me until I was older . . ." The girl grew very serious during her story. She held her large, almost black eyes steadily on the ears of her horse, and although she felt her friend's eyes on her she did not turn her head. "I thought about it all night," she said, "And I wanted to tell you before you leave for Neetha."

Thalionmel rode on in silence next to her friend. One could see by the movements of her brows and mouth that she was thinking and searching for the right words. "Does it matter if you are the daughter of a countess or a maid?" she asked quietly. "You are the same person as before, Zulhamin, my dear friend and sister . . . No, don't look so serious. Let's have a race instead. Whoever reaches that elm over there first wins." She pointed to a lone gnarled tree about two hundred strides away. "What do you say? Are you in?" Zulhamin reluctantly nodded, then she tossed back her hair.

"Fine," she said, "but I get to count. On three. One—two—three!" On the last word she struck the flanks of her horse with her calves and pressed her body as closely as she could to the animal's neck. "Go, Dari, run!" she called. "Faster, faster!"

Whether Zulhamin had a better start, or her horse was faster, or Thalionmel held back, the younger girl reached the tree well ahead of her sister, so that after she struck the tree she had time to turn her animal around and wave her arms in triumph. "I won! I won!" she yelled out of breath.

"Yes, you won," confirmed Thalionmel happily. "You ride like a child of the desert, like a Tulamidian princess . . ."

"Perhaps I am a Tulamidian princess," replied Zulhamin. "I have a Tulamidian name after all. Perhaps my mother was a foundling of noble birth, and raised by peasants. I thought about it last night and it's possible . . ."

"Oh, what you think about when you're supposed to be sleeping . . ." Thalionmel smiled and shook her head. "But you're right. It is possible."

"And my father—I mean my real father," continued Zulhamin, "because Uncle Foxfell can't be my real father, since he doesn't recognize me and I don't even know him—so, my real father is a Tulamidian prince, kidnapped by a black magician and held in his tower. And that broke my mother's heart. In any case, I would be a Tulamidian princess, and that's why I want to be a dancer."

"Do you really want to be a dancer?" Thalionmel

looked carefully at her friend. "Are you serious about that?" Zulhamin nodded energetically.

"Of course, I'm serious. I want to be a dancer like the one in the book. Why do you ask?"

"Because . . ." The older paused thoughtfully. "Because I have an idea, but I don't know if I should mention it. If I tell you about it and awake hopes in you that may not be realistic, then you will be disappointed and even sadder."

"I don't understand what you're talking about," said Zulhamin, her lower lip trembling, "but I'm beginning to get sad now."

"No, no tears, not now, please!" Thalionmel struck her left hand with her fist.

"Then tell me what your idea is," insisted the younger girl as she mimicked her friend's gesture. Although tears shimmered in her eyes and were ready to flow, her round, red lips were open in anticipation. "Tell me!" she repeated.

"Fine," began Thalionmel, "but remember, I can't grant or promise you anything." Zulhamin nodded seriously, and the elder continued, "There is a dance master in Neetha who teaches dance and grace to clergy and novices in the new Temple of Rahja . . ."

"Grace?" Zulhamin raised her brows in question.

"Grace is when one moves charmingly," explained Thalionmel. "Perhaps . . . perhaps, you can apprentice with the master. I think that you're graceful and that you can move very charmingly even now without lessons. And if the dancer in Neetha agrees, then she may take you as a student. Then we could both live and study in Neetha, and see each other more often. Not as often as now, of course, but once every seven cycles of Praios."

"Do you think she would take me?" Zulhamin asked, and now her eyes shone with excitement and joy.

"I don't know, little sister, I really don't know," replied Thalionmel. "I don't know if the dance mistress would take you as a student, or if my parents will allow you to become a dancer. I don't even know if you're going to be allowed to ride to Neetha, but I do know that I would be exceedingly happy if we both lived and studied in Neetha, and I knew that you were always close by." There was an awkward silence as she lowered her eyes, then she shook her curls and smiled roguishly at her friend. "Then I wouldn't have to write to you, and you know how I don't like to write. If you were to stay here you would expect a letter from me twice a moon, and if you came along I would be free of that worry."

Thalionmel turned her horse and galloped back to the forest path they had left for their race. She felt redness in her cheeks from talking with her sister, and it was with relief that she felt the cool wind on her face.

"Wait for me!" she heard her friend holler behind her, but she didn't want to wait. Sooner or later Zulhamin would catch up, and her cheeks would seem red from the wind and not from the admission of feelings.

At almost the same time, the girls reached the path through the fields that lead to the road to Shilish. The day had grown warmer and the air flickered over the light-colored dust of the path. A thick hedge of wild roses and blackberry brambles obscured the children's view to the south, but as they turned on to the road they saw a figure about one hundred strides away. He was walking south near the forest between them and the path to the village of Morlak, a small hamlet just outside the baron's lands.

"Let's see who has the best eyes and can tell first who's coming," suggested Zulhamin. Thalionmel nodded.

"It's a boy," she said after a while.

"How can you tell?" the younger wanted to know, but Thalionmel shrugged like her mother.

"You're right, it's a boy," confirmed Zulhamin, as they closed in on the wanderer, "and he's under ten."

"And he's not from Brelak," the elder added.

Now the girls were about seventy strides behind him. Suddenly Zulhamin bounced with excitement in her saddle. "I know who it is!" she called. "It's Pagol! I win again!"

"Pagol? The saddlemaker's son from Morlak?" asked the friend. "He must have brought my belt. Come on! Let's catch up with him, eagle-eye, so he can tell me all about it."

The girls spurred on their horses, but before the distance between them and Pagol's slight figure had closed by more than twenty strides, two boys burst out of the forest on his left. They jumped on the unsuspecting traveler. The attackers must have been twelve or fourteen, and they weren't from Brelak, either. Thalionmel and Zulhamin did not recognize either of them. "By Rondra, two against one!" cried Thalionmel as she drove her heels into her horse's flanks.

The young robbers had their eyes on Pagol's small purse. While the larger one had the boy's arm behind his back and his head forced into the dirt, the other sat on Pagol's kicking legs and swiftly undid his belt with a dagger between his teeth. The saddlemaker's son hopelessly tried to free himself from his attackers, but the more he resisted, the harder they pulled on his head and twisted his arm. Pagol moaned and cried, but it seemed no one could hear him.

At the sound of the approaching horses the waylayers turned their heads and saw the girls galloping toward them. The larger of the two attackers dropped the boy's head and felt around the dust. Suddenly he had the dagger in hand. Slowly he stood up with Pagol's belt in his left.

"Hey, riffraff, get out of here!" called Thalionmel. "And drop the belt, boy!" But before her last word was finished a rock hit her in the forehead. Her tender white skin burst open and a red rivulet ran down her face, disappearing into the collar of her shirt. The girl flinched at the sudden pain, but she did not stop her approach. Now she was only a few strides off. She stopped her horse and leapt out of the saddle before her sister could stop her.

"Careful, Zulhamin," called Thalionmel when she saw the larger figure reaching for another rock. Pagol raised his head slightly at the mention of the trusted name. "Help me, Baroness, help me!" he whimpered. A kick in the shins made him cry out.

"Look at that, a royal doll," growled the boy with the dagger as he crouched down and approached Thalionmel, clenching Pagol's belt firmly in his hand. "We'll see what we can get from you." He held his weapon ready to attack. His accomplice was also standing and weighed a rock indecisively in his hand.

"Let's get out of here, Rupert, this is too much for

me," he hissed. Then, as he ran off, he threw the heavy rock at Zulhamin who was standing in the middle of the road not knowing what to do. The rock just missed the girl, and she screamed as it flew past her ear.

"Wretched dog!" yelled Thalionmel and she wanted to run after him but the armed boy was in her way. He fiddled with the dagger and flashed an ugly smile, which showed that he was missing his two front teeth. Thalionmel stood her ground with her legs slightly spread and her torso leaning forward. Her fists awaited her opponent's attack. As she stood there with her lips tightly pressed, eyes squinting, and muscles shaking under the exertion, she looked like a wild cat ready to pounce.

"No, Thalionmel, don't do it. He has a knife!" Zulhamin pleaded, but her sister ignored the warning. She approached the younger boy, and they began to face off with slow, careful steps. Neither looked away for even a fraction of a second, so as not to miss even the slightest movement of the other. The boy named Rupert had his mouth open but his smile was frozen into a strained mask. A fine thread of saliva ran out of the corner of his mouth. Thalionmel's lips, in contrast, formed a thin, slight frown, and the delicate nostrils in her chiseled nose flared with her heavy breath.

Suddenly the dagger shot out. Thalionmel anticipated the attack and leapt aside. While she fell, she kicked her opponent's leg so that he stumbled. Although Rupert was able to catch himself with his right hand, he lost the dagger in the process. Nonetheless, she underestimated the skinny boy's abilities, and in the last moment Rupert was able to extend his right hand toward the dagger and just grasp it with his finger tips. The girl needed both hands to hold her opponent's arm to the ground. Just then her opponent dropped Pagol's belt and drove his left hand firmly into her blond curls. Painfully he pulled on Thalionmel's hair and bent her head back. The girl groaned and loosened her grip for a moment. That seemed to be what Rupert was waiting for. His dagger darted out and for a moment it looked as if it would poke out Thalionmel's wonderful eyes. Thank Rondra the girl was able to turn her head at the right moment so that the blade just grazed her cheek and ear.

But the boy did not hold his weapon tightly enough and with this powerful motion he dropped it again. The dagger flew high over Thalionmel's body and landed within the reach of Rupert's left hand in the road dust.

"Zulhamin, the dagger," Thalionmel called to her sister, who was watching the fight in tears. But before Zulhamin could get to the weapon, Rupert released his opponent's head and reached for the dagger.

As soon as Thalionmel's head was released it snapped forward and her forehead struck the boy so hard in the nose that he was paralyzed with pain for a moment. In a flash the girl used this brief moment of inattention. She grabbed Rupert's stringy hair with both hands, lifted his head, and slammed it with all her power into the ground. "Go to Boron," she hissed.

The boy moaned, blood flowed out of his nose and cracked lip. Although Rupert tried to fend off his opponent's attacks, his limbs no longer seemed to obey him. He helplessly pulled at her clothes and kicked up road dust.

Thalionmel raised Rupert's head again to smash it to the ground, and again she muttered, "Go to Boron!" Her third and fourth strikes were even more powerful than the first two, but before she could raise his head a fifth time, the girl felt a hand on her shoulder. "Stop Thalionmel! You are killing him," she heard her sister say.

Thalionmel released Rupert's hair. Only then did she seem to notice that the boy no longer resisted. Motionlessly and with eyes closed he lay on the ground, only his weak breath proving that he was still alive.

The girl stood up. She was out of breath and looked blankly at what she had done. Rupert moaned and rolled to one side. She turned away.

"The rat's still alive," she said mostly to herself.

As Thalionmel approached her friend with staggering steps, Zulhamin shrunk back in disgust. She had never seen her sister like this before. Her hair was dusty and disheveled, her clothes torn and bloody, and where the dagger and rock had injured her, there were dark red crusty streaks in her face. But more than the wounds, the strange look in the familiar face repulsed Zulhamin, because she did not understand. "Oh, Thalionmel," she stuttered.

Thalionmel looked around as if she did not know the area and was looking for a familiar landmark. Her eyes caught sight of her sister, wandered across the horizon, and landed on Pagol who was crying and crouched at the side of the road. "What's wrong with him?" she asked suddenly. "Is he injured?"

"I don't know," sobbed Zulhamin, then she bent down and silently handed the dagger to her sister. Thalionmel took it and stuck it in her belt.

"What's wrong, Pagol?" she asked again.

It turned out that Pagol's shoulder was dislocated. His face and knees had abrasions from the gravel in the road, and his shin had a bloody bump, but after Zulhamin gave him her colorful, braided belt as a sling for his arm, he agreed to be helped up on Thalionmel's horse. The boy's second biggest concern was the money in his purse. He counted it again and again until he was certain that not a copper bit was missing.

Zulhamin wanted to treat her friend's wounds and had already torn a strip from her clothes to do so, but Thalionmel refused to let her. "Those are only scratches," she said, "you don't need to bandage them!" Then she swung into her saddle in front of Pagol.

"Shouldn't we take care of him?" suggested Zulhamin, her eyes moving from the injured attacker to her sister. The boy was able to roll to the side of the road. He lay there in a ball with his hands on the back of his head and blood coming out between his fingers.

"You can pull out a weed, but it will grow back," replied Thalionmel and she spit on the ground. "Mount up, Sister!" With those words she turned her horse south toward the path to Morlak, which was only fifty strides off.

※ ※ ※

The eighth hour was almost over, and the evening arrived with gray and purple in Brelak. Just as Durenald decided to take up the search for the girls, Goswin, the saddlemaker, his brother Helme, and the two sisters came riding into the yard.

It was late because Thalionmel and Zulhamin repeatedly had to tell the saddlemaker's family the story of the attack, and Goswin's wife, Alena, insisted that she wash Thalionmel's wounds and that the children be rewarded for their daring intervention with a bowl of hearty soup. Finally, Thalionmel asked to leave, and Goswin and Helme armed themselves with daggers and whips to accompany the children to their parent's manor.

When the foursome reached the place of the attack there were only a few dark drops of blood on the dust as evidence of the fight. Rupert was gone, as Zulhamin noted with relief. Although the men had discussed in detail how they would take the boy into custody and present him to the baron, neither made any attempt to look for him when they saw he was gone. That was fine by Zulhamin, who thought there had been enough revenge taken. It was impossible to see what Thalionmel was thinking. With a straight face the girl searched the road and the forest, and only for one moment did the triumph she secretly felt flash in her eyes.

※ ※ ※

Durenald rushed toward the four riders who had just turned into the gate where Elgor was holding his lord's favorite black horse. When he saw his daughter with her cuts and disheveled clothes, but apparently in good health, and the adopted daughter, who seemed to be unscathed except for the missing strip from her clothing, the anger and worry about his children turned into a feeling of endless relief and thankfulness. "Peraine, I thank you," he mumbled as he closed his arms around his daughters who had jumped out of their saddles as soon as they saw him and were now talking rapidly.

The baron heard three reports of what had happened. Each was different in content and speed and they flowed over him like rain. Finally, with a smile, he took the girls by the hand, thanked Goswin and Helme for accompanying them home, and showed them the way to the kitchen where Titina had prepared them a meal. "Now go in the house," he turned to the children. "The baroness is sick with worry."

Kusmine had watched the scene from the dining room window after she heard the horses and voices in the yard. Her tall, slender figure was wrapped in a loose house coat of light gray Brebak silk. Her straight blond hair fell to her shoulders which gave her stern appearance a hint of girlish charm. When she saw how her husband rushed to the door with the girls, she strode back to her place at the head of the table and calmly awaited the threesome.

But at seeing her daughter with her open wounds, so that half of her face was covered with fresh blood and the other half was covered with dry brown streaks, it was difficult for her to maintain her composure. "Come here, Daughter," she said extending her hand to Thalionmel. "Let me have a closer look at you. Then tell me how this happened. No," she turned to Zulhamin, who began to rattle off the tale in a high voice, "your sister should tell the story first, uninterrupted, and then we will listen to your report, and no one will interrupt your story, either."

And so, for the fifth or sixth time that day, the girls told the story of what happened that afternoon on the road to Shilish near the crossroads at Morlak. Durenald listened, with a furrowed brow and an occasional shake of the head, to his daughter's brief report and then to the long, detailed, lively story told by their adopted daughter. Kusmine looked at the older and then the younger. Only when Zulhamin said, "and then she beat the boy's head into the ground so hard that I thought she wanted to kill him," did she look up at her husband.

"Now you have to go to bed, children," she said after the younger was finished. "Have Titina make you dinner. You, Thalionmel, will have to let Susa take care of your wounds. If they aren't bandaged they will reopen. You know that you will have a scar on your cheek, not a disfiguring one, but something that will be seen your entire life?"

"I know, Mother," the girl said, and a blush came

to her cheeks. "But before I go to Susa allow me to make a request. I promised it."

"Well, what is it?" Kusmine raised her brows in question.

"I promised Zulhamin," began Thalionmel, "that I would ask your permission for her to accompany us on the trip to Neetha. She rides very well. And I told her about the dance mistress—she wants to become a dancer. And I heard that my sword is here."

"You want to be a dancer, my dove?" interrupted Durenald as he took Zulhamin's hand. The girl nodded energetically. "And you want to go to Neetha and live with the sharisad and apprentice with her and leave Auntie and me here alone?" Zulhamin nodded again but as she understood her uncle's words her expression of happiness turned to one of dismay. "Don't look so angry, dove," Durenald grasped the child's chin. "All fledglings leave the nest. That's the way life is and the old ones have to accept that. You still have some time to consider it, just as Auntie and I do." Then he smiled and turned to his daughter. "Your sword, sheath, and belt are on your bed. Tomorrow we will see if it is as good as it looks. And now go to bed, children. May Boron grant you a good night's sleep."

⚜ ⚜ ⚜

That night both girls lay awake for a long time. Thalionmel proudly felt the herbal compress that Susa made for her temple, ear, and cheek. Scenes from the fight with Rupert flickered in her imagination, and she asked herself if she had pleased the Goddess. "Perhaps I should have killed the boy and not listened to my sister," she thought. She wanted to ask her mother about that tomorrow. She took her sword to bed with her, and as she slept it lay in her arm like a little girl's favorite doll.

Zulhamin imagined that she was a student with a beautiful but strict dance mistress. The instruction hall was darkened, and there were colorful wall hangings in the room; bandurria and flute players sat on low pillows just as they did in her book. But the beautiful picture faded out again and again and an image of Uncle and Auntie alone and sad at lunch appeared in its place.

Durenald and Kusmine were also unable to sleep, because there was a lot to discuss. In the end, they agreed to allow Zulhamin to travel to Neetha. And if she was fit after the long ride, Kusmine wanted to present her adopted daughter to the dancer Shahane.

☙ ☙ ☙

At daybreak three days later, Kusmine and her two daughters embarked on their journey to Neetha.

6

THALIONMEL PACED BACK and forth with her hands behind her back. The room was small and sparsely furnished. A sole lectern stood beneath a high, narrow window covered with parchment. On the opposite wall three stools formed a row, and on the east wall hung a very large devotional picture.

The girl stopped in front of the painting and examined it, as she had already done several times during the past hour. "Perhaps it will happen this time," she thought. But nothing happened.

The painting featured a life-sized woman with alabaster skin and long, curly blond hair protruding from under a shiny gold helmet. The warrior's armor and splints were also of gold, which accentuated her short tunic made of leather strips. The woman stood barefoot with her legs apart and a two-handed sword over her head. The golden blade extended the imaginary axis through her symmetrical figure. "That must be Rondra's blade," thought Thalionmel. "It's probably gold plated, since solid gold is too soft for blades." A lioness with shiny, red-tinged fur crouched between the woman's legs, ready to pounce. Her teeth were bared, exposing enormous fangs. The sharp claws of her front paws were also prominent. The lioness stared steadfastly at Thalionmel.

Her eyes moved up the woman's perfectly muscular legs, her none too full breasts, and her uniform face. Unlike the lioness, the woman showed no emotion. Her face was a lovely oval with a well-shaped nose, red lips, and large blue eyes under arched, dark brows. Like the cat, the woman also seemed to be looking back at Thalionmel.

Red and yellow flames encircled the warrior so that it looked as if she were on fire. The rest of the picture was dark purple, like a stormy sky. Thalionmel stepped a few paces to one side to see if the two pairs of eyes would follow her and discovered to her astonishment that she could escape neither the ambivalent warrior's blue eyes, nor the angry yellow-green stare of the lioness.

"Why is it that the Goddess and the lioness follow me with their eyes no matter where I go? Is there divine magic in the painting?" No, she did not think so, because then she would feel something different. It must be a trick by the artist, just as the gold on the picture was not really painted with gold dust. She had examined it carefully. When the next to last student was called out and she was finally alone in the room, she took a close look at the picture. There was no gold on it, only yellow and brown and white and even a little bit of green and blue. And the surface was not entirely flat, either. In some areas the paint was thicker than in others. Here and there she could even see brushstrokes. Thalionmel liked the picture, she found it beautiful and moving. Just as she thought the pictures of the former garrison commanders in the dining hall were beautiful and impressive.

Thalionmel thought it odd that at this moment she was impressed by the artist's ability, rather than carrying on a silent dialogue with the Goddess. But she could not pray. She had tried for more than an hour without success. She could say the words in her head, but she did not feel moved; she did not experience the strange hot feeling in her solar plexus that she occasionally felt during the common prayer in the classroom. "Goddess Rondra, fill me with your spirit," she said in a steady voice. "Grace my limbs and give me strength. Enter my heart and give me courage. Join my soul and give me anger. My body is yours, and I will sacrifice my enemy for you. Red blood, holy blood, blood, cleanse me, so be it."

It was as Thalionmel expected, she felt nothing inside. "I don't sense her presence," thought the girl, "yet I should feel her more than ever when I'm looking at her image. She's not with me, she's not looking on me with pleasure. She's not with me and I will fail the examination." Thalionmel sighed.

At eleven she was the youngest of the three candidates for the temple examination that Tsa. Cassim had just celebrated his thirteenth cycle of the Twelve, and Silvana would soon see her twelfth. Generally, twelve was thought to be the best age for the exam. However, the young priestess, Yasinde of Feyhacht, who instructed the garrison students in the Rondra cult, had no reservations when Thalionmel asked to take the examination early. Thalionmel prepared herself thoroughly. She embraced the most important tenets of the cult and memorized them, she participated in the evening prayer, which was only mandatory for students over fourteen. She fought to the brink of exhaustion in every fencing lesson, and she began to keep a diary in which she recorded her achievements and disappointments.

"It was probably presumptuous to take the examination so early," the girl thought. "I won't know the answers and my comrades will laugh at me when they hear I failed. Now it is too late and

Yasinde will soon open the door. I see my mistake. I absolutely wanted to be the youngest in my class to pass the examination, and that was false pride. I wanted to see the temple from the inside, and that was curiosity. I wanted so much to wear the silver pin with the leaping lioness, so that the priests in the foyer would see that I had permission to enter the temple, and that was childish desire for recognition."

As Thalionmel stared into the Goddess's eyes she intended to be ruthless with herself during the evening confession. "Goddess Rondra, I do not ask you to come to my aid because I'm not worthy," she mumbled. When she looked away from the Goddess's image to look at the light cast on the floor to determine how long it had been since Silvana had been called in for the examination, she noticed that the door to the room was open. She flinched when she saw a dark-haired, middle-aged priest observing her. He was wearing a mail shirt and the blue and white temple robe. She had never seen the man before, nor had she heard him come in, so she did not know how long his black eyes had been watching her.

The priest must have noticed, Thalionmel was sure of that, and she resented her ridiculous tendency to be startled. Her heart began to beat wildly as if she were in battle. To complete the embarrassing picture her cheeks blushed. "Thalionmel of Brelak," the priest said plainly, "I am here to bring you to the temple examination. Follow me!"

Well, now it was time, and there was no way out. Either way it would be over in half an hour. Thalionmel almost felt relieved when she realized that the end was not far off. She mechanically placed one foot in front of the other and rolled her tongue around to moisten her mouth. Her lips and mouth were so dry she feared she would be unable to speak a word.

The girl followed the priest in silence, careful to maintain the proper distance behind him. The dark, strict man would certainly ask her the most difficult questions, but she knew Yasinde liked her, so she could hope for some pity. "Pity?! Favoritism?! What kind of ridiculous and unfitting thoughts are these, as if they mattered! I should prove in the examination that I know enough about the Goddess's cult and have the maturity to enter the temple," she thought. "What does that have to do with pity? Well, apparently I don't have the strength of character and maturity, because I'm hoping for pity."

The priest stopped in front of a heavy oaken door. After knocking twice, he opened it and stepped aside, followed by Thalionmel. The girl heard the door close behind her and the priest's heavy steps echoed away down the hall.

She stood in a room similar to the previous one, only it had two windows. The blinding light caused her to squint. Below the windows two priestesses and one priest sat at a simple table. At the left Thalionmel recognized Yasinde, who was scrawling some notes on parchment. She had briefly looked up as Thalionmel entered, but she quickly returned to her notes. The woman in the middle, on a raised armchair with detailed carvings and gold, must be the Honorable Gunelde ter Bersker. She was in her late forties, tall, with short brown hair and narrow-set green eyes. On her right sat a pale blond priest of Yasinde's age, mid or late twenties. He was slight for a warrior of Rondra, the girl thought.

Thalionmel took a soldierly bow when she entered the room, now she was standing at attention about three strides in front of her examiners. Her heart beat wildly as she waited for the first question. The temple leader and the blond priest carefully examined the girl. Yasinde put her quill to parchment and looked intensely at Thalionmel.

"You are Thalionmel of Brelak?" the high priestess asked after a moment.

"Yes, Your Honor," the girl replied in a slightly hoarse voice. She chose to focus on a point between the priestess's brows, so that she would not have to look into her strict gray eyes, though seeming to do so.

"How old are you, child?"

"Seventeen cycles of Praios ago, I turned eleven, Your Honor."

"That is young for the examination," the priestess remarked softly, as if to herself, "You must not say 'Your Honor' after each question."

"Yes ma'am, Your Honor." Thalionmel bit her lip as she saw Yasinde smile out of the corner of her eye.

The first questions were very simple. They were about conduct in the temple, the words one uses to invoke the Goddess, and the correct form of address for the priests. Then the Honorable Gunelde asked Thalionmel to speak about her life. She wanted to know odd things, such as if there was a brook in Brelak, how many people lived in the manor, and which crops her father planted. She listened patiently to how Thalionmel had a sword in hand at three, and that she learned to ride shortly thereafter, but these facts did not seem to interest her especially. She did not ask much about Thalionmel's academic progress either; instead she asked detailed questions about her relationship to her adopted sister.

Thalionmel was beginning to wonder when the examination had begun. She estimated that half an hour had passed. "Cassim and Silvana were not examined this long. I'm probably being examined more thoroughly because I'm the youngest. If the priestess asks me questions about the church history or the Holy Order of the Theater, I'm sunk. I did not prepare for that."

"Who do you hate the most?" interrupted the voice of the temple leader. The question came so suddenly that the girl almost replied, "Quendan."

Quendan was a fellow student. He was thirteen and so dirty that it was repulsive to practice hand-to-hand combat with him. He was her partner in wrestling and boxing. Quendan had pimples on his chest and shoulders, and more than once while they were locked in wrestling his pus had gotten on Thalionmel's hands. He spoiled hand-to-hand combat for her and caused her performance to be below average. The boy also combed sugar water into his hair, a habit which was almost more repulsive to her than the pussy pimples. Quendan had written several emotional love letters to Thalionmel over the past six moons, all of which extolled his parent's wealth and his advantages. Yes, Quendan was the most despicable person Thalionmel knew, and she hated him with all her heart. Yet her answer was, "The Nameless One." It was her first lie of the examination. she did not know the Nameless One, and did not understand how everyone could hate someone they did not know, but because everyone hated him and feared him, she assumed that it was the answer that Honorable Gunelde wanted to hear. It was the first time the high priestess smiled.

"That's right, Thalionmel," she said. "One must hate the Nameless One. Now you can go."

Thalionmel stood there as if she had been struck by lightning. Failed! It only took a few seconds for her to realize it and then her lips began to quake. The girl bowed to the examiners and then turned to go. "Don't cry," she ordered herself. "Just don't cry!" As she reached the door she heard the voice of the high priestess behind her. "Follow the hall to the left, until you reach an empty room. There Knight Odil will grant you a pin and let you into the temple through the side door. Rondra be with you, child."

The girl walked to the room as if she were in a dream. A moment ago she thought that she had failed because of her obvious lie, and now here she was, about to look at the Goddess. For years she had desired to see the Temple of Victory from the inside. Now she felt uneasiness, almost panic at the prospect. The Honorable Gunelde may not have recognized her lie, but one cannot fool the Goddess. "Goddess Rondra," she began to pray, "from now on I want to conquer my hatred of Quendan. And I will hate the Nameless One to such a degree that the lie will be a truth."

She had reached the temple nave. His Honor Odil

smiled at her, and although his black eyes seemed to examine her quietly, he seemed much less strict and disturbing than he did only half an hour ago. "Rondra be with you, Your Honor." Thalionmel made a slight bow and the priest returned the gesture. Then he affixed the shiny silver lioness pin to her blue wool garrison student shirt. Thalionmel really would have liked to take the pin off and look at it in peace, but thinking it would be inappropriate, she merely glanced at the new emblem on her uniform.

"Thalionmel of Brelak, you will enter the temple through this door only this one time," explained Knight Odil gesturing toward an opening covered with heavy blue fabric, "that is unless you decide to join the order." He smiled again, softening the seriousness in his face. "The side door is reserved for the clergy and when you enter or leave the temple in the future you will use the main door. You have shown through the examination that you are prepared to enter the house of our Lady, so don't be afraid to do so. Lady Rondra is expecting you. You need not only love and honor her, but also fear her and strive for her. Never wake her anger, for her divine wrath is more powerful than the human mind can comprehend."

Although Thalionmel had heard these and similar words often, now it seemed that she understood for the first time that the ways of the Twelve were incomprehensible. The realization that no mortal could comprehend the Twelve, neither her nor the Honorable Gunelde; neither the Sword of Swords in far-off Perricum, nor the most experienced Rondra warrior. No one would understand more of the Lady than the edge of her little toe nail. That excited her. She felt how each tiny hair on her body stood up on end, and the more they did the more her uneasiness subsided.

"I'm ready, Your Honor," she said with a voice that was foreign to her. The priest pulled the curtain aside.

"Welcome to the house of the Goddess," he said, "Rondra be with you, Thalionmel of Brelak."

The first thing Thalionmel noticed when she opened her eyes, for she had them closed when she entered the room, was the brightness in the enormous hall. She had expected weak lighting similar to that of the garrison's dining hall, where candles were lit even by day so that the teachers and students could recognize the food on their plates. Here in Rondra's Hall of Victory, countless torches hung on the walls and on the columns that supported the ceiling. "It could hardly be brighter in the house of sublime Lord Praios," the girl thought. The light from the torches was reflected and magnified by a wealth of shiny weapons, shields, and helms decorating the temple's walls. "Who cleans and polishes the many hundred weapons? Is it the job of the novices or Rondra's servants?" she asked herself and immediately thought the question inappropriate, because in the meantime her eyes were fixed in the same direction of all the other eyes in the hall.

The statue of the Goddess stood in the middle of the temple, exactly under the enormous dome in the temple ceiling. Thalionmel could not say how many strides high or wide the temple was, she only knew that it was the tallest and widest hall she had ever seen. Even the statue exceeded her expectations. It was made of a light yellow stone, probably marble, without any decoration of gold or paint, she determined with surprise. Even though it was without colors, the girl thought the statue seemed to move a bit.

Thalionmel had not yet ventured from where she first stood. She was still one or two steps behind the door that led to the living quarters of the clergy. She still did not move. She let her eyes wander across the statue.

The Goddess had her profile to the girl, because the stone statue faced the main entrance. Thalionmel's eyes were even with the lower edge of the decorated pedestal on which the statue stood. In order to see the feet she had to look up slightly. She could see the right foot. She wore a light sandal, exposing the toes. In spite of its size, it was a very delicate toe. "The edge of the baby toe nail," thought Thalionmel, but she did not know what to make of this stream of thoughts.

The Goddess wore a sleeveless, flowing gown that fell almost to the floor near Thalionmel. Thalionmel was surprised that, other than the sword on which her right hand rested and the winged helmet, there was no other sign of her warring virtues.

The girl looked at the statue for a while before she noticed why the folds in the gown seemed to move as if with the Goddess's breath. It was because of the numerous light sources that illuminated the statue. In addition to the torches and candles in the temple, the pale light of the cool Tsa morning streamed in the arched windows of the dome and poured pale blue brightness over her head and shoulders. When a cloud went by, a torch went out, or a draft made the candles flicker, it seemed as if the gown rustled or the Goddess moved her arms or brow.

Even the dead stone seemed alive, and Thalionmel asked herself if it was because of its pale color, which was like a fair Tulamidian's skin, or because of its surface. The marble of her gown was smooth and matte like fresh linen, but where it represented her skin it was polished and shiny.

Finally, the girl gathered the courage to circle

the statue, but she maintained the same distance from it. At this hour of the day there weren't too many believers in the temple—there were only about two dozen men and women. Almost all were proudly wearing the symbols of their warriorhood. Thalionmel was embarrassed by her simple student's uniform and her age. She was the only child in the temple. She noticed a young novice in the aisle of the temple who was busy replacing the burnt-out tallow lamps and torches, but he was certainly fourteen and wore a sword on his belt and a golden band around his forehead.

No one even noticed the girl as she silently approached the believers standing or kneeling in a semicircle in front of the statue. Most of them were in intense silent dialogue with the Goddess, but some were mumbling their prayers so loudly that Thalionmel could clearly hear them as she walked by. To one side of the group stood a tall, emaciated woman warrior in a well-worn tunic. Her eyes were closed and in her hoarse voice she sang out a chorus of "Praise you, Lioness" with her hands extended to the ceiling.

When Thalionmel reached a point on the axis between the main entrance and the statue she went down on her left knee. She leaned back and looked up at the Goddess's eyes, which seemed to stare into the unseen distance. "Goddess Rondra, fill me," she began to pray silently. Only then did the girl see that the Goddess was wearing armor over her flowing robe. Her protection enclosed her shoulders and chest like a collar and ended in a double arch beneath her breasts. A fine pattern of scales was chiseled into the stone and the closure was fashioned in the form of a lioness's head. Her powerful neck rose majestically from the collar of armor. Curls framed the edge of her helmet, but the Goddess wore her hair in a braid down her back so that not a strand disturbed the line of her column-like neck.

Her chin and her slightly parted lips were soft and full, but her straight brows undermined any impression of softness that the chin or mouth created. The Goddess had her left hand on her hip and her left leg appeared naked between the folds of her gown.

"Red blood, holy blood, blood, cleanse me, so be it," mumbled Thalionmel and suddenly she noticed to her shock and dismay that she had said the words of the prayer without the full attention of her heart or mind. She lowered her head, closed her eyes, and tried again in her own words. "Goddess Rondra, incomprehensible warrior of the sky, forgive me my shortcomings and let me be your worthy servant," she prayed.

Thalionmel kneeled before the statue for a long time. She tried to think of nothing, to hope for nothing, and to feel nothing, not even the dull pain in her knee, which slowly turned to numbness. She wanted to be an empty vessel for the divine spirit. Suddenly something touched her shoulder and a sweet shock went through the girl. When she opened her eyes she saw the old woman, whose tunic had brushed Thalionmel's shoulder. The old woman looked at the girl with still, black eyes. White wild hair framed the dark face that seemed so familiar to Thalionmel. As she tried to remember how she knew the woman, she nodded a brief greeting, turned, and left the temple.

Then Thalionmel rose and began to slowly stride across the temple. Now she looked at the weapons on the walls and observed the inside of the halls from various angles. Lastly, she approached the base of the statue because she had noticed that the pedestal was decorated with a relief that she now wanted to examine closely. The front side showed a roaring lioness, the symbol of the Goddess, and the sides were decorated with pictures from battles. On the left side she saw an army of courageous warriors in a battle against a superior force of enormous enemies, and Thalionmel guessed that it was an image from the Battle at Trollzack. The right side depicted the four deities: Lord Praios, Efferd, and Ingerimm, as well as Lady Rondra. They stood above a sea of human and other forms, an image from the Battle of Brig-Lo. The image on the back was difficult to interpret. It showed high seas, lightning, and stormy clouds. In the shapes of the waves the girl thought she saw two wrestling forms, but she was not certain. Sometimes she saw them clearly and at other times they disappeared. "Perhaps it was an image of the Goddess's works and anger," thought the girl, "or perhaps it showed the marriage of the Goddess to Efferd, ruler of the sea." She decided that she would ask Yasinde about it.

As Thalionmel left the temple the eleventh hour was half over. The girl was happy that there was still a little time remaining before the common midday meal at the garrison. At this moment she just wanted to be alone. She felt strangely empty as if she had fasted for a few days and spent a sleepless night. The latter was true. "If only Zulhamin were here," she thought.

Her sister was the only person Thalionmel wanted to be with at this moment. Although she wanted to be alone, at the same time she felt an urge to tell a trusted friend about her first visit to the temple. Zulhamin was still her dearest friend. She had not grown very close to any of the other students. And just as she loved none of her peers, none of them loved her. "Quendan's courting was not love, and probably not even liking," she thought. He probably hated her as much as she hated him.

He had to know that he tortured her every time he tried to be near her. Quendan was the last person on ethra that she would tell about the examination and the Goddess.

All at once the girl felt deeply sad and as lonely as the loneliest person in the world. She aimlessly wandered through the streets full of people rushing about, bargaining, laughing, and arguing. She felt the sadness grow heavier and heavier on her soul. She blinked to drive the unwelcome burning tears from her eyelids when suddenly she saw Pagol.

"What is little Pagol doing here all alone in Neetha?" Thalionmel thought in surprise, as she blinked again. The boy stood against a wall along the harbor and looked out to the sea. The girl saw immediately that he was sad, but she could not say why she knew. "He's probably here with his parents and got lost," she thought. Although she had never thought of the saddler's son as her friend or playmate because he was so young, she was glad to see an old acquaintance.

"Hey, Pagol, what are you doing here?" she called as she ran towards him. The boy did not see her, and he did not even seem to have heard her. Now she was standing next to him and tapped him on the shoulder. "Hey, Pagol," she said again and the boy turned around. It was not Pagol. Thalionmel had never seen the boy before.

"Oh, excuse me," the girl said, blushing. "I confused you with someone else. I thought you were a boy I used to know." The boy's face did not look at all like Pagol's. He was older, perhaps ten and his pale face and short nose were covered with freckles. Just as the girl wanted to turn away she noticed the welts on the boy's naked legs. Some were fresh and red and some were older and blue. Thalionmel was surprised that she had not noticed them right away. The boy was freezing in a thin shirt. He shivered and his thin arms and legs were covered in goosebumps. "Why were you whipped, boy?" she asked instead of leaving.

The boy looked at her suspiciously, and for a moment it looked as if he wanted to run away. "He's probably a pickpocket and because he is so young they just whipped him instead of cutting off his hand," thought Thalionmel. Her curiosity was piqued. She had never met a real thief. "You can tell me, I'm a warrior and not a gossip like Quendan," she said encouragingly.

The girl expected a look of respect and was very surprised when the boy spit in the water with a look of disrespect. "You're lying," he replied, "you're not a warrior, you're too young, and you don't have a sword." Thalionmel felt her anger rising. The little urchin dared to call her a liar! She glared angrily at him, and made a fist. "You dare call me a liar," she wanted to say, but then she noticed that he was right. "I'm not a warrior, yet," she replied coolly and without theatrical pathos, "but I will be one soon, and then you'd better not call me a liar." The boy did not respond. He looked the girl over from top to bottom, then he looked back out to the sea. "Do you ever want to sail away, you . . . warrior?" he said after a while and pointed to a three-masted ship on the horizon. "I want to go to sea as a cabin boy."

Thalionmel thought about it. "I don't know, I've never thought about it," she replied. "Anyway, I have to finish school first. But why do you want to leave? Are they after you?"

The boy looked surprised. "Who would be after me?" he asked.

"Well, the guards or the people you stole from. Tell me, how does one become a thief and what is it like?" Thalionmel forgot that just a few moments ago she had wanted to punish the boy for his unfitting behavior, and now she smiled and looked at him, expecting an exciting tale. A real thief stood before her in flesh and blood; a thief, perhaps the member of a legendary guild of thieves, who would tell her of his dangers and adventures.

But the boy remained silent. He was silent so long that Thalionmel thought he had not heard her question. She was just about to repeat it when he began to speak.

"If you have never had enough to eat," he pronounced softly, "and you go to the bazaar and see a roll on the floor of the baker's stall, would you pick it up?" Without waiting for the girl's reply he continued, "And if there wasn't one there, would you not try to knock one from the pile with your sleeve as you walked by?"

Thalionmel wrinkled her brow a little and looked at the three-masted ship on the horizon as she thought about the boy's question, but he spoke before she could answer. "No, you wouldn't, because you are training to be a warrior and warriors are honest folk." There was much bitterness in the boy's voice. He made a fist of his right hand and struck the wall again and again. "And I'm sure you have enough to eat at the school, because rich people don't send their children to a school where they'd have to starve."

"We practice fasting and hold religious exercises," Thalionmel wanted to add, but she did not get the chance. The boy looked at her with a combination of curiosity, hatred, and admiration. "If I were as big and strong as you and went to the warrior school, then I would hit you, because you insulted me by calling me a thief," he said with his voice shaking. "But maybe I wouldn't. It would be a shame for your beautiful face." He suddenly turned away and strode off.

"Hey, wait!" called Thalionmel, almost unintentionally. The boy stopped and looked at her questioningly, and she said words that she had not wanted to say. "Please excuse me for accusing you of being a thief. Do you accept my apology?" The boy nodded and Thalionmel extended her hand to him.

Neither child knew what they should talk about or where to begin, so they just walked silently around the harbor. When Thalionmel caught a whiff of the fish stand, she noticed how hungry she was. The common meal had already begun and unless she hurried, her comrades would have eaten everything. She could explain her lateness with a long stay at the temple and a walk lost in thought. Everyone would understand.

When these thoughts went through the girl's head she felt her cheeks blush, and she saw out of the corner of her eye how the boy noticed this and tactfully turned his head. "What kind of strange, little fellow is he, both annoying and amazing at the same time, to be able to read my dishonorable, dishonest, and faint-hearted thoughts. Not only did he notice my shortcomings, he did not use it to his advantage," she thought.

Recognizing an opponent's weakness and not using it to your advantage, was seen as particularly honorable in battle against a knight, expressing the knightly quality of charity and forgiveness.

Thalionmel had often heard this phrase, but never had it seemed so appropriate. "Are you hungry?" the girl suddenly heard herself asking. The boy nodded.

"I'm always hungry," he said matter-of-factly. "Why do you ask?"

Thalionmel did not know. Did she hope that the boy would pull a loaf of white bread and fresh goat cheese out of his torn shirt and offer her some? "I'm hungry, too," she said. "And if we are both hungry, then we should eat something." She looked questioningly at the boy and he looked back with surprise. "Does that mean you have money and are going to buy us something to eat?"

Money? The girl already had every reason to blush, which angered her. Money! How did she think that she could get something to eat without money? Because she had always had enough to eat, and she never had to do anything to get it? And why did she mention food to this starving child? Because she knew in her head that there was hunger and misery in the world, but she had never felt it in her heart?

Full of expectations and hunger, the boy looked at Thalionmel. He opened his mouth a little bit as if he were ready to chew. "I do have a little money, but not here. It's at school," stuttered the girl. Angrily she thought of the silver and copper coins in the trunk in her locker. Although all students had to keep exact accounting of expenditures, no one would have had anything against alms at the temple.

At Thalionmel's words the boy's mouth closed to a small line and his expression seemed to be somewhere between disappointment and hate. She nervously patted her body as if to prove to the boy that she had no money, or in the unreasonable expectation of finding a hidden coin, but then her finger found something hard and round, and before she knew what she was doing, she had the button in her hand.

Her student's uniform was simply tailored and of plain blue fabric, without decoration or detail, but the buttons on her leggings were made of pure silver. "That's silver," said Thalionmel. "We'll be able to get something to eat for that, don't you think?" The boy reached for the button, looked at it carefully, bit on it, and gave it back to the girl.

"You want to trade your button for food?" he asked in surprise. "What will you say when they ask you what happened to it?" Thalionmel was just thinking about that and because she did not have an answer she shrugged. "You should think about that," the boy said as she subconsciously walked toward the good-smelling fish stand. "Perhaps you can tell them that someone stole it in the crowd, or that—"

"Don't you worry about what I will tell them,"

Thalionmel interrupted him sharply. "But I don't think I will lie."

At the fish stand, the boy asked for the button and had Thalionmel wait a short distance away. For a brief moment the girl thought that the boy wanted to take off with the loot, but he turned around and winked at her. Then he gave her a lesson in haggling. His loud negotiations with the fishmonger ended after the button changed owners several times, then finally disappeared into the man's purse. The fishmonger took two large, flat pieces of bread, split them in half, and then placed a fried fish in each. He used the other half as a lid, gave them to the boy, and then put something else in his hand, which immediately went into his trouser pocket.

The boy must have been terribly hungry, because even as he walked toward Thalionmel with his precious load carefully balanced, he could not keep himself from taking a few greedy bites from the top one. When he reached the girl he handed her the lower one without saying a word or interrupting his chewing and swallowing.

Thalionmel was also very hungry and she began to enjoy the sandwich. The two children walked silently through the harbor alleys as they chewed. At some point the girl felt an elbow in her side. He was gesturing at his pocket and when she reached in she found a few copper bits—the change. When she realized what it was, and that he wanted to give it to her, she put it back in his pocket.

Then the boy told Thalionmel the story of his life.

The boy had been a scribe's apprentice for the last six moons. The master was a horrible and miserly man. He let his few apprentices work to exhaustion and did not feed them sufficiently. Even the smallest oversight, such as a misspelled word or an ink spot on the parchment, or even the request for more bread was punished brutally.

His life used to be better, he said. But that was when his mother was still alive. His father was a servant in the Temple of Praios, and his mother used to wash and mend the priests' robes. Two years ago she suddenly fell sick and died. After that, his father was not himself. He stopped taking care of himself, his job, and his son, and sought comfort in Boltan and beer.

He had almost gambled away all their meager savings and possessions when an event occurred that changed the boy's life. One evening his father met a friendly and well-traveled Tulamidian in his favorite tavern. The man invited him to play a game of Boltan, and at first it seemed that his father would win back all his lost riches. There were stacks of silver crowns and copper bits piling up in front of him . . . until the tide turned and the dice no longer fell to his father's advantage. Then the dark-skinned stranger started winning. He won so much, the boy assumed the Tulamidian must have been using black magic. And so the impressive stacks shrank until father lost not only all his belongings, but had also given the stranger a promissory note for a staggering amount.

The boy would not talk about how his father paid his debts. Thalionmel assumed he did so dishonorably. In any case, one morning the father told the boy that he was going away on a trip, took him to the scribe, and left a few coins as tuition.

Because the boy could write well, he thought he would be well taken care of by the master. How wrong he was showed in the welts on the boy's body. They had been inflicted for absences, and the longer he stayed away, the worse the punishment. He said that he finally ran away for good yesterday, and that he was thinking about signing on to a cog or shivone as a cabin boy, but he had not yet dared. He did not know what to do and asked for her advice.

The request came as a surprise to Thalionmel, because she could not stop thinking about the punishment from his master, which lay ahead.

The children sat on empty beer barrels in a brewery's yard and looked out at the sea. No one noticed them and the warm Tsa sun shone on their backs as they enjoyed the play of colorful sails on the blue-gray water.

"I think you should become a scribe, if you can write as well as you say," Thalionmel finally said. "I don't write very well, but that doesn't matter. Cabin boy just isn't the right job for you, if you will forgive me. You're a bit too small and delicate for that. In addition, I've heard that the conditions are by far worse on ships than with the worst master. Although I don't recommend that you go back to your master. He seems to be a horrible person." She stopped to think and the boy remained silent as well.

"Why don't you go to the Praios School?" she asked.

"To the Praios School?" The boy looked at her questioningly. "That costs tuition, don't you know that?"

"If you sign up as a novice, then they will take you as you are, and if you decide—" The girl bit her lip as she noticed she was about to advise the boy to do something dishonest, but the boy was already shaking his head.

"I can't. I haven't heard the calling, and you can't lie to them. 'Priests can see into your head,' my father always said."

Thalionmel realized that she ought to head back to the garrison. It occurred to her that every year there were a few students at the garrison school whose parents weren't noble or wealthy. They were the children of simple peasants or craftsmen. They were taken because they showed talent and desire, and did not have to pay tuition. "At my school there are students who are poor and don't have to pay tuition, perhaps that is also the case at the Praios School," she said with hesitation. "They can join the garrison after they graduate if they want to, but they don't have to." She paused before continuing. "If you learn the arts of a scribe at the Praios School, like calligraphy and drawing decorative boarders and plants and animals as every good scribe should, then you could offer your services to the temple to thank the priests and Lord Praios for their generosity."

The boy drummed with his feet against the barrel, as he thought about what the girl had said. "You think I should go to the temple school and ask if they would take someone like me?" he finally said. "But they will know me as Ettel's son."

"If your father did something wrong, it is not your fault and no one will blame you," replied Thalionmel. "Tell the priests about your life, just as you told me, and then show them an example of your work."

"You mean now?" interrupted the boy.

"Why not?" said the girl, "and if you don't want to go alone, I'll join you."

Thalionmel had spoken without thinking. She had to go back to the garrison. It was already into the fourth hour, and if she were on time for the religious exercises, her punishment would not be too severe. But now she had promised to accompany the boy, and she had to do so. She wanted to, and suddenly it was clear to her that she was enjoying this strange adventure, the freedom, and the disobedience. "I can speak for you," she said, "and probably better than you because of my position and age, and they say I'm well spoken." The boy nodded.

"Then let's go to the temple," he said sliding off the barrel.

As the two walked to the Temple of Praios, Thalionmel told the boy about her life. She began at the present with the lashings and arrest she expected, and she avoided using the word fear, but did admit that it made her uncomfortable. Then she spoke of the loneliness she had felt after leaving the temple, and the details of her first visit to the house of the Goddess, which was so strange and disappointing. She talked about the examination, the lie and Quendan, and she only stopped when they reached the bazaar in front of the temple.

Here Thalionmel suggested that they take some refreshment before inquiring at the temple. The boy agreed immediately. He seemed to be hungry again, and the girl wanted to have some time to collect her thoughts and choose her words for the priests. She counted their money. It was not much, but the boy was good at bargaining and quickly returned with a snack of sufficient beer and millet bread.

When they reached the temple, Thalionmel did the talking. It was her turn to use the correct words, and say her name at the right moment. Soon the children were standing in front of the priest. With a pounding heart and a steady voice Thalionmel presented his case. She did not lower her eyes once, even though the priest's eyes were more strict and intense than those of the Honorable Gunelde.

"Such horrible and unfair punishment cannot please Praios," she ended her speech. "That is why I ask you, Your Honor, to take this boy and disregard his origins and poor clothes." The priest nodded thoughtfully.

"No, my daughter, a person should not be judged by his clothes," he said finally. "You are correct, but I do suggest that you take a closer look at your own. You are missing a button." He smiled at Thalionmel and the girl blushed.

"Now come, my son, follow me," the priest said turning to the boy. "We will test you and then decide on your application. You, my daughter, should go home and pray for your soul." He gestured for the boy to follow him, and then turned to go.

The boy seemed confused. It all went so fast.

He looked hopelessly at Thalionmel.

"Good luck, Boy, and may the Twelve bless you," Thalionmel said, extending her hand. The boy did not understand the gesture. He patted Thalionmel on the shoulder.

"Farewell," he said with a hoarseness in his voice. "I hope we will see each other again."

※ ※ ※

Thalionmel did not hurry back to the garrison. Her steps were heavy and slower the closer she came to the dark building. She had not often been late. Only a few times at home and only once during her nine months at school, and the punishment awaiting her would be the worst she had ever known. She was afraid. Very afraid. And the knowledge of her shortcomings did not lessen her fear. It made no difference that she knew that the punishment would be over almost as soon as it began and that she could use the days in jail for thinking. The fear remained.

Thalionmel decided to tell Sergeant Birsel the truth and leave out no details. She would just not mention the strange boy. She did not want to give the appearance that she had made her mistake out of charity.

When the girl reached the door to the sergeant's

quarters she realized that she had not asked the boy for his name, nor did he know hers. She wondered if she would ever see him again.

Then she knocked.

7

THE NOON MEAL had just ended, and Sergeant Birsel sent for Thalionmel to give her the letter. The parchment with the broken seal proclaimed *To Thalionmel of Brelak, student at the Margrave's Garrison of Neetha*. When the girl recognized her mother's handwriting her heart jumped with joy. A letter from home! She blushed as she always did when she was terribly excited (or ashamed). She thanked her superior and teacher with a brief bow and waited to be dismissed, feeling like she was about to loose her soldierly demeanor and posture. Luckily, Sergeant Birsel didn't seem to notice. The burly, forty-five-year-old woman yawned deeply and then waved at the girl to move on. After another bow Thalionmel carefully slid the precious parchment into her shirt, for a warrior should carry nothing in her hands but a weapon, and left the dining hall. As soon as the heavy door closed behind her, she hurried down the dark hallway, anxious to go to her hideaway where she would secretly read the latest news from home.

"Today is my lucky day," she thought. "After the lunch break we will fence with the two-handed swords; and tomorrow is another good day, since it's the third Praiosday of the moon, and I will be allowed to go visit my sister, Zulhamin."

The thought that the letter could contain bad news did not even cross the girl's mind. It would be like all the other letters she had received from her mother since she enrolled at the school sixteen months ago. First would come general greetings and blessings, then some advice and warnings in spiritual and secular affairs, the latest gossip from Brelak, and, after the farewell, it would have a cheerful footnote from her father, counterbalancing her mother's harshness.

When Thalionmel reached the end of the corridor, she looked around with her heart pounding from running, joy, and excitement. She did not want to be seen going up the steep, narrow, spiral staircase that lead to the roof of the house.

In the attic Thalionmel had a secret hideaway where she went whenever she wanted to be alone. She missed the pond in Brelak where she used to sit among the reeds, unbeknownst to anyone but her sister, and as she climbed the steps she felt increasingly homesick. "But I'm so happy about the letter, how can I be sad?" She stopped for a moment to think. "No," she decided, "I'm not sad. Longing and sadness are not the same thing, even if they leave the same hot feeling in my chest and a burning behind my eyes." She continued on her way up the dark spiral staircase. After a few steps it grew lighter and she knew that she would soon be three-quarters of the way to the top.

The small window near the top was not much wider than an embrasure. Its sole purpose was to fill the staircase with light, because there was nothing to defend in the middle of the garrison. Thalionmel lifted herself up to look out the opening. She sneezed as a ray of sun tickled her nose. During the midday break, it was quiet in the yard. She noticed a few soldiers and servants sitting in front of the horse stable engrossed in dice. In a shadowy corner of the kitchen garden, a few boys and girls busily plucked chickens for tomorrow's meal, and on the distant battlement she made out the silhouettes of some of her fellow students on guard patrol. Thalionmel would have liked to sit in the window and read the letter, but it was too narrow to be comfortable. After one more look around she continued up the steep stairs as quickly as she could. She was anxious to read the precious news.

The attic used to be a storage area for wheat. Now,

since the new storehouse had been built, the attic was unused. Only the remains of a winch on the wall gave a clue about the garret's past. The last days had been very hot and humid, and Thalionmel hesitated for a moment before she opened the hinged hatch. When she put her head through the opening, the heat and the lack of fresh air almost took her breath away. She had second thoughts about retreating to the cool staircase, but her desire for absolute privacy made her continue. Stepping into the attic she felt her skin grow stickier and within seconds small drops of sweat trickled down her back.

The attic was in surprisingly good shape. The rafters and ridge beam were of heavy stone oak, blackened by age, but free of rot. Only a few of the wooden shingles were missing, just enough to light the room and give the floor an odd pattern of yellow stripes and spots.

Avoiding any extraneous motion, Thalionmel slowly went to her secret spot, her steps heavy as if she were wading through water. She shoved four loose shingles aside to let a rectangle of light shine on the planks. The additional opening in the roof took away none of the heat's laming power and not a whisper of fresh air stole in as she had hoped. Only the dust particles and a yellow spider with green splashes seemed to loom above the heat; the dust was dancing happily in the sunshine and the spider was nimbly wrapping something into a cocoon with its eight legs.

After Thalionmel dried her hands on her leggings, she carefully pulled the letter from her shirt and peeled off the ribbon with the rest of the seals. Before she unrolled the letter, she wiped her forehead with her sleeve so that no drops of sweat would soil it or make it illegible. There were two full pages, she noted in surprise before she began reading.

Brelak Manor, the fourteenth of Efferd

Dear Daughter! May our Goddess Rondra always be with you and guide you on your way!

Thalionmel held the parchment closer to her eyes because the blazing light and the strange burning in her eyes from her sweat made it difficult to recognize the small letters and she blinked as she continued.

How are you, my dear child? Are your body and soul healthy? Your dear father and I pray daily for your health, because we hear so seldom from you. Please let us know if you need more money to pay a courier, and keep track of your expenses. Your adopted sister Zulhamin, as you well know, receives less allowance than you do and she has enough to send a messenger twice a month.

Thalionmel was overcome with a sense of guilt as she read her mother's critique of her writing habits. It had been over a month since she had dropped a note to her dear parents. She thought of home often and sometimes the longing was so strong that it was almost physically painful. At the same time she felt no desire to reach for her writing utensils. Ink and quill always angered her. They were her enemies, unlike the sword that was so steady in her hand. If she could only get her hand used to holding a quill. Alas, each time she sat down to write to her parents, her mind would suddenly draw a blank at the sight of the empty parchment. Ashamed, she continued reading.

If you prefer taking your money to the temple instead of using it for a courier that is honorable, and we certainly don't want to chastise you for that, but remember that the Goddess prefers a pure heart and honor to shiny coins.

Thalionmel felt like she had been caught. How did her mother know that she had done that more than once?

When giving alms it is difficult for a child like you to know what to do. Ask the priests and follow their advice. Enough said about financial matters. I also want to remind you to practice hard and to always obey the rules of our Goddess and your teachers and superiors. Have you already been introduced to the two-handed sword? If so you will have noticed that the use of this weapon is more difficult and takes much more practice than the regular sword. Please send us an exact accounting of your progress in your studies soon.

"I will certainly do that, dear mother," thought Thalionmel. "I will write tomorrow, I promise." Then she continued to read.

Before I get to the actual business of this letter, I want to tell you what has happened in Brelak since my last note. Be strong, dear daughter, because these are sad tidings that I must tell. Susa Westfahr, our loyal nanny, went to Boron three cycles of Praios ago. The unhealthy and hot winds from the Khom desert had poisoned her blood and took her strength. There was nothing we could do to save her. We even sent for a doctor from Neetha, but his bloodletting and tinctures came too late for the poor thing. The fever was too strong and within a week it claimed her body and soul. We buried her yesterday, and the entire village cried. It was a beautiful service and your father spoke and prayed almost as if he were a priest of Boron.

Thalionmel lowered the parchment and looked through the opening above to the blue Efferd sky. Something wet ran down her cheek and she did not know if it was sweat or a tear. Her good nanny was dead and she would never see her again. Her mind understood the meaning of the words, but her heart did not. Just four months ago, during her last visit home, Susa was alive and well. She had proudly shown her new blue apron and bonnet that father gave her for her tsafest. Now, in two months, when she would go home for her mother's tsafest, she would find the nanny's room empty. "We all have to die some day," she thought. "Susa, my parents, Zulhamin, that's the will of the Twelve." Again she felt the moisture on her cheeks and the burning in her eyes. "I would have liked to see her one more time, to hear her say 'Child, you have grown, you'll be bigger than the lady someday.'"

The girl looked at the spider's web. The spider was gone, presumably hiding behind the beams waiting for its next victim, only the cocoon hung in the middle of the delicate web. "You will die, too, you pretty green trapper," Thalionmel thought defiantly. "You just don't know it yet." Reluctantly she returned to her reading. She squinted as she continued.

But the untimely death of poor Susa is not the only bad news I have to report. Good old Master Gisbrecht, my fencing tutor, has tasted Rahja's wine for the first time, and he will follow his fiancée, a merchant woman from Pertakis, to the north soon. As you can see my child, nothing stays the same. I'm not looking forward to finding a new teacher, because over the course of the years I have come to enjoy Master Gisbrecht's company and fencing style. But I must have a new teacher, so I will stay nimble and won't be overcome by laziness. Otherwise all is well in Brelak. Three children were born—the Daskes had a boy, and the Lechdans had twins. Elgor was kicked by the new stallion, but it's nothing serious. And your father and I are well, for which we must thank the Twelve. Now I will turn to the real purpose of my letter.

That was the end of page one. The second page contained much smaller writing and Thalionmel had to hold it close to her eyes to be able to read it. For a moment her concern about Susa's death gave way to curiosity.

Do you remember Zordan Foxfell? He is my half brother, my father's bastard son, your uncle, and probably your adopted sister's father. You have seen him but once when he presented you with the pretty wooden figures that you enjoy so much. Recently, he paid us another visit to Brelak Manor. We had not heard from him for more than eleven cycles of the Twelve. In fact, we had already suspected that he was in Boron's arms. Anyway, he did not pay us a visit to catch up with what's happening in our family. He was purely interested in financial matters, which it took us a while to discover, although his true motives were poorly hidden behind his colorful turns of phrase. I gather that he had his eyes on my small inheritance, a small piece of land in Malur. He also intimated that it would behoove me to pay him a small annuity should he get into financial trouble.

It's not easy for me to tell you what you need to

know. Your Uncle Foxfell is not a good person. He is a gambler and philanderer who neglects the warring arts, as well as any other honest work. He has dealings all over the world, but I don't care to know the details. His profits would be sufficient if he didn't squander everything in games and pleasures, of which I want to know even less than his business affairs. You should know that he not only wasted my father's generous inheritance while he was still alive, but also rode a precious race horse to death. He even denies that your father and I gave him fifty ducats a few years ago. The bitterness my half brother's dealings and words awoke in us was horrible, but it is not the reason for telling you these bad things about him.

Dear daughter, Susa Westfahr's sudden death teaches us that Boron can call on each of us at any time. Golgari could be sent for your dear father or me tomorrow, in the next moon, or at some other unexpected time, because the ways of the Twelve are incomprehensible to us. That is why your father and I decided to make arrangements for our death, as far off as it may be. We want to do it in writing and seal it so that there can be no misunderstandings or illegitimate claims. As our biological daughter, you would not only be the primary mourner, but also the primary heir. Now read carefully this summary of our will. The entire document would be too long for this letter.

Zordan Foxfell is excluded from our inheritance. For

reasons mentioned above, he will not receive anything. Your adopted sister, who went by her mother's name, Plotz, shall from now on be called Zulhamin of Brelak. After our death, the lands in Malur shall be hers, as well as a yearly annuity of sixty ducats from the earnings in Brelak. That shall be paid to her regardless of her earnings in dance, so that when the inheritance is divided by five, three parts will be yours, and two parts will be Zulhamin's. Also, your father and I grant you the opportunity to contest our will, but know this: It would disappoint us and it would disappoint the Twelve if you were hard-hearted toward your sister.

"What are you accusing me of, Mother?!" thought Thalionmel almost angrily. "Me hard-hearted toward Zulhamin? She is my sister. What is mine is hers. Why I would share Brelak Manor with her and everything that comes with it when . . ." No! She did not want to think about it, not about her parents dying nor about the inheritance. She did not want the money, and it seemed sick and unnatural to think about the family fortune while her parents were still alive. Uneasily she returned to the letter.

I have to tell you one more thing about Zordan Foxfell. My half brother told us he will be spending the near future in the south of Lovely Field. Because we did not part in anger or feud, it may be that he returns to Brelak as soon as he finds his purse empty. I would not deny him admittance, for he is my brother and only living relative. But I have to warn you, it is likely that you will meet your uncle during your stay at Brelak Manor. Beware of him. You could find him appealing. He is handsome and knows how to be flattering and speak courteously.

"A handsome man? Never!" determined Thalionmel. "I could never fall for a rogue who rode a horse to death. Nor do I find courteous tongues particularly appealing." Her mother's letter ended here. After the closing, a short note from her father followed.

My most precious little warrior! Accept this embrace from your old father and the request to write to your lonely parents a little more often. The Twelve be with you, dear child. Once again, our good Lady Peraine blessed us with the prospect of a bountiful harvest. The wheat has grown tall and the apples, pears, quince, and beets are plump and standing or hanging, as the case may be. The harvest will be here soon. The doctor says I am too fat, although he doesn't put it quite in these terms. He advised me to enjoy lighter cuisine, so that I will no longer be bothered by shortness of breath. Anyway, the upshot is that I have to fast, and I don't know if that will be very pleasurable for our Ladies Travia and Peraine, good old Titina, and myself.

Many happy greetings from your loving father, Durenald of Brelak.

Thalionmel let the sheet glide to the ground. The

heat had tired her and the letter with the sad and strange news also did its part. The least of her worries was that her father's figure was a bit too round and that he would have to avoid the pleasures of the palate, although she was not completely indifferent to his plight. As long as Thalionmel could remember, her father had never said no to a good meal. She closed her eyes and clearly saw him before her, praising Titina's culinary arts with a glass of wine in his right hand and a goose drumstick in the left, his forehead beaming with perspiration and eyes shining with pleasure; chiding mother for eating "daintily like a sparrow" rather than reaching "like a soldier." Perhaps he would grow melancholic or grumpy from fasting, she thought.

After Thalionmel read the letter a second time, she placed the sheets on top of each other, stroked them flat, and folded them twice. Then she got up to get her secret letter collection from its hiding place.

The collection of private documents was in a folder of dark wax cloth that measured about fifteen by twenty fingers. It was jammed between the beams just a few strides from where she sat. Thalionmel had to reach to grab it, and her moist fingers slipped on the waxen cloth the first try. Annoyed, she wiped the burning sweat from her forehead, dried her hands, and tried it again, but this time she pulled so hard the cord that held the packet shut broke, and the contents landed on the dusty floor.

Thalionmel stomped her foot. She could have cried from anger. All her treasured letters, soiled and dirty! She stood still for a moment and watched the dust settle on the floor and parchment. Then she began to collect the pages of various sizes. It was tedious and dirty work, and when Thalionmel finally carried her treasures over to the light she felt the grimy layer of dust and sweat on all of her bare skin. Now she would have to bathe before fencing lessons. First, however, she had to order the letters without damaging them with her dirty fingers any worse than they already were. She paused for a moment to think. Then she leaned her head to one side and pulled off her shirt. She turned it inside out and used the damp linen to wipe off her hands and face. A glance through the opening in the roof told her that she still had more than an hour before class started. She could complete her work without having to rush.

It turned out that there was less damage than she thought. Most letters could be returned to their original condition by dusting them off. Sixteen moons of the past were piled up before Thalionmel and now and again she had to smile when her eyes caught a familiar line. "I can't allow myself to get caught up in this!" she said to herself. "Otherwise I will never finish in time."

It was not difficult to put the pages in chronological order, because all of the letters from Brelak were dated. Whenever a note carefully written in an unpracticed hand fell out, her heart cramped with grief. It was from Susa and it said, *My dear pett! It is lonlie her without you and your dear sister. May the twelf watch over you! Your Nany Susa Westfahr.*

Thalionmel closed the folder. She tied the ends of the broken cord and made a bow, but instead of getting up to take the package back to its place she stayed still and continued looking at the floor. There, just a few steps away she saw a letter she had not collected. She could tell by the size and color that it was not from Brelak, but she did not recognize the writing. "It must be from Zulhamin," she thought. But that couldn't be, she had not missed any of her sister's letter. With a sigh she stood up and was glad that she had not yet put her shirt back on. When she picked up the sheets and held them up close to identify the handwriting, she was surprised at first, but then she shook her head and smiled as she remembered. It was addressed *To the blonde girl, whose name is perhaps Talimall of Brekla.*

Thalionmel had not thought about the boy for

all those moons, yet when she recalled the strange afternoon in Tsa she saw the pale, dirty, freckled face clearly before her and she wondered how she could have completely forgotten him. The letter was beautifully written, with decorative initials on every line. And it was thanks to this letter that she spent only one day of her three-day sentence in detention. Quendan, her archenemy, had given the letter to Sergeant Birsel and reported what little the boy had said at the gate.

The corporal punishment, of course, could not be undone, but Thalionmel found five strokes with the Brabak cane to be fair and reasonable for her inexcusable absence and the intentional damage to her student's uniform. At least that's what she believed then, as she took the punishment with her teeth clenched. Only with the last stroke was she no longer able to suppress a soft moan, which she remembered with shame.

Before the girl put the letter with the others, she read the lines again which she had almost completely forgotten. *Dear Patron*, read the salutation, and she smiled to herself at the unusual formulation. Patron. Only a scribe's apprentice could think of that. After the usual blessing followed news that the boy had passed the exam and was accepted as a student at the Temple of Praios, as well as an extended thank you for her help. The letter ended with a compliment of Thalionmel's intelligence, beauty, courage, and a farewell. There was no signature. Back then Thalionmel wondered if the boy had forgotten it in haste or if he wanted to keep it secret. Now she was certain that it was the latter, for a practiced scribe, who forms letters so cleanly and delicately, and writes such pleasing sentences, would not make such a mistake.

Since he never asked, Quendan did not know the boy's name either, although he immediately realized who was meant by "Talimell of Brekla." After all, the boy had offered a good description of her appearance and manner. Then Quendan ran to the Sergeant and told her what he knew and showed her the letter.

Just a half hour later Thalionmel was summoned by Sergeant Birsel, who handed her the letter with an angry expression and demanded an explanation from her. The girl was so overjoyed to find out the contents of the letter—less about the thanks and beautiful words, than about the boy's decision to finally run away from his evil master—she beamed with happiness and her voice was cheerful as she gave her report. After a warning never again to omit any facts from a report, she was released. "You could have spared both of us the punishment, Thalionmel of Brelak, if you had told the whole truth from the beginning," the sergeant said. "In any case, your honor is restored and now you may go." Her superior's last words were soothing for the girl's soul, because she had spent the night awake worrying about her honor.

"Yes, yes, my honor," thought Thalionmel with a sigh, carefully cleaning the parchment and placing it with the others. "It's not that simple. I'm never certain that my deeds are truly honorable, and even less so with my thoughts." She noticed that the heat had begun to make her sleepy, and that her thoughts were becoming as slow as her movements. If she stayed in the attic any longer, she would spend the first hour of instruction with the two-handed sword half asleep. And so, after carefully putting away the package, she descended.

⚜ ⚜ ⚜

When Thalionmel entered the fencing hall, her hair was still moist and sticking to her head. She was one of the first. Only Praiodane and Quendan were waiting with rosy cheeks for the class to begin. With a quick nod of the head she greeted her classmates and joined them, but she stood far enough away to make it clear that she did not want to talk to them. She stood comfortably with her weight on her right leg and her right hand on her hip as she awaited the arrival of Sergeant Birsel and the other students.

But Quendan ignored the girl's body language and went up to her. He was not as disgusting as he used to be, she had to admit, and ever since she had made fun of his hair in anger, he stopped using the sugar water in it. Now his red-brown hair fell straight and thick almost to his shoulders. He had less pimples now, too. There were only a few pale purple marks on his forehead to remind her of his earlier skin problems.

"Where were you?" he whispered. "I looked for you in the writing hall because I thought that you might want to answer the letter, but you were neither there nor in the dormitory."

"Where are the two-handers?" replied Thalionmel, hoping to change the subject. As soon as she had entered the hall she had eagerly looked for the weapons, but to her disappointment there were only wooden sticks of various length against the wall.

"What?" Quendan looked at Thalionmel in surprise. "The two-handed swords? Oh, we will probably have to get them from the armory ourselves. Or we will practice with the wooden swords over there against the wall. Anyway, you didn't answer my question. Where were you? Was there bad news from home?" Quendan seemed more concerned than curious, but regardless Thalionmel did not really want to talk to him. She looked past him with her mouth drawn tight.

"My nanny died," she finally said quietly.

"I'm sorry to hear that." Quendan lowered his head and kicked at the ground. He secretly reached for the girl's hand and gave it a quick squeeze, but Thalionmel pulled it away and crossed her arms in front of her chest. "Why are you sorry?" she asked gruffly. "You didn't even know her."

"I'm sorry for you," Quendan said turning away. Without changing his expression he stood between the girls and looked, as they did, at the door.

Thalionmel knew that she had hurt her comrade's feelings. It had been her intention, as though she could make her worries less by passing them on to him. "It's his own fault," she told herself, "because he spied on me and asked curious questions." She did not have much more time to reflect, because just then the rest of the students entered the fencing hall. They arrived one by one or in small groups. Delicate Fenja was already fourteen, but she had to fence with the eleven- to thirteen-year-olds because of her size. Close on her heals was dark Brin, in his usual good mood and sloppily buttoned shirt. Then came Gaftar, Erlan, and Parionor who were engaged in a hot debate about the new game from the north, Imman. Next came the twins Efferdane and Eboreus, of good form and so alike that if they were the same sex it would have been impossible to tell them apart, followed by the

Tulamidian merchant's daughter, Palmeya, and her suitors, Leomar and Raul.

Shortly after the students entered, Sergeant Birsel stepped into the hall with a two-handed sword on her back. It grew quiet. The boys and girls quickly took up their places according to height and stood at attention. They greeted their superior in unison, "Rondra in greeting, Lady Sergeant!"

"Rondra in greeting!" she replied and then inspected the students with her arms crossed behind her back. She looked long and hard through her amber-colored eyes at each one of them, from head to toe, without giving a hint as to her assessment of appearances.

Inspection was the least pleasurable part of the class, because no one knew if they would be struck with the crop in the sergeant's belt for even the smallest oversight and then punished with expulsion from class or, even worse, writing an essay.

Thalionmel had taken little time to get herself and her clothes in order. She stole a glance down to see if she would discover anything that might catch her superior's attention.

"Thalionmel of Brelak!" The girl flinched, albeit barely noticeable as the dark voice called out her name. "Is there something on the ground that is more interesting than my fencing lesson?"

"No, Lady Sergeant!" Thalionmel tried to stand

straighter and not blush as she returned her superior's gaze.

"Then why are you looking at the floor instead of straight ahead as required?"

"I was checking my shoelaces, Lady Sergeant."

"Why didn't you check them before class?"

"I did, Lady Sergeant, I just wanted to be sure."

Thalionmel felt the embarrassing redness climbing into her cheeks and she only hoped that her comrades would not discover it. Sergeant Birsel inspected the girl for a while and then she gave her well-worn speech on the soldierly virtue of discipline, the foundation of the military. Without looking away from the girl, she spoke of the horrible consequences of a lack of discipline in the field and she told the old tale of the guard who was to blame for the death of the entire battalion, because he fell asleep on watch. Then she turned to the subject of self-control and the power of will: the sisters of discipline, before coming back to the issue at hand—poorly tied shoes, followed by the subject of poorly tied splints. While on the subject, the sergeant also remarked that someone, who sloppily buttoned his shirt, could hardly be certain of the proper placement of his armor. "Isn't that right, Brin Exbreaker?"

"Well, now she got around to poor Brin," thought Thalionmel with relief.

"Yes, ma'am, Lady Sergeant," he replied. His voice

sounded a bit hoarse, and it was not loud, but clear enough to understand, but the sergeant held her left hand behind her ear and leaned toward the boy.

"I can't hear you, Brin Exbreaker," she thundered.

Although Brin, who was almost three fingers smaller, stood four people down from her, she could feel the boy cringe. The twelve-year-old's voice was changing, and after he cleared his throat he repeated, "Yes, ma'am, Lady Sergeant," and it sounded high and shrill. For a brief moment a satisfied smile crossed the sergeant's face, but it was gone so fast that Thalionmel wondered if she had really seen it.

"So you agree with me," the soldier continued, "that someone who buttons his shirt badly would also be careless with the fitting of his armor?" She fixed her eyes on the boy with her brow furrowed.

"Yes, ma'am, Lady Sergeant . . . I mean . . . I . . ."

"Do you agree with me or not, Brin Exbreaker? It's up to you."

"Poor Brin," thought Thalionmel. Sergeant Birsel was apparently having one of her worse days. The sergeant was from Grangor and suffered under the heat. Whoever was her victim on a day like this had to ask the Twelve for mercy. Uneasy silence hung in the fencing hall, because it was not clear if Brin would be the victim. The gifted boy had clearly been Sergeant Birsel's pet for the last moons, so it could all be show. At any moment the superior could fixate on the spot of dirt on Gaftar's cheek or on Praiodane's sloppy legging laces, because she saw them, too.

"I meant to say . . . Lady Sergeant, I mean . . ." His last words jumped an octave. Embarrassed, he grew silent. But Sergeant Birsel gave him no time to collect his voice and thoughts.

"Brin Exbreaker," she railed into him, "we don't want to waste the day Rondra and Praios gave us listening to your stuttering. Because it seems that you cannot decide, you should take the time this evening to write about discipline in general and correct soldierly uniforms in particular. I expect," her voice grew a bit louder, "twelve cleanly written lines on this topic by tomorrow."

Twelve lines! By Rondra, that was a lot. Thalionmel was ashamed at the relief that Brin, not she, was punished by having to write an essay. "It's easier for Brin to write than for me," she assured herself, "and a badly buttoned shirt is much worse than a glance at the ground."

"At ease, soldiers!" Sergeant Birsel called suddenly. "Let's begin with the class." With these almost friendly words the tension eased among the thirteen students. Some exhaled audibly, others scraped their feet on the floor and fiddled with their hair or clothes. There was nothing more to fear today, except for a painful stroke of the crop for a fencing or posture error.

"Today's lesson will be an introduction to the history, meaning, and use of the most noble of all weapons—the two-handed sword," Sergeant Birsel began as she undid the ties. She showed the students the nine-span-long sword, which they were allowed to hold one by one.

Thalionmel was the third-largest student and one of the first to hold the impressive weapon in her hands. With a self-assured smile, she noticed how difficult it was for Eboreus and Quendan to lift the sword over their heads. When it was her turn, she had to admit that she also was unable to do so. Even a regular sword was too large and heavy for a student their age, and the two-hander weighed almost twice as much.

"Soldiers, take note," Sergeant Birsel said after all the students had seen and held the sword. "Now that you have all had the queen of weapons in your hands, listen to its history."

Thalionmel was disappointed. She had hoped that after the examination they would take up practical instruction. Even a practice fight with wooden swords would have been better than a lecture. But as soon as the teacher spoke her first words, her disappointment faded. Sergeant Birsel's lecture imparted new information and moved the girl's heart. She spoke of the Goddess Rondra, who created the first two-handed sword through her divine will, and she explained how it became her favorite weapon. The sergeant spoke of the Battle of Brig-Lo, quoting the holy scriptures, saying, "The Goddess herself mowed down half of the forces of the heathen Hela with one swift stroke of her powerful flaming sword, sending them back to their home beyond hell."

Sergeant Birsel interrupted her lecture to explain to the students that the term "flaming sword" in the ancient text meant a "flamed sword," and began to describe the form and advantages of such a blade. Thalionmel knew this already. She had carefully studied her mother's weaponry books, so for a brief moment she let her mind wander. She pictured the battlefield at Brig-Lo and the merciless armies at war. The warriors were a dark mass of moving bodies, just as threatening as the black clouds gathering on the horizon. On a far-off hill she saw the horrible, heathen Hela, her arms above her head and surrounded by bolts of flashing light, which she used to command her lowly creatures. Then in the middle of the fight, she saw the Goddess—powerful, white, and blazing, with a golden blade in her right hand. The picture faded and suddenly it was no longer the Goddess wading through the sea of bodies, but Thalionmel herself. She held the two-handed sword high over her head, ready for its deadly strokes . . .

What was that? Thalionmel cringed at the blasphemous image in her head. She did not call it up, at least not intentionally. Was it her punishment for daydreaming during class, or perhaps a test? Confused she shook her head to be able to think and listen clearly.

Sergeant Birsel had come back to the original subject, the divine origins of the two-handed sword. "So now you understand, students," she continued "that a two-hander does not belong in the hands of a mercenary. Such blasphemous atrocities are unheard of in Lovely Field, but there are reports of mercenary troops in the Central Empire who fence with the two-handed sword. These godless amateurs, as I call them, are not punished for their shameful act, but are instead paid double, and call themselves double mercenaries." She snorted and looked for approval from each of them. The students nodded.

"It's correct to nod, soldiers," the sergeant continued, "because only a knight, a warrior of standing or academic training, may wield a two-handed sword! And to see a commoner sitting on an old nag in full armor . . ." she paused briefly to give the students a chance to cough or giggle politely, ". . . should be as ridiculous to us as the sight of a mercenary with a two-handed sword."

Then Sergeant Birsel continued on about knightly duels and honor, but this part of the lecture was not satisfying to Thalionmel because it did not answer her questions.

"Enough theory, soldiers. Now let's turn to the practical part of our lessons." With these words Thalionmel was wide awake and stood at attention, although it was not required. She watched intently as Sergeant Birsel gave a demonstration of the postures, grips, strokes, and attacks. Instead of a dry presentation, she engaged an imaginary opponent in an impressive display similar to the Tulamidian shadow fight.

Anyone looking at Sergeant Birsel immediately saw that she was a very strong woman. She had a short neck with well-defined muscles, a broad chest in comparison to her medium height, and large hands and feet, as well as prominent muscles on her arms and legs under a layer of fat. Watching her stride across the yard and hearing the fabric of her leggings scrap, no one would dare challenge her.

It was even more surprising to see Sergeant Birsel in her shadow battle. Her powerful movements were smooth and had more in common with a dance than with a fight. After just a few moments she had broken into a sweat. Her short brown hair stuck to her head, and the fabric of her uniform was dark under her arms, breasts, and spine.

The sergeant's face was so red from the heat and exertion, a stranger would have thought that she would soon have a stroke, but anyone who knew her was acutely aware that her powers were far from waning. After a while her breath came irregularly, but there was still enough for her to give the required explanation of her demonstration. Even if she had whispered, the students would not have missed a word. Holding their breath, they stood amazed by their teacher's sword dance, and each one tried to memorize the names and movements of her hands, arms, and legs. Side step, attack step, cross turn, oxen stroke, side turn, thunder slap, hammer, crab walk, Rondra's blitz . . .

At the end of the demonstration the students clapped and stomped their feet in appreciation, as was customary only at the end of class. For the first time that day the sergeant smiled as she wiped the sweat from her brow.

For the following instruction the students were each given a wooden stick sized to their height. Only at closer inspection did Thalionmel see the sticks had hilts, but that was all they had in common with real weapons. Then they practiced: the crossways grip around the large diameter so as to cut in front of the body, then the side step, right front, left front. The students only practiced this one movement, again and again until the praiosdisc approached Efferd. By the time the class was dismissed, no one had yet mastered it.

Sergeant Birsel told the students that they would practice with heavier and heavier swords over the next few years, until their muscles were strong enough to bear a real two-hander. "To become a good sword fighter takes five cycles of the Twelve," she ended her fencing class, "for the two-hander it takes seven."

Thalionmel could well believe that.

☙ ☙ ☙

Late at night Thalionmel awoke to a mild pain in her stomach. She could not remember eating anything bad, so she was surprised. But the sticky wetness between her legs told her that it had happened for the first time. She calmly got up, and did what she had been told to do; and as she laid back down to rest she felt strangely light and proud as if she had passed an examination.

8

THE ROOM WAS decorated in Tulamidian fashion: lengths of dark red and pink fabric stretched out from the center of the room like a tent ceiling; on the walls hung plush carpets and precious silk tapestries depicting animals, hunting parties, and star-struck couples in flowering gardens. There were bouquets of colorful feathers and silk flowers in glass urns and a golden cage was filled with hopping and fluttering birds of all colors. The windows were hung with heavy curtains. Small, inlaid lacquer tables with silver goblets and engraved brass dishes for sweet and salty delights were arranged so that the four men could easily reach for refreshment.

They had made themselves comfortable on low divans covered with brightly embroidered fabric with golden threads. A Moha girl sat in front of the fireplace, which had heated the room almost too well. She was thirteen or fourteen years old and wore only a loin cloth, silver bracelets, and strings of shells, wood, and glass beads. She tended the fire by occasionally adding a piece of wood or fanning it with a miniature bellows. Across from her reclined a tame, young leopard. When it turned its head to follow the languid movements of the men or the flutter of the birds, the bell on its collar gently rang.

In addition to the fire, numerous candelabras of various heights illuminated the room. There were sparklers from Thalusa with red, blue, and violet flames tingeing every object with an iridescent glow.

The room was full of scents. The girl occasionally added an incense of rahjawood and bits of aromatic resins to the fire. The fresh green smoke of the intoxicating tobacco mixed with the sweet heaviness of the dream resin made for a somewhat overpowering, but completely harmonious perfume. The sounds were just as rich as the smells: the gurgling of every puff of the bulbous water pipe as the eldest man enjoyed his tobacco; the singing and chirping of the birds; the silver ringing of the bells and bracelets; the soft clattering of shells and wooden beads; the muffled men's voices; the soft, slightly nasal quality of the flute; and the sweet sound of the bandurria.

"Say, honorable Sir Achtev," said the oldest man, a Tulamidian in his fifties and dressed like the other men in their native costumes of loose-cut, richly embroidered silk burnus. He turned to his neighbor on the left, "What is this dream resin made of that you enjoy so much? It seems to make one sleepy."

"Oh no, dearest Sir Tuleyman," replied the man. "It does not make one sleepy. It relaxes the body, but it awakens the mind." He took a deep puff from the long pipe in which a glowing lump of resin burned and dreamily watched the delicately winding smoke rise from it. "As far as I know," he said after a pause, "dream resin comes from the dried juice of the Maraskanian. It's an intoxicating melon mixed with ground aquaforte seeds." He was silent for a moment. "They say it increases a man's power," he added with a giggle.

The oldest man joined in the laughter. "Well, then I won't need to ask you for a puff, dear Sir Achtev, because no woman that I have ever been with has had reason to complain." He smiled contentedly and rubbed his goatee. "Holy Rahja has always been good to me, even though I'm no longer the youngest and have nine grandchildren." He thoughtfully puffed on his water pipe. "And now, good Tsa willing, I will soon have a tenth."

The man named Achtev, a slight man in his late twenties with well-balanced features, pursed his lips and whistled in recognition. "Congratulations, most honorable Master Tuleyman, on the satisfied women and numerous grandchildren, as well as on your daughter's or daughter-in-law's blessed condition."

"It's not that far along yet," replied Tuleyman. "First they have to be married, in a custom which I'm sure you are familiar with from home, Achtev." When the youngest had called him "most honorable master" in the last round after the usual exchange of courtesies, he had shown that he had exhausted the possibilities, and the eldest had the right to return to the plain form of address. Tuleyman returned Achtev's smile and sighed heavily. "Well, now I'm counting on my little Neraida, the joy of my old age, the light of my darkness, the flower of my oasis."

"Don't sigh, Tuleyman, future father-in-law to my brother," added the Tulamidian laying to Tuleyman's right. He could have been a bit older than Achtev, but he was younger than the fourth man reclining on the divan with his eyes closed, either asleep or contemplating. "Did you not yourself select my brother to be Neraida's husband, and did my father not pay you a good price for her?"

"A daughter like Neraida cannot be bought with gold, horses, or camels, Nazir. My Neraida is the perfect daughter: beautiful, smart, obedient, and attentive, and she will be the perfect bride. But as much as it pains my heart to lose her, it also pleases me that the long-standing business relations between your father and myself, dear Nazir, will be deepened and strengthened by the marriage of our children." He took another puff on the water pipe, and wished to pass the mouthpiece to Nazir, but he smiled and shook his head, gesturing toward the long pipe on the delicate stand on the table next to him. "I think I will try a bit of dreaming our hostess prepared for us," he said and clapped his hands. Instantly the Moha girl turned her head, and as if she knew the man's wishes, she approached him with a glowing coal from the fire. When she reached Nazir, she went down on one knee and took the pipe from its stand to light it. After two deep puffs, the dream resin glowed evenly, then she smiled and silently passed the pipe to Nazir.

"May I ask from whence you hail?" Achtev sat up slightly and smiled at Nazir and Tuleyman. "I just heard you call your doubtlessly perfect daughter, Neraida, most correctly the flower of your oasis. Now I'm wondering if you meant the Oasis of Terekh, where I married my youngest sister—a jewel like your daughter, a modest, yet polished diamond—to a rich hairan." Achtev reclined again and puffed at his pipe and continued to smile. Attentively his light gray eyes, a rare color for a Tulamidian, wandered between Tuleyman and his future son-in-law.

"You praise your sister with well-chosen words, Achtev," said Tuleyman. "A modest, yet polished diamond." He slowly repeated the words with his eyes half closed, as if he wished to taste them. "That is a lovely image, a poetic turn of phrase, that I will note, with your permission." He opened his eyes and looked at Achtev questioningly. "But that does not answer your question. No, we are not from Terekh. Our oasis is much further to the east. Can you guess which one?"

"Birsha?"

"Not far enough east. Guess again."

"Al'Rifat?"

"No, now you're too far east, Achtev."

Tuleyman broke out in high laughter. He dropped the pipe's mouthpiece and held his stomach in his hands as he shook with laughter. Large tears rolled down his blushing cheeks, and he wiped them off with the back of his hand, as he finally caught his breath. "You must guess further south. Try again."

Achtev participated politely in Tuleyman's laughter, and did not give any clue that he might find the game annoying. He wrinkled his forehead in thought but before he could suggest another place, Nazir brushed his future uncle-in-law's shoulder and whispered, "You don't find this game enjoyable, do you Achtev?"

"I think it's very enjoyable," he replied and

laughed as if in confirmation. "I love solving puzzles. May I guess again? Are you from Keft perhaps?"

"Yes, we are from Keft. How did you know?" Tuleyman shook with laughter again and this time Nazir joined in. "He figured it out," he snorted. "He actually did."

The merriment woke the fourth man who slowly opened his eyes and looked around the room. For a moment his eyes dwelled on the Moha girl, but then his eyes fixed on Nazir, who was still giggling. His black eyes looked at Nazir through half-closed lids—to the point of rudeness, had he noticed—but Nazir was entirely focused on the difficult task of smoking while laughing.

The fourth man was handsome and in his late thirties, with a long braid of black hair wound down his back. He turned toward Tuleyman and Nazir. "Keft, you say?" he began after a moment when the laughter died down. "One hears odd tidings from Keft. The place harbors heretics and false prophets who are up to no good."

"You should not believe everything wandering musicians say," replied Tuleyman. "There was a single heretic, but he was given his just punishment moons ago."

"Tell me more," he said with curiosity. "Who was it and what type of heresy did he engage in?"

Tuleyman furrowed his brow. "Blasphemy is not

a very pleasant topic for discussion and neither is burning at the stake, but I do want to answer your question. The heretic was a confused old man who preached that a new god would soon appear."

"A new god?"

"So it was, brother," added Nazir with flashing eyes, because he, in contrast to his future relative, found the events back home in Keft interesting and worthy of conversation. "I saw him myself. He stood on the roof of the Temple of Praios and preached. His voice resounded like a gong, and you could hear him in all of Keft."

"The performance seemed to make quite an impression on you." The man with the braid smiled and looked up past his drooping eyelids at Nazir. "And his words must also have made an impression on you?"

"Not at all, brother," replied Nazir, glancing at Tuleyman. "His words were so disgraceful that the Seven-Horned One must have been whispering in his ear. He said that a new god would soon appear and that he would be more magnificent and powerful than the Twelve, who would have to serve him; and from that point on, all the people would have to follow the commandments of the new god."

"That's enough, Nazir," Tuleyman placed his well-manicured, hairy black hand on the younger man. "The gentleman does not want to know all the details." Despite the protest of the other man, he continued.

"To summarize, the old man was captured by the Praios priesthood and tortured to retract his statement, but he would not, and it was ordered that he be burned to death." He put his fingers on his temples and closed his eyes.

"Seeing as though you don't like this topic, please tell us a bit about your business, Tuleyman," said the man with the braid as he twisted his mustache. "You trade in horses, do you not?"

"Trade, yes, but we also raise them," Nazir answered for his grandson. "We crossbreed Elenviners with our Shadifs to get a breed that has the passion of our horses, yet the robustness of the northern animals. The Northerners, with whom we have successfully traded for more than ten years, prefer stronger and larger animals than we do. And you trade in gold?" He looked at the stranger.

"Red gold is what it's called," the man smiled to himself and gestured at the light-eyed Tulamidian. "But it is my friend and brother who does the trading. I am currently trading in pieces from Golden Land and magical artifacts. From time to time the value of gold can be improved upon, if you know what I mean," he giggled, "and we have combined our talents for now."

"Red gold . . . Moha slaves?" Tuleyman opened

his eyes and looked intensely at the stranger, almost in disapproval.

"Well, each man serves Phex as best he can, but we will stick to our horses, right Nazir?" who nodded and was silent for a moment.

"What is keeping our delightful hostess?" Tuleyman said, breaking the silence and changing the subject. "I have been waiting for moons to see her dance again. I have to admit that Mistress Shahane's performance means almost as much to me as the visit to Rahja's House, where I will take my tithes tomorrow."

"They say that she is over thirty," said the man with the braid as he turned and gestured for the girl to pack him another pipe. "Isn't that a little old to kindle the spark of Rahja in men's hearts?" He leaned back again, took a deep puff on his pipe, and held the smoke in his lungs for a long time before he exhaled through his nose.

"Oh, brother, those are the words of a man who has not seen Shahane dance. Shahane is perfect in all womanly ways. She is sweet like a ripe date, fiery like a Shadif, bubbly like a Bosparanjer, beautiful like Madamal, and as graceful as a blade of grass in the breeze." Tuleyman shook his head and clucked his tongue. "The maturity and experience only enhances her appeal. Believe me brother, she dances like sweet Rahja herself."

"I'm still more anxious to see her students," the man with the braid laughed. "Budding blossoms please me more than mature flowers."

"Do you mean blossoms like this one?" Nazir gestured at the Moha girl who took the men's inspection without blushing. "She is rather pretty, but she could be a bit lighter," replied the man with the braid without lowering his voice.

"Then I wasted my money on you, brother," said Achtev with a laugh. "You can wash a Moha as much as you like, but she will still have copper skin. But Shahane has Tulamidians and northern women, so you may well find what you like. Where is she anyway? Go to your mistress, girl, and ask her how much longer we will have to wait for her passionate performance."

The young woman got up, but before she reached the door, the damask curtain parted and two youthful beauties entered the room. They were eleven or twelve years old and both were of delicate build. One wore her long black hair in a pony tail and the other had brown curls to her shoulders.

The girls were dressed like sharisads, the Tulamidian dancers. They wore ribbons and flowers in their hair, silver bracelets and anklets with bells, and long, full skirts of petal-like fabric, one the color of fire and the other the color of the sea. They wore fringed scarves around their narrow hips and beaded bodices that were cut so that their budding breasts seemed just a bit fuller.

As soon as the girls entered the room, the men stopped talking and carefully looked at the little beauties' figures and costumes. The man with the braid sleepily brushed the hair from his forehead and reached for his wine goblet. Tuleyman set aside the mouthpiece of his now extinguished water pipe and locked his hands behind his neck. Achtev and Nazir kept their eyes on the girls while secretly reaching for the confection tray.

The musicians stopped playing. They were waiting for their cue to start the performance, which would come after the girls had greeted the guests in the Tulamidian tradition and taken their bows. They took up their positions, one stride apart, one the mirror image of the other. Following an invisible command, both girls simultaneously raised an arm, the dark girl's left and the other's right as their hips began to sway. The dance had begun, and the music came in louder and more rhythmic than before.

Anyone who has ever had the pleasure to see a sharisad's performance in a hairan's tent in Tarfui or a house of delights in Khunchom will remember the pleasure until the day he dies. He will always associate the words "Tulamidian dance" with a feast for the soul and senses. The girl's offering for their mistress's guests was far from such a sensual delight.

They kept the beat and delicately moved their hands and feet, but the performance had a stiff and rote quality to it. The fact that they made no mistakes only served to emphasize that impression.

The young girls smiled prettily as they spun, swayed their hips, and bent their torsos dramatically backwards, but their smiles seemed fearful and fixed with the heavy makeup on their eyelids, lips, and cheeks. The swaying and circling hips did not go with the immature figures, and as charming as the dance was, it lacked the lightness and teasing, the tempting and promise of pleasures to come, which only a mature body and an experienced soul can evoke.

That was the opinion of the gentlemen as well. Tuleyman could only suppress a hearty yawn with difficulty. Achtev leaned back on his cushion and listened to the sound of the bandurria and double flute with his eyes closed. Nazir ate candied fruits, and only the Tulamidian with the braid followed the presentation attentively. With the final chord, the girls bowed before their intimate audience, and the men clapped politely but half-heartedly. Only one mumbled, "Delightful, truly delightful!"

There were three more solo performances before the Mistress Shahane stepped onto the dance floor herself. After the children, a fourteen-year-old girl danced. She was graceful and coquettish but not always in time to the music. Then a sixteen-year-old with red hair and the pale skin of a northerner demonstrated her talent, followed by a very young Tulamidian with black hair in tiny braids.

Finally came Mistress Shahane herself. Jumping and spinning she whirled into the room, and immediately all four men were as awake and attentive as anyone could be after enjoying wine, dream resin, and intoxicating tobacco.

Mistress Shahane was tall for a Tulamidian and in her mid-thirties. Her hips and breasts were full, but she had a small waist. He skin was smooth and pale like alabaster and she shimmered with oil heavy with the scent of rose petals. In the previous dances the bandurria player kept time, but now the other musician switched his flute for a dabla and took over the bass. Soon the duo's music had a heating effect.

Tuleyman had not exaggerated. Shahane danced like Rahja in the flesh.

※ ※ ※

Barely past the curtain, she began to spin, ever faster, until her feet barely seemed to touch the ground and the little bells on her jewelry rang out, high and silvery above the drone of the dabla and the raspy sound of the bandurria. She took off one brightly hued gossamer veil at a time from her hips, stomach, neck, and arms, and carefully let them fly through the room so that each of the men could catch one.

Mistress Shahane was not bare under the veils, because a good dancer knows that nudity does not awaken the senses as much as the hint of it. Her blood-red silk skirt was embroidered with silver and gold, and cut so that when she spun it formed a fluted disc and rose high enough so that one could just see almost all of the dancer's perfect legs for a brief moment. The skirt had high slits to the hip and when a slower movement followed the passionate entrance, now and again a light-colored thigh appeared through the aromatic fabric.

Shahane emphasized her hips with a belt richly decorated with fringe, glass beads, and small golden coins that swung, whipped, and danced with her every movement. The belt was so tight that it pinched the flesh of her stomach and hips, and this too was an artful trick because an unadorned body would not show the small erotic movements. The shiny, flashing belt ornaments played off the pulsing flesh, creating an almost magical effect, drawing the eyes of the observer back to his point on her body.

The colorful sparklers lent the scene a magical light that gave the dancer's every movement a new shade, sometimes in time to the music, sometimes syncopated, so that Lady Tsa would have also enjoyed the presentation.

Yet it was Lady Rahja, and she alone, who blessed Shahane's dance. The gossamer of the luxurious clothes, the artistic and acrobatic ability, the cool calculation and planning in the progression and form of the dance—everything cried out with a spirit of desire.

None of the men could say how long Shahane had danced at the end of the performance. After the first sound of the drum and rippling bandurria melody, each man began to dream for himself. Whatever fantasy the dream evoked, the dancer always remained Shahane.

Tuleyman dreamed that he took Shahane home and made her his fifth, Travia-blessed bride. His obedient wives took her to the bridal tent and there she danced for him alone. And while she danced he felt how his aging manly powers were reborn, and before the dance was over, he and Shahane had celebrated their marriage on Rahja's altar.

In Nazir's dream Shahane took the form of all the women he had ever possessed until she finally became wild, young Achmad'sunni, whom he desired desperately. He wanted to take her, but smiling and spinning she always got away. Then he caught her with his rope. She turned and wriggled, but the knot grew tighter and tighter until it finally cut deep into the white flesh of her arms and breasts. Her brows were raised in pain and her lips open in a cry of pain, and she gave herself to him . . .

Achtev, the slave trader, dreamt of an enchanted forest. The objects in the darkened room became trees, and the dance floor was transformed into a moonlit clearing where delicate winged fairies danced in the round. A beautiful queen, sad and lonely, twirled in the middle. When she saw Achtev she lit up and passionately reached for him. "Come to me, lover," she murmured, as the wind blew away her veil.

The fourth man dreamt of Shahane alone. He saw her dancing form, but as she turned, bent her body, and swung her hips, her clothes fell off and the womanly body grew increasingly younger until suddenly the twelve-year-old girl she once had been stood before him. There was no hair under her arms, her breasts tiny swellings, and there was just the first fuzz between her legs. Shy, but knowingly, the younger Shahane looked at his aroused manhood approaching her secret lips . . .

And then, at some point, Shahane's dance was over. The mistress's performance did not end with a sudden drumroll or a wild twist, it seemed more as if the music and Shahane's movements gradually became more quiet, softer and more reserved, and as the dancer stopped in a graceful pose, the four men returned from their dreams. Numbed, they stared at Shahane before they dared to break the almost devout silence with their applause and bravos.

The dream herbs had reddened their eyes, and they were breathing heavily, as if they had physically exerted themselves. Achtev pulled a silk scarf from the folds of his burnus and politely blew his nose, and Tuleyman discretely wiped a tear from his eye.

"Brilliant, dearest Mistress Shahane," he mumbled, "Truly brilliant. I think you are getting better every time, if that is possible. But it seems to me that your dance has never been as rahjaesque, captivating, and moving as today."

"Thank you for the compliments, dear Tuleyman," replied the dancer, smiling as she sat down on a low chair the Moha girl brought. Her chest heaved with quick, deep breaths and a small trickle of perspiration wound down between her breasts, but her voice gave no hint of the exertion. "Please bring me my robe, Tiri-Pequi," she said to the girl who was returning to her place by the fire, "and a goblet of wine and a pipe, the refreshment will do me good."

After the girl laid the red silk house coat around Shahane's shoulder's, fastened it carefully, and straightened it, the dancer seemed transformed. Her seductiveness melted away and when she turned to the men her tone was business-like and friendly, like a beautiful and clever merchant woman who likes to negotiate. "And now, my dear gentlemen, tell me honestly, how did you like the presentation?" She smiled and looked from one to the other with her brows raised.

For a brief moment there was awkward silence, then Tuleyman cleared his throat and spoke.

"Dear, honorable Mistress Shahane, you danced like the Goddess, so sensual and moving, that I almost forgot the dances of your students, but they were, if I rightly recall, very dear and refreshing." He paused and stroked his beard. "Yes, very dear," he repeated. "One immediately recognizes a good school." He nodded thoughtfully before continuing. "But in comparison with you, dearest Shahane, they pale, like the dreams in the night against the rays of the sun. They are still pure lambs, children, and they may touch a man's heart, but they will never excite it. Right, Nazir?"

The other man nodded thoughtfully. "I don't see it quite like that, future uncle-in-law. Except for the first two they were all of marrying age, and I say freely that I truly liked the redhead and the charming wild young thing with the braids. They awoke other feelings in me as well."

"Well, I like to hear that," said Shahane. She took

a wooden pick with a candied cherry from the glass confection tray, and tasted it with the tip of her tongue, but did not bite it. "Can I hope then that you will engage one of them?"

"But," Nazir began a bit awkwardly, "the marriage will be in Keft, and that is very far away indeed. Actually, we were hoping to invite a dancer from Keft or Unau." He looked for help from his future uncle, who poked him in the ribs with a laugh.

"Oh, you simpleton, you are thirty-one, twice a husband, a father of five, and still as innocent as a virgin." Tuleyman laughed so hard that tears ran down his cheeks, and it took a long time for him to catch his breath and continue. "You are not supposed to engage her as a dancer, dumb boy, that was not what our delightful hostess meant. No, for a small gift in gold, she will be very friendly to you. Right, dearest Shahane?" He winked at the dancer and licked his lips.

Nazir blushed. "How much for the girl with braids?" he asked suddenly and louder than intended, which caused Tuleyman to shake his head in disapproval. But Shahane overlooked the small faux pas and turned toward Nazir after licking the cherry again. "There are no limits placed on your generosity, dear Master Nazir, give as much as you think appropriate, but remember that my house is not a house of pleasures like one can find down at the harbor. My girls are select beauties and trained in dance and grace. They are also experienced in the arts of Rahja. And . . .," she looked deeply into the young man's eyes for a long time, "Aischa knows a game or two she likes to play . . ."

But Nazir was clearly too intoxicated or confused to fully comprehend the sense of Shahane's words or the amount expected, because he pulled at his uncle's sleeve and murmured something in his ear. Tuleyman answered just as quietly. Then, while both men whispered, nodded, and exchanged hand signals, but before Nazir came to a decision, the man with the braid turned to Shahane. "It is my wish and desire, dear mistress, for one of the little beauties we first saw to be very friendly to me, and I will return her kindness with generosity." He lifted his heavy eyelids as far as he could and looked anxiously at the dancer.

Shahane shook her head with a smile of apology. "Unfortunately that is not possible, dear master," she replied. "Can I not direct your attention and desire to Duridana, who was the second to dance. She's a pearl, a feast for the eyes, soft as a calf and just fourteen." But the man shook his head.

"No, I don't like Duridana. She may be beautiful, but she is too ample for my liking. With your pardon, I can hardly believe that she is only fourteen. I think she looks closer to sixteen. Why can't I have one of the little ones? Preferably the one with black hair."

"But, dear master, I told you that's impossible. Forget those two!" Shahane furrowed her brow, and finally bit the cherry from the pick and carefully chewed it.

The man got up from his divan and made a fist. "Why can't I have the cute black-haired girl? Answer me. I have just as much money as the others."

"Dear master, I don't think that I owe you anything, but I will answer your question." Shahane's voice had grown a bit sharper but her features were smooth again, and she smiled at the guest. He now sat straight up and stared at the dancer's forehead. Suddenly he pressed his two fists together and mumbled something in a strange dialect.

Shahane raised her brows and shoulders in a shrug and continued, "Perisel and Zulhamin do not belong to me. They are only my pupils, from noble and rich houses and their parents pay good tuition."

Suddenly she grabbed her head, shook it, and stared wildly at the man. "What are you thinking, Master?" she hissed. "How dare you try something like that in my house!" The man flinched and lowered his head.

"Forgive my audacity, I think I'm drunk," he said plainly.

"You are violating Travia's laws, Master," the

dancer replied strictly. "But I will forgive you and attribute your impetuousness to the intoxication." She reached for her goblet, stared at it for a moment, and put it back down without drinking. "But listen to my three suggestions carefully. Never do it if you have had wine, intoxicating tobacco, or dream resin. Never do it to a person who knows as much as I do." Her lips curled into an ironic smile. "And thirdly, never try to force love. Lady Rahja will not look kindly upon it and the pleasure will become adverse." She looked intensely at the man with the braid as if she expected some sign of regret or agreement, but he did not seem to hear her. He looked in Shahane's direction, yet not at her face, somehow he looked right past it, right at the bare breasts of the Moha girl, who was standing next to her lady's chair with a tray of confections. Shahane noticed and again curled her lips into an ironic smile.

"Then give me the Moha!" the man said abruptly and almost curtly.

"I thought she was too dark for you," added Achtev with a giggle, but no one heard him.

"Tiri-Pequi is my friend," replied the dancer. "I cannot give her to you. If you want her, then ask her yourself if she wants to oblige."

The man got up so quickly that the leopard clawed at the fluttering burnus. There was a brief tearing sound as the claws tore into the silk. The man turned around, kicked at the animal without hitting it, and gathered his garment. With a wrinkled nose and flashing teeth he hissed, "Ask a slave for permission? I can't believe it!" as he strode out of the room.

Shahane's voice followed him, "Dear Tiri-Pequi, would you please accompany the master to the door and show him the plate where he can leave his contribution for the hospitality and entertainment?"

"It would be my pleasure," the girl replied in accent-free Garethi.

⚜ ⚜ ⚜

It took a while for Zordan Foxfell's eyes to grow accustomed to the light of day once he was on the street. Blinking, angry, and aroused, he walked toward the harbor where he hoped to find relaxation and quiet at a house of pleasure. Not too far from Shahane's house a pretty, slender, blonde girl in a blue uniform walked past him. His eyes followed her as she went by. Little did he know that he was looking at his niece, Thalionmel, who was on her way back to the garrison school.

9

"YOUR ADOPTED SISTER is a dancer, Baroness?" asked the armed man as he turned to his young charge.

"My *sister*," corrected Thalionmel, "wants to be a dancer. She is only eleven and still apprenticing with the famous Mistress Shahane, but I think she dances very well for just beginning her third year of training." The girl squinted into the distance and thoughtfully wiped the sweat from her brow.

The Rondra sun burned mercilessly down upon the three riders as they rode north along the small, dusty, hedge- and tree-lined path between the harvested wheat fields and pastures of goats and languid cows chewing their cud. Since they had left the protective forest two hours ago, the heat had risen almost unbearably, but neither the two men nor the girl allowed themselves to complain about it.

Like her two escorts, Thalionmel wore light leather armor. The gauzy woolen undershirt stuck to her body and she was relieved that the men had convinced her to wear a straw hat instead of a helmet. The hat was the type worn by local farmers when working in the fields. "I hope we get home soon," she thought, "I'm beginning to melt." But she knew that she would have to sit in the saddle for two more hours and talk cheerfully, if need be. The heat was also tiring the horses and to make them go any faster would have been despicable cruelty.

Initially, Thalionmel was upset and felt embarrassed in front of her fellow students because her parents had sent the two armed men as escorts, but now she was glad to have them. It was easier to suffer with company. Both men were meritorious warriors in the Brelak citizen's militia, and she had met them before. They were both suffering as much as she, but neither the serious blond Gisbrecht, who led, nor the red-bearded Answin at her side gave any hint that the midday sun was the slightest annoyance. To the contrary, Answin, whose face had become almost scarlet over the past hours, tried to distract the girl from the strain of the ride by keeping the conversation as charming and elegant as was possible for a peasant's son, while Gisbrecht strained and focused silently on the apparently superfluous task of looking for threats of danger.

At the ninth hour the travelers broke off from Neetha, and now the praiosdisc was past its apex by one hour—the hottest time of the day. Of course, it would have been better to have left earlier, thought Thalionmel, but she could not leave the city without a long good-bye to her little sister, who was bed-ridden with an attack of the Brabak gooseshingles and thus denied the much anticipated trip to Brelak.

Oh, how sorry Thalionmel felt for poor Zulhamin, who was pale and covered with reddish yellow pox. Suffering from a fever, Zulhamin had difficulty fighting back the tears and sobbing. The girl wanted so badly to come along. "It's only the gooseshingles," she complained, her small face upset. "It's not a very bad disease, and I would certainly get better at home faster than I will here."

But Mistress Shahane and the healer who was called in had no mercy. Even Thalionmel had to agree that her sister was unfit for the tiring ride. "Only nine days, my little lamb," the sharisad said and Zulhamin gently brushed the moist hair from her forehead. "Then you will be better and allowed to follow your sister. But until then you must listen to the healer and stay in bed."

"In nine days Auntie's tsafest will be over," Zulhamin protested and sniveled. "I have not written her a letter, because I did not know that I would get sick."

And then the tears, which had been held back for a long time, began to flow, and Shahane carefully brushed the girl's hot, moist cheeks. "Don't worry about that, little lamb, last night I wrote a letter explaining everything to your foster parents, and as far as your gift is concerned you can either send it along with your sister or hand it to your auntie in person later. She will not be any less pleased by it, just because it arrives a little late. A nine-day delay is not that tragic! Imagine you had broken your foot and could never dance again, now that would be truly bad." Then she left the sisters alone in the room together.

"Your mistress is right," Thalionmel said when the girls were alone. "The gooseshingles are not a real tragedy. Remember when I had them one year ago and had to stay out of class and the temple for two weeks? Don't look so sad, tell me instead what you want to give my mother, and then I will tell you what I am giving her."

"It's not the pox, and you know that." Zulhamin made her little hands into fists and repeatedly struck her blanket. "I'm not a sissy nor a lamb. I was so excited about riding with you and I really wanted to see Auntie's face when she unpacked my gift."

"What is it, won't you tell me?" Thalionmel asked, and Zulhamin made a move to get out of bed. But her sister gently pushed her back on the pillows. "No you can't get up, you know that. Tell me where I can find the present and I will give it to you without looking at it."

It turned out that Zulhamin's gift was a miniature portrait showing the girl in the clothes and pose of a sharisad. Thalionmel held the picture close to her eyes and looked at it carefully. "How can anyone paint so small and exact?" she said, impressed. "It looks a lot like you, now I think that it looks very much like you, but that you are even prettier in real life. How did you pay the painter?"

"I have saved twenty-one crowns since I started my apprenticeship with Mistress Shahane," Zulhamin replied. "The other girls and I recently danced at that wedding I told you about, and I earned three crowns and seven bits for my dance."

"You didn't tell me about the money," Thalionmel interrupted her sister in surprise, "but please continue."

"Well, that's all. Together with my savings it was enough to pay the painter. Do you think Auntie will be pleased?"

"And how!" Thalionmel's response was so fast and convincing that Zulhamin smiled for the first time that morning. "And what are you giving Auntie?" she asked with her eyes shining with fever.

"Oh, now that I have seen your present I'm almost ashamed of my small gift." Thalionmel blushed and pulled a rolled parchment from her saddle bag and handed it to her sister. It was covered with neat writing in red ink, but it was not artistic. Only the decorated heading and decorative scroll of Rondrian symbols showcased some ability.

"The Sword of Swords says—" Zulhamin began to read aloud, but her sibling interrupted her.

"You don't need to read it. It's a commentary by the Sword of Swords about a holy book of the Church of Rondra, and I spent almost every night over the past days in the library copying it. Well, it isn't anything special, but perhaps mother will be pleased a bit that I took on this tedious challenge."

"Of course she will be pleased, and I think that it turned out very beautifully, especially the calligraphy in the heading and all the little swords, helmets, shields, and lionesses. I didn't know that they teach you calligraphy and drawing at your school." Again Thalionmel blushed.

"We don't learn it per se. Quendan had a few drawing lessons as a child, and because he can draw so well, he helped me."

"Because he's in love with you he helped you," Zulhamin giggled and corrected her.

Thalionmel was glad that she could cheer up her sister a bit that morning by telling her a few humorous incidents from the daily routine at the garrison. Although kindness usually put her off, she pulled herself together and kissed Zulhamin's hot forehead when she said good-bye. "I know how to really kiss," her sister whispered. "Fiona showed me and maybe I'll tell you someday."

"Really kiss, as if I didn't know how that works," thought Thalionmel as she recalled her sister's farewell words. "You cross noses and press your lips together and stick your tongue in the other person's mouth, disgusting!" She snorted at the memory of her first and only kiss, which Quendan had demanded as payment for his help, and she shuddered in disgust.

"Are you not well, Baroness?" Answin's voice interrupted Thalionmel's thoughts. "There is a tree over there where we can rest for a bit. That would certainly be good for you."

"Why? Do you think that I need a break, Answin?" The girl was truly surprised.

"Well, I think I just saw you shiver, and anyone who is cold on a hot day like this desperately needs a break." The armed man's sweaty brow was furrowed in worry and he looked intensely at his charge, but Thalionmel just laughed.

"Don't look so worried, Answin, I'm not cold and I'm not sunstruck, either. What made me shudder was the memory of something absolutely disgusting, but I cannot tell you what it was. Let's talk about something more beautiful." She looked invitingly at her companion.

"Well, now you have piqued my curiosity, Baroness. Did you recently see a worm creature, smell a basilisk, or dream of a demon?"

Thalionmel shook her head and laughed. "No, no, no! Much more disgusting than all of that, but I can't tell you."

"Grant me one more guess, Baroness. Last night a spider crossed your bed, a really big one with hairy legs."

"But Answin, I'm not afraid of spiders!" Thalionmel feigned anger, furrowed her brow, and shook her head slightly, as honorable Yasinde often did when a pupil gave the wrong answer.

"I am," Answin admitted with a grin. "I can't imagine anything more disgusting than sharing my bed with a big, fat, hairy spider." And then they both laughed so heartily that Gisbrecht turned around in surprise.

"The path through the woods is in bad shape," the young woman remarked, suddenly changing the topic. "If something isn't done soon, next year everyone will have to take the long way through Shilish. That would be very tedious, don't you agree?"

"I agree," sighed Answin, "there is always a lot to do, but never enough money." He raised his shoulders with open hands like his lady did.

"Why isn't there enough money? The forests around Neetha belong to the margrave and, as far as I know, he has as much gold as Kohm has sand. He could use some of it to maintain the path, or even better, make it a road." It filled Thalionmel with satisfaction and pleasure that she could talk about serious issues like an adult. Answin wrinkled his forehead thoughtfully and wiped the sweat from his eyes.

"Well, as far as the count's money goes, Baroness, he does have lots, but certainly not as much as you think." Thalionmel wanted to add that her mentioning of the margrave's gold and the desert sand was just a metaphor, but Answin spoke so thoughtfully without pausing that she swallowed her comment. "And tell me," he continued, "who benefits from the road? The margrave? No, it's as useful to him as he is interested in it. It's only good for those of us in Brelak, and maybe for those in Morlak and Wyrmheath . . ." He paused again, but this time Thalionmel had nothing to add.

"Yes, the road is important for us," the armed man continued. "But we are too few to maintain so many miles and we can't do anymore than cut off a presumptuous young tree or slice off an annoying branch from a bush when we are on patrol." He sighed heavily. But he had dropped a good buzzword. And because of the patrol they talked about the citizen's militia and the robbers and waylayers, and this topic engaged the two until they reached the first cottages at the edge of Brelak.

※ ※ ※

The first thing that Thalionmel noticed as she led her horse into the welcome cool dark stable was a noble chestnut gelding with a blond mane and tail. It had not been there on her last visit.

Elgor smiled widely when he saw the girl and made a deep bow as he offered immediately to tend to her piebald, but Thalionmel politely turned him down. "Thank you, Elgor, but I have to do this work myself. It is not only my parents' wish, but my own. And in addition, if I weren't in school now, I would be a knave and would not only have to care for my own horse but that of my lord, so I really do have it good."

Thalionmel laughed cheerfully and began to whistle a tune that was popular in Neetha as she took off her horse's saddle and baggage. In truth she didn't want to do the work, not only because she would have liked to rest after the tiring ride, but especially because she could hardly wait to greet her beloved parents. As she had ridden along the gravel path that led in a curve around the manor house to the yard behind, she had sneaked a glance at the dining hall windows. Her parents stood there, the figures distorted and unclear because of the round bull's-eye glass, but they were identifiable. Thalionmel also thought she had seen her father leap into the air with joy and wave wildly, but she had returned the greeting modestly as befit a warrior.

It was Durenald who could not contain himself. The girl had hardly dried the sweat-drenched coat of the horse when he stormed into the stable, grabbed his daughter from behind and spun her around. He held her far from him to examine her as he breathed heavily and smiled. "Let me see you, little warrior," he said puffing, as his impressive stomach heaved with happiness and exercise. "I think that you are bigger and more beautiful than last time, but it will still be awhile before you are as big and beautiful as your dear mother."

Suddenly Durenald pulled his daughter to him and wrapped his arms powerfully around her childish figure. Thalionmel was only able in the last moment to turn her head to the side so that her father's kiss fell on her cheek and not her lips. "How are you, my dear child?" He puffed in her ear. "I have missed you so much. And where is your dear sister? Did she choose to visit old Danja or Lechdan's ninth child?"

"Thank you, dear father, I'm fine, and I hope that you are well, too," replied Thalionmel, as she carefully unwound herself from the hug. "Poor little Zulhamin isn't doing so well. We had to leave her back in Neetha because she came down with the gooseshingles two days ago. Mistress Shahane wrote a letter to you and Mother, explaining how she came down with the illness and extending the healer's opinion that there is no need to worry. It seems that the shingles will be gone in nine days and then Zulhamin can come back to Brelak in good health. But say, what a lovely gelding that is. I don't know him yet, but I think you have made a good buy."

"That's not my horse. The gelding belongs to a guest." Durenald scratched his head and made a worried face. "The poor dove, so she has a fever and scratchy pox, and is certainly much sadder than I am." The baron sighed and shook his head in worry. "And she won't be at your dear mother's tsafest tomorrow. What a pity!"

Thalionmel took her father's hand and gave it a quick squeeze. "Don't be sad, dear father, Zulhamin will be better again soon." Now she sighed too and looked almost reproachfully at Durenald as she continued, "This morning I had to console my little sister, and now you, and soon Mother, although she will probably not show as much of her disappointment. And I miss Zulhamin myself, and I would have rather brought her along than have left her behind."

"Mother, yes..." Durenald nodded. "Let's go to her, come!" He turned to the exit without letting go of his daughter's hand, but she protested.

"Wait, Father," she said laughing. "I'm not done with Alrik!"

"Nonsense, child, today Elgor or the stable maid will look after her. Elgor!" he turned to the stable master. "Take care of the baroness's horse. She's released from her duties."

"Do you think that will be alright with Mother?" Thalionmel wrinkled her brow as she followed her father to the yard, and he nodded energetically.

"I think so, little warrior! She has awaited your arrival with such suppressed impatience that we should not make her wait any longer. You know it is bad manners to make a lady wait. But go to your room first and wash up, and put on some nice clothes. We have a guest and you should make the best possible impression."

"Who is it?" the girl asked. "Someone I know?"

"No, I don't think so, or at least you would hardly remember him, and he would also have difficulty recognizing you. You did meet once, but that was a long, long time ago. Well, can you guess who it is?" Thalionmel did not need long to think.

"Uncle Foxfell, perhaps?"

"Congratulations, warrior, you are right." Durenald bowed before his daughter and extended an elegant leg despite his full form. "You are not only beautiful and brave, my lady, but smart as well." Then he gave his daughter his arm to accompany her to the back entrance.

༜ ༜ ༜

"So, Uncle Foxfell has come to visit Mother on her tsafest, or rather, to fill his empty purse. We'll see," thought Thalionmel, as she ran the wide-toothed ivory comb through her unruly curls. "The handsome, horse-killing, sweet-talking man that I'm supposed to be wary of. He's not a good person, and I should make a good impression on him?" The girl did not know what to think of that development. "I will not dress up like a doll, that's for certain!" She finally decided on a plain, sleeveless tunic that fell to her knees and tied sandals. It was an outfit that seemed appropriate for the weather and in its simplicity was not an insult to the Goddess.

"What will I talk about with my uncle?" Thalionmel wondered. She walked to the dining hall where she knew refreshments awaited her—cool beer, compote, and salty millet cakes. She looked forward to them, almost more than to seeing her mother, she admitted to herself. It would be stiff and formal, if a stranger was present. "But in the next three weeks I will have many opportunities to be alone with

Mother. We will talk, ride, fence . . ."

The girl was especially happy about the fencing, because even after more than two years at the school, her mother was still the best teacher. Her reserved praise made Thalionmel even more happy than the even rarer complement from Sergeant Birsel. "Perhaps I will be able to beat her this time," she thought. "Mother will be forty-three tomorrow and that is a ripe age . . . Rondra, forgive me for my arrogance. Of course I will not be able to beat Mother. She may be old in years, but her powers have remained young. They never learned the two-hander in Vinsalt, only attacks and defenses, and I will be able to show her what I have learned and teach her something."

Their first meeting was nearly as formal as Thalionmel had feared, even an outsider would have thought so. As coincidence would have it, Kusmine had also chosen to wear a tunic that afternoon. Hers was of the finest snow-white linen with a bit of black embroidery at the neck and hem. It was also a bit longer than her daughter's. The tall, white figure of the baroness casually leaning against the chimney immediately caught the girl's eye, and although Thalionmel intended to approach her mother with measured steps and a soldierly, plain expression, she could not help but quicken her pace and smile when she saw her beloved mother.

Kusmine's eyes lit up when she saw her daughter and a gentle blush came to her cheeks, but she did not rush to the child, instead she casually raised her right hand to receive the kiss. After the customary greetings were exchanged, she gave her daughter a conspiratorial wink. "You look good, my child, we will speak later. Now greet your uncle."

Thalionmel did as she was asked. She had already observed the slender, delicate man as she entered the room, but now she could get a closer look. Nothing about him seemed extraordinary. She did not think he was handsome or ugly, attractive or repulsive, and she was almost a bit disappointed that his appearance, voice, and manner did not wake any feelings of repulsion in her as she had expected. Politely, but without any real interest, Foxfell asked about school, her talents, and progress, and she answered him just as politely. She praised his horse and expressed happiness that he seemed to have made the trip to Brelak without any difficulties.

That ended the initial conversation between uncle and niece, and the three adults continued the conversation where they had left off when Thalionmel entered. They spoke of the state of the world, the relations between the old Empire and Gareth, as Foxfell was want to call the Central Empire's capital, and Megbilla and far-off Brabak, as well as rumors that the kalif in Mhanadistan or Mherwed—

Thalionmel had difficulty keeping these foreign names straight—was planning an attack to expand his empire. They spoke of the latest invention, a crossbow with secret mechanisms that let a bolt be reloaded quicker and fly faster . . .

Zordan Foxfell, the well-traveled guest, was asked about the news in the world by Durenald and Kusmine, and so he did most of the talking, even if it was not his intention. Because the parents seldom asked anything of their daughter, to get her opinion on a topic or see how the news had been taken in Neetha, Thalionmel had a long opportunity to observe her uncle. "He doesn't really look like a horse killer," she thought. "I can't see anything horrible about him. But his eyes look a little tired, as if he were not truly interested in the topic at hand." She wondered why Foxfell looked so different from her mother, but he was only similar to Zulhamin as much as people of Tulamidian heritage would be.

When the girl thought of her sister, it became apparent to her that neither her mother nor her father had mentioned her in the presence of her uncle. It seemed to be an unspoken arrangement, and she decided to keep it as well.

The afternoon turned into evening almost imperceptibly. At some point a boy and a girl in white but slightly soiled aprons carried in plates and dishes for the evening meal, and only when they had left the room did Thalionmel realize that they were two of Lechdan's numerous children.

The girl ate without great pleasure. The small snack and the heat had staved off her hunger and, in addition, she was a bit disappointed that her first day home had gone so astray from how she had hoped. She followed the conversation casually, looked out the eastern windows as the blue of the sky turned to a leaden hue. Soon the western windows showed the last of the sun's rays, and she saw how differently her parents enjoyed the meal and she waited to be given a signal that she could leave the table.

Almost every time Thalionmel looked at her uncle their eyes met. Although Foxfell seldom turned to her, she felt as if she were being watched or inspected. "What is there about me worth staring at, that's what I would like to know?" she thought uneasily. "I brushed my hair and put on clean clothes." She did not like how her uncle looked at her, he was invasive and bored at the same time. She was glad when her father finally got up and offered a prayer of thanks to Travia and Peraine.

"Would you like to accompany me, warrior?" the baron turned to his daughter. "I want to stretch my legs after the satisfying meal. And I don't think that you have seen the young olive trees I planted this year. I will not get to see them bear, but your grandchildren will find them very useful and will have a magnificent grove for strolling." Thalionmel nodded eagerly and father and daughter left the room together.

"Don't be sad, child," said Durenald when the door closed behind them. "You will have many chances to speak and practice with your mother over the next few weeks. And believe me, she would rather be with us than in an unpleasant conversation. But Zordan Foxfell is her brother, or rather her half brother, and because he asked her for a private audience on his arrival, she can't very well turn him down."

"Is it about money?"

"About money, about his inheritance, whatever ..." Durenald's voice was a bit curt, but soon his good-natured personality shone through again. "Whatever it is," he continued, "it's better that they are talking about it today and clearing it from the table, so that we will be able to celebrate tomorrow in peace and harmony."

As Durenald and Thalionmel walked down the gravel path the praiosdisc had just disappeared below the horizon. There was not a breath of wind and although the eighth hour had just begun, it was hardly any cooler. In the west, delicate violet clouds hung in the rosy sky and a leaden wall of distant rain rolled in from the east so that the bushes and trees glowed eerily in unnatural colors.

"What do you think, Father, will it thunder?" Thalionmel asked, after she had enjoyed the strange scene in silence. Durenald nodded thoughtfully, "I don't know, my child. For a real thunderstorm we need moody Lord Efferd and wild Lady Rondra. Although he has his rain clouds ready, none of her storming can be felt, and I can't hear the pounding of her horse's hooves." As if to chide the baron just then there was a distant clap of thunder, and Thalionmel laughed. "Well, good," admitted Durenald, "her storm riders are coming, but she is still far away and she won't reach Brelak before midnight."

As father and daughter meandered through the village, it grew ever more quiet. At the beginning of their walk they had heard a few cows lowing to be milked in the distance, pigs squealing as they awaited their slop, and through open house windows they heard people talking, arguing, and laughing. Even the birds greeted the sunset from the treetops with their evening song. Yet, as Durenald and Thalionmel climbed up the narrow field path to the new olive grove all was silent.

The two strollers also lowered their voices as they exchanged news about Brelak and Neetha. Durenald was puffing as he spoke because the humid air and climbing the path tired him a bit. Thalionmel caught herself finding her father's heavy breathing annoying, but she could not convince him to turn around or rest, so she took over the conversation.

"Do you want to know what Zulhamin and I are giving Mother for her tsafest?" she asked. Durenald nodded and she gave all the details about the wonderful miniature picture her sister had commissioned and described the unbelievable likeness and fine brush strokes that were so minute that they did not seem like individual strokes, even if one held the picture a half span in front of one's eyes. Durenald said, as he breathed heavily, that he could not see anything either one half or even a whole span from his eyes and that he would have to use his polished crystal to look at the art work tomorrow.

"Oh, you won't get to see it tomorrow, Father. Zulhamin wanted to give it to Mother in person upon her arrival in nine cycles of Praios. She is so excited about seeing Mother's face when she opens the portrait, and I did not want to take that away from her." Durenald nodded understandingly. Thalionmel continued and told about her comparatively small gift, which had cost her a lot of sweat and trouble, and when she finished the baron put his arm around his daughter's shoulders and gave her a squeeze. "You are two good children and both of you please your old parents," he was moved as he mumbled.

When they reached the olive grove, Thalionmel was amazed how lonely each of the delicate trees seemed. But her father explained to her that these one-and-a-half-strides-tall saplings would turn into magnificent trees and that they would need plenty of room not to crowd each other.

"It will certainly be a fabulous grove," the girl said without true conviction, and then they both fell silent to await nightfall.

When the last frog song echoed away, the crickets ended their chirping love songs, and the washed-out colors faded to night, Durenald and Thalionmel made their way home. Not a single star was able to find a hole in Efferd's heavy clouds, and because the shutters were closed on the few cottages where there was still a light burning, father and daughter hurried to reach the manor before they were surrounded in complete darkness. It was still very warm, although cooler than earlier in the day. It was more humid and once the sky opened up over the far-off Etern Mountains and they saw Rondra's wild warrior, Thalionmel felt her hair stand on end because of an invisible force.

The girl was glad to reach the manor and see the few lights on, and hear that the yard and building were filled with the busy sounds before the quiet of night. Voices carried out of the library. It was her mother and uncle, and Durenald suggested that they go by and finish the evening with a glass of wine. As they neared the room the girl noticed the talk between the siblings was more heated than normal conversation. They could clearly hear what was being said although the door was closed. Wrinkling his brow, Durenald remained silent and wanted to leave, but Kusmine's voice rang with anger through the door. "We've been talking about this and nothing else for two hours, Zordan, but you can't change my mind. Our last will is signed and sealed and in a safe place. And I will not reach into our treasury to pay your debts. Twelve ducats is all I have. I cannot give you any more."

"Your miserliness will cost me my life, you disloyal sister!"

"Twelve ducats and not a bit more, that is my final word."

Thalionmel expected the door to fly open and her angry uncle to storm out, but it grew quiet. "Now we have unintentionally overheard their conversation," said Durenald, aware they were in the wrong, "and you have been witness to an ugly scene. Come, child, let's go in and perhaps your friendly smile will smooth the waves, and we can spend the evening in the harmony I so desire."

Although Thalionmel did not at all want to be

in her uncle's company, she followed her father without question. She did not know how she would be able to smile after having heard what she was not supposed to. But it was easier to do than she thought, because as soon as they entered the room, Kusmine clapped her hands together and smiled. "There you are! You came just at the right moment," she called. "Our conversation just ended. Come, sit with me, dear husband and daughter, and let's talk. Robak! Rooobak! Where is he, he should bring us some wine."

"Let me get the wine, Sister," Foxfell interjected as he busied himself putting a purse in his inside pocket. "I have two bottles of the finest mulled wine from Thalusia I brought for your tsafest, but now it seems like the right moment."

It did not take long for Foxfell to return with two bottles of dark red wine, and this brief moment was the only one during which Thalionmel could speak freely with her mother, as she would often later recall. She got four silver goblets out of the cupboard and put them on the table in the midst of the seating. As her uncle opened the bottles to pour she wondered why the corks came out so easily but she did not think much about it.

"Truly a noble grape, Brother-in-law, very spicy . . ." Durenald stated with the expression of an expert after one sip. "But let us now drink to this togetherness, that I attribute to Travia's grace," he lifted his goblet, "and may Lord Boron grant us all a quiet night and good dreams."

At the mention of the dark god, Foxfell briefly lifted his heavy eyelids and a strange smile crossed his face, but no one other than Thalionmel noticed. The girl had not ever drunk much wine, because she usually preferred beer, so she did not empty her glass in a single draught like her parents did. Instead she took a careful taste. She found the wine to be sweeter and heavier than the local varietals. The spice in it had a slightly bitter aftertaste that evoked a medicine she took when she had gooseshingles. So she just sipped it and smiled as she turned down her uncle's offer to pour more.

Foxfell did not seem to drink much himself, because he was so busy keeping his hosts' glasses full. His glass remained almost untouched all evening.

Just as Durenald had hoped, it was a cheerful gathering. Seldom was he in such good spirits, and Kusmine also seemed to forget that just a few moments ago she had been fighting with her brother. She laughed often and loudly, she pinched her daughter in the side and pulled at her hair, sharing anecdotes from her student days, and at Thalionmel's request her parents took turns telling the story of the beginning of their love.

But at one point everyone grew tired. Foxfell was

the first to discretely yawn and soon the others followed. "Your wine is not only sweet and spicy, Brother-in-law," Durenald said, wiping the tears from his eyes. "It also goes to the head and I think I'm a bit intoxicated. I will probably sleep so well tonight that not even Lady Rondra's thundering army will wake me."

"You're right, dear husband," added Kusmine. "I'm tired too, and I think we should go to bed so that we can be rested to celebrate my tsafest tomorrow. Sleep well, all of you, and may Boron be with you." She nodded at her brother and gently kissed her husband and daughter on the forehead. That ended the evening's drinking and everyone retired to their sleeping chambers.

10

THALIONMEL HAD DRUNK barely more than half a glass of wine, yet she was tired and fuzzy as she went up the staircase to her chambers, followed closely by her uncle. "It must be the heat and humidity weighing so heavily on my head and limbs," she thought. "I can't think or see clearly. It makes every step toilsome."

"Sleep well, Uncle," she said as she reached the half-landing and hallway leading to her chambers. She made a quick bow and started to turn around when her uncle's piercing eyes caused her to hesitate.

"Going to bed so soon, young warrior?" Foxfell asked with raised eyebrows. "That would be a pity. I have a present for you, and I have wanted to give it to you all day. I keep thinking that I have seen you before. I was hoping that you could help me remember where that might have been."

"That was twelve years ago." Thalionmel closed her eyes as she mused. "But, by your leave, I cannot recall it."

"I can, dear niece, but I do not speak of that encounter; and although you were a darling child in swaddling clothes, you made a much greater impression on me that one time I saw you in the blue uniform of a soldier." Foxfell started to walk toward his room as he spoke. Then he grew silent and gestured invitingly for the girl to follow.

Without hesitation Thalionmel proceeded in his direction. "What present does my uncle have for me?" she thought as she walked the short distance beside him. The hall was dimly lit by the two carefully shielded candles the uncle and niece carried. Catching sight of their shadows, the girl had to giggle at what she thought was a fox fleeing from a lioness. Climbing the steps had been difficult, but now she felt especially light, as if she were walking across a springy meadow.

"Take a seat, beautiful niece, and join me for a drink," Foxfell said as they entered the room. He reached for an open bottle on the shelf, but Thalionmel shook her head.

"Thank you, Uncle, but I think I've had enough for one evening."

"You speak very wisely, almost like my doctor, who has urged me to drink wine only in moderation." Foxfell put the bottle back and busied himself with his saddlebag. He pulled out a long, wooden box.

"That's why he drank so little," thought Thalionmel, "it was his doctor's orders. It would certainly be better for Father if he were more moderate in his enjoyment of wine. His cheeks got redder and redder as he drank and he also seemed to sweat, but that might have been the hot, humid air—"

"If wine does not agree with you, beautiful warrior, then try this," Foxfell's voice interrupted the girl's thoughts. He handed her a delicate little pipe with smoke curling from the end. Thalionmel had hardly noticed him pack and light it.

She shook her head again. "Pipe tobacco always makes me cough, Uncle."

"It's not pipe tobacco. It's something special, a connoisseur's delight from Al'Anfa. Grant me the pleasure of sharing it with you. It will refresh your mind and body." Thalionmel wrinkled her nose as she sniffed at the pipe mistrustfully, but since her uncle smiled encouragingly, and repeated what a pleasure it would be for him to share the rare, noble treat with such a smart, beautiful, and courageous guest, she finally gave in. As she accepted the carved ivory pipe, she brushed her uncle's hand and shrunk back. But Foxfell only laughed.

"I don't bite, pretty niece, and I don't have any

horrible diseases. Listen up! You have to take a deep puff, inhale the smoke, and try to keep it in the lungs for as long as possible. Two or three puffs are enough, and then you will feel new energy flowing into your limbs and mind, which are heavy from wine."

Thalionmel nodded. Carefully she put the mouthpiece between her lips, took a little puff, and immediately exhaled the smoke.

"No, no, you didn't listen!" Foxfell's voice sounded a bit impatient. "You can't just waste this precious smoke! You should inhale, deep and heavy, and don't be afraid, it won't be harsh."

The girl blushed slightly at her uncle's words. "Silly cow!" she thought. "You're behaving as if this is your first smoke. What will your uncle think of you? That you're a sissy and afraid to cough?" She puffed decisively, filling her lungs deeply with smoke and, according to her uncle's instructions, left it there until she had to take another breath.

Thalionmel had hardly exhaled when she noticed to her surprise that she felt strangely happy. The tobacco tasted good, much better than pipe tobacco, and it did not scratch her throat, nor did it make her want to cough. The slight numbness from the half goblet of wine had been washed away.

"Well," she said, looking straight at her uncle, "was that right?" As he smiled and nodded, she took another puff before handing back the pipe.

Foxfell smoked with deep inhalation. "Do you think it tastes good? Does it agree with you?" he asked, looking at her through half-shut eyes.

"It tastes good, Uncle, and I feel much fresher than I did just a few minutes ago." She looked back at him, smiled, and reached for the pipe as soon as he extended the mouthpiece to her. After two more puffs, Thalionmel noticed to her disappointment, the embers were extinguished. So she sank back down into the chair to experience the newly acquired freshness in her mind and body. "I haven't felt this good all day," she thought, "and here I am, sitting with the uncle I barely know or like, yet I'm happier than I ever was before."

Thalionmel looked around the room. Although only two candles were lit, she could see everything clearly, even a spider web in the corner behind the armoire and the dust under the bed. "The maid is not very thorough," she thought, and contemplated telling her mother about it, but then the thought slipped away.

The room was in a state of comfortable disorder. Among the writing utensils and parchment on the table there was a jumble of personal objects, combs, flacons, and brushes of various shapes. Some items of clothing were carelessly spread around the bed, one of which was a yellow burnus with a long, carefully darned tear. "The seamstress went to great lengths, but the thread she used was a bit darker than the fabric," Thalionmel thought, "and one can see each individual stitch."

"Aren't you curious about your present?" Thalionmel heard the far-off voice of her uncle. She turned her head. He was sitting there in his chair, just as he had been sitting this whole time, looking questioningly at her. His face seemed much closer than before, and at that moment, she could see a certain similarity to her mother. Although his nose was substantially larger than hers and had bigger pores, the shape was similar. So was the chin, only it was broad and masculine. Thalionmel thought that it should be shaved again because the dark beard was already showing above the skin and continued to grow as she watched it.

"Did you ask me something, Uncle?" Thalionmel said in a voice that sounded so strange and hoarse to her that she giggled in embarrassment. She listened until the echo of her words and laughter faded, then she tried it again. "You should shave, Uncle. Your facial hair grows so fast." Yes, she recognized her voice, although the echo was irritating. "One can tell that you never went to an academy or garrison school, otherwise you would have learned to be neat." She laughed loudly and Foxfell joined in.

"How are you feeling?" he asked.

"Good, Uncle, very good indeed." Why was her uncle yelling at her? He was sitting only a stride or two away. She didn't know exactly why his voice was so loud.

"Well, I'm glad you're so concerned about my appearance. Now, may I honor you with my gift?"

A gift, yes. Thalionmel had heard that word once before that evening. She could not say what that had to do with honoring, but her friendly uncle would certainly explain that to her.

"I'll have to ask you to turn around so that I can wrap my gift for you." She understood every word he said, although he was whispering. Obediently, she stood up and turned her back to him.

The sound of rustling was so loud, it almost drowned out the crashing of the waves and the splashing of the Chabab river. "Don't rustle so loudly, Uncle, I can barely hear the waves."

"The waves? What are you talking about, child?"

Thalionmel had already forgotten. "Waves," she thought, as she looked at the things on the table that were flickering with the candle light. "'Waves,' a pretty word." The bristles on the brush grew and moved. The teeth of the comb bent apart and pulled together, and the parchment floated up and down as she breathed. The girl breathed evenly and tried to bring her breath into rhythm with the movement of the papers. Then she would be able to read them, although they were facing the other way.

Kusmine of Brelak, was written on one. *Kusmine of Brelak, Kusmine of Brelak, Kusmine of Brelak, Kusmine of Brelak* and *Durenald of Brelak* was on the other *Durenald of Brelak, Durenald of Brelak,* again and again. "My parents have written Uncle a very strange letter," thought Thalionmel. She could also write letters like that without spilling ink or wracking her brain. Perhaps it would please her parents to read their names so often, because she herself enjoyed reading them. Now she carefully read every line of every page.

While Thalionmel read the letters, they eventually became transparent and she could read the sheet below that was half covered by the others. It was not written by her parents. It seemed to be written by a scribe, for she did not recognize the handwriting. "I will have to keep breathing evenly so that I can read everything," she thought. She breathed carefully and read:

Our last will and testament: We—Durenald, Baron of Brelak and Kusmine, Baroness of Malur and Brelak—have made the following decisions in the case of our deaths. Our tangible and intangible property shall be split in equal parts by our daughter Thalionmel and my—Kusmine of Brelak—half brother, Zordan Foxfell.

Should our daughter Thalionmel not yet be of age at the time of our death, we hereby appoint Zordan Foxfell as her guardian. In addition, Zordan Foxfell shall administer the fief of Brelak as well as our daughter's inheritance and strive to expand upon it—

"You can turn around now," her uncle's voice interrupted her reading. The girl did not have the opportunity to think about the meaning of the strange letter, for as soon as she turned around she forgot about it.

Zordan sat as he had before in his chair, smiling and holding out a box to Thalionmel. A blue satin ribbon was wrapped around it and the ends were tied in a bow. The silk glittered in the candlelight as Thalionmel took the package. She touched the bow gently with her finger, and new light and colors were wondrously created. "How lovely," she mumbled. "Absolutely lovely."

"You have to open it, dummy, that's just the wrapping. Come here, I will help you." Foxfell patted his thighs and Thalionmel sat in his lap. She was not certain if she had ever sat on anyone's thighs.

"Yes," she recalled, "when I was younger." Her father had often let her ride on his legs. Each tsafest he put her on his lap and helped her awkward little fingers untie the packages and ribbons. Now her uncle put his arm around her and guided her hand as she destroyed the bow. She was sorry to ruin the fabulous creation, but she was happy cuddled up against her uncle's chest.

"Now open the box and see what I brought for you." Thalionmel carefully opened the lid and a high squeal of pleasure escaped her lips. On a bed of red velvet lay a delicate dagger of silver and gold, the curved blade richly decorated and the hilt inlaid with red, blue, and green jewels. The light reflected in them, creating a cascade of colors that truly exceeded the bow's glory.

"Can I touch it, Uncle?" the girl asked out of breath.

"Naturally, my darling. It belongs to you," he crooned.

But Thalionmel hesitated as if she were afraid the wonderful object would dissolve or turn into a regular dagger if she touched it. Finally, she tapped at the colored stones with her finger, and then she took the dagger in her hand. She carefully ran her finger along the blade, but there was no cutting pain, and her skin was untouched. "It is not sharp at all," she determined to her amazement.

"Do you like my present, little niece?" asked Foxfell. Thalionmel nodded.

"It's wonderful," she mumbled.

"Then you should thank your good uncle for it."

"Thank you, Uncle," the girl said without taking her eyes off the dagger. She had just discovered that something was moving inside the stones. She held the weapon close to her eyes for a long time, looking into the jewels. What was it? She had to know what was moving in there! Suddenly she realized there were tiny figures hopping and waving at her, trying to speak to her, but before she could find out what the little people were trying to tell her, she felt her head being grasped and saw her uncle's shiny eyes.

"I want a thank-you kiss."

Thalionmel closed her eyes, pursed her lips, and started to reach for her uncle's forehead, when she felt something warm and moist forcing its way into her mouth. She pulled away and dropped the dagger. "I don't like to kiss like that," she said as she got off his knees.

A dark shadow crossed Foxfell's features. "I will teach you to like it," he murmured angrily. Then, smiling again, he continued, "Dance for me if you don't want to kiss."

"But Uncle, I can't dance. Zulhamin is a dancer, I'm a warrior." Thalionmel uncomfortably shifted from one foot to the other.

"That's wonderful for Zulhamin, whoever she is, but you can dance, too. All little girls can dance. Watch me, and I will show you how." The girl looked her uncle in his black, shiny eyes, and as she watched them, he spoke quietly to her. "Trust me and do as I tell you. I'm your friend, your dear uncle who loves you." A slight shudder ran across her scalp, resounding through her skull and into her brain, so she knew that he was speaking the truth.

"Now spin around," he continued. "Do you hear the music? It's slow, and you should spin slowly, too, so that I can see you clearly and you won't get dizzy." Indeed, as her uncle mentioned the music she heard it—soft, dramatic sounds accompanied by a distant drum. She enjoyed spinning and seeing how the room spun, and all the objects in it became shiny streaks around her.

"You're a beauty dancer from Brebak," she heard her uncle's far-off voice say in the rhythm of the drum.

A beauty dancer? Thalionmel had never heard of such a thing, but she liked the idea, and her uncle would certainly soon tell her what that meant. "You're very beautiful," continued the muffled, distant voice. "You're hot from dancing. You want to remove your garments, they are confining and conceal your beauty. Toss them aside."

"I'm hot from dancing," thought Thalionmel, "very hot indeed. My uncle is right." Relieved, she removed her belt and let it fall to the floor. With the leather band no longer constraining her she felt a bit better, but she was still hot and would soon start to sweat. She could feel the first drops of sweat coming out of her pores, moistening the linen, and making it as heavy as winter wool. The garment bound her and squeezed her chest, making it difficult to breathe. She had to remove it quickly. Without interrupting her dance, she pulled the tunic up over her head and held it for a while in her hand, until it slipped from her fingers.

"That's beautiful, very beautiful indeed," said the distant voice again, but this time it was so close and quiet that Thalionmel thought her uncle whispered the words in her ear. She turned her head, but he was not there next to her. He sat in his distant chair, smiling and circling around her. "That's beautiful, but it's not yet perfect," the voice continued. "The loincloth covers your most beautiful parts, it's ruining the image of perfect beauty. You have to take it off to be free and happy."

Free and happy, free and happy, rang out the echo, almost louder than the original voice, and Thalionmel hummed along with the words. The words went well with the lute and dull rumble of the drums, whose rhythm her feet had taken up on their own. She was glad that she could dance so well, but her dance was not perfect and only when it was perfect could she be truly free and happy. The girl's hands wandered to the knots that held the ends of the cloth. Joyfully she smiled as she tugged at them.

Soon freedom and happiness would be hers . . .

Finally, the cloth came off and fell between her feet. Thalionmel continued to spin around, oblivious to Foxfell's audible gasp. One more turn and happiness would certainly be hers. But what was that? Something was wrapped around her foot and trying to stop her. She kept turning but its grip grew stronger so that she fell out of step and almost stumbled. Swaying she stopped, endlessly disappointed and indescribably sad.

The room kept spinning, but its dance grew slower and slower. Something golden floated by and came to a shaky stop on the window sill. "A golden oval. I have to free myself from the loincloth and start the dance over from the beginning," thought Thalionmel, but she could not take her eyes from the golden object. Something pale was reflected in its polished surface. It was a small, pale figure, and as the girl carefully walked up to it the figure moved.

The golden object was a small brass mirror, as Thalionmel now saw, and the pale figure in it seemed to be a human. It was a thin, pale, naked, girl who seemed vaguely familiar to her. "That's me!" she cried out in shock.

The lute song stopped, the drums became distant thunder, and Thalionmel began to shiver. "Where am I?" she thought, "And why am I naked?" Slowly she turned around. She saw a table, armoire, bed, and finally a chair, where a man with a black braid sat with half-closed eyes. A crooked smile played on his face as he looked at her. She recognized the man, it was her mother's half brother, her uncle Foxfell. "What am I doing naked in my uncle's room? How improper! By Rondra, what happened?"

Her thoughts were a jumble. Unable to move she stood there staring at Foxfell.

"What's the matter, child?" she heard a voice, which seemed foreign yet somehow familiar. "Are you dizzy? Come sit on my lap and rest. You are pale, my little one." It was her uncle who spoke. His grin was more crooked now. Invitingly he slapped his hands on his thighs, a gesture that confused the girl, because she recognized it but did not know why. "Don't be afraid," her uncle continued. "I'm your friend, your dear uncle . . ."

"I'm your friend . . ." There were those words again. The girl had heard them before and she had felt a strange tickle in her scalp. Now there was no tingling. Confused, she scratched her head, looked at her uncle, and wondered if he really was her friend. She refused to believe it. He did not really know her. He was a gambler and a horse killer, and he had made her take off her clothes. "That's why I'm naked." She knew suddenly and as the thought became reality, she blushed.

"What did you do, Uncle?" cried Thalionmel. "Did you put me under a spell so that I would undress?" She stomped her foot, but as she sensed the floor giving in she stopped insecurely and stood there swaying. "You're not my friend at all. I think you're a bad person and I will tell my parents everything tomorrow."

As quickly as the soft floor would allow, the girl ran to the door. Alas, her uncle was already there, grabbing her by the chin, and forcing her to look at him. "You won't tell them anything, dummy. You will sleep . . . sleep . . ."

☙ ☙ ☙

Tap . . . tap . . . went the black knight's feet. Only a few more steps until he reached her. Thalionmel raised the two-hander over her head and so did the knight. Tap . . . tap . . . The knight mechanically raised and lowered his feet, but he didn't seem to be coming any closer. Now he grew paler, almost translucent, but his steps sounded as they did before. Tap . . . tap . . . tap . . . tap . . .

It took a while for Thalionmel to awaken completely. Her head hurt and she was freezing. A cold draft blew across her body. She must have forgotten to lock the shutters and windows before going to bed, because the wind opened them and the shutters were slapping up against the house. Clap . . . clap . . . clap . . . clap . . .

The girl got up quickly and locked the window. "Yes, the thunder is not far off," she thought. As she leaned out to reach for the shutters the wind tossed her hair. A beautiful bolt of lightning with branches and angles appeared for a moment and the landscape flashed in white blue light, followed by a powerful clap of thunder.

Thalionmel rubbed her aching forehead. She remembered drinking some wine, and apparently it did not agree with her. Her throat was parched, and she could hardly swallow. She lowered her hand and coincidentally brushed her stomach, then she realized that she was naked. "That's odd," she thought, "I must have forgotten to put on my nightshirt." She had vague memories of colors, music, and a glorious dagger from the darkness of her dreams, but they were so unclear that they faded away before she could catch them.

Thalionmel felt around for her clothes. She would have to go to the kitchen to get some beer or water before it became impossible to swallow. The tunic she wore the day before was not where it should have been, so she felt around in the darkness for her saddlebags, which contained her comfortable suede knickers and a blue linen top. If she had not had such a piercing headache, she would have found what she was looking for faster. Only when she went to put her leg in the shorts did she notice she was wearing sandals, and again she was puzzled.

All the lanterns on the wall had gone out, and even the torches on their brackets were dark, so the girl carefully felt her way in the darkness to the stairs. The wind had grown stronger and whipped around the house and through the trees making their leaves rustle. "I'm glad it's no longer so hot and humid," thought Thalionmel as she slowly went down the stairs. "My head is throbbing enough as it is." Just at that moment a powerful clap of thunder shook the manor. There were several aftershocks, then there was nothing but the whistling of the wind and distant rumblings.

The girl's thirst had grown almost unbearable. She had never been so thirsty. "Perhaps I'm only dreaming that I'm thirsty, and if I go back to my room, instead of getting water, everything will be fine." She did not know what would be best, so she paused to think. She had just left the last step and stood in the hallway that lead to her parents' private study and chambers.

Indecisively, Thalionmel stood at the foot of the stairs and could not determine if she should go back up to her room or down to the kitchen. A faint light at the end of the hall caught her attention and silently, almost unaware of what she did, she walked toward it. The light was coming from the study, through the cracks around the door. As she approached, it seemed to be flickering, but she was not sure and felt her way further along the hallway.

The next clap of thunder came not without warning. Just before the crashing blast shook the manor, a bolt of lightning reflected through the small open window in the stairwell, casting the hall in a brief ghostly light. Thalionmel saw everything as if in a dream: the polished wooden floor, the lit woodcuts between the torch holders on the wall, the heavy closed doors, and the one that just opened from the study as the thunder made the girl flinch.

Then the darkness of night surrounded her again. No, it was not entirely black, because the rectangle at the end of the hall was surrounded in a faint yellow light. In this light, which Thalionmel believed to be a candle or an oil lamp, she saw small furniture, all sorts of little objects, and a small man—or rather a puppet, because the room behind the door truly reminded her of a puppet theater she had seen with Zulhamin at last year's fair in Neetha. "What a strange performance," she thought. She had to blink to see straight. The weak light and the distance made the figures fade in and out of focus.

Everything in the room had been turned upside down. Folios had been pulled from the shelves; the drawers of armoires, chests, desks, and writing stands had been pulled out and the contents haplessly spread among the precious books on the floor. The treasury's lid was open and the little man was busy filling gold and silver coins into a leather satchel. "He'll be caught soon," she thought, "and then there will be a great sword fight. That was exactly what happened at the puppet show."

The little man, supposedly a Tulamidian, had his jet-black hair in a braid. He was wearing dark clothes, and his mouth and nose were hidden behind a cloth as if he was anticipating a sandstorm sometime soon. As Thalionmel attentively watched the action on the tiny stage, she could hear Robak quickly approaching. "He's probably checking if all the shutters are secure," she thought, "because it won't be long before it starts to rain."

The little puppet did not seem to notice anything. He was busy gathering the coins and interrupted his work only to inspect the lid and sides of the chest. Just then Robak came up the stairs. There were a few distant rumblings of thunder which drowned out his steps, so that he had already reached the hall when the last of the thunder faded. When Thalionmel saw the light from his candle she pulled back into the shadows. She could not say why, but she did not want to be discovered.

"By Phex, what's going on?" the lackey mumbled

as he passed the girl. "The lord is up working so late ... but no ... no ... by the Twelve!" He ran and almost reached the study. At that moment the disguised man looked up and saw Robak. In a flash the puppet was at his side. There was a gleam of silver in the lightning.

Then it was quiet and dark, and the scene changed. The Tulamidian held the lifeless body of Robak by the shoulders and dragged it into the room. Uneasily he looked around, stopped to listen, and reached for the oil lamp on the table. "Strange," thought Thalionmel, as he blew out the flame, "to make it even darker for himself and harder for me to see."

In the darkness, she could not observe what the little man was doing now. Thalionmel heard the crunch of breaking glass, and saw that the little Tulamidian reached for the satchel and candle before turning to the door. Gesticulating as if he were casting a spell on the shelves, table, and armoire, he walked out of the room. Finally, he threw the candle in the room and hurriedly strode down the hall—straight toward her.

"No, he hasn't seen me," thought Thalionmel as the Tulamidian with the flowing robe rushed past her. At that moment, he was no longer a puppet, but a finely built man, and the weak scent of wine and herbs that rushed past with him reminded the girl of something long ago. However, she did not have any time to contemplate this, because a fascinating show began on the little stage. All over—on the floor, the walls, the furniture, books, and parchments—little flames began to dance, and within a few moments these jagged flames became a spectacular wall of blazing fire.

All her hair stood on end and the girl almost fell over as thunder and lightning struck so close she thought that the divine breath had touched her. Through the doors and walls she saw the flash, glowing white, fantastic and evenly jagged, like an enormous flaming sword. She did not know how long the image lingered, but it faded with the cool wind.

Thalionmel shivered as the sudden draft blew past and began to pull strongly on her clothes and hair. "Yes, now the storm is here," she thought. The storm had certainly arrived. It whistled around the house, tugging at the shingles and shutters so that the noise seemed quiet in comparison to the distant rumblings of thunder.

Slowly, Thalionmel began to realize what was happening around her. A blaze filled the room and the flames reached for the neighboring door, assisted by the wind through the broken windows. Hungry tongues of flames licked and hissed, and it did not take long for the wood to begin to glow. The door burst open with a crash, but the girl did not hear it in the roar. "Fire—fire—soon the whole house will be on fire," she thought, standing frozen in horror until one clear thought came to her, "My parents! Where are my parents?" Thalionmel wanted to yell, but her tongue was unable to make a sound. No, it wouldn't matter if she cried or kept silent, she would not be able to wake her parents. She knew that for certain. They were fast asleep, drugged from the wine her uncle had given them.

And now the images from the night before came together in her mind's eye. Some things were clear and simple, other images did not fit, but one thing was certain—horrible Uncle Foxfell had stolen gold, murdered Robak, and started a fire. Now her parents would burn.

The girl was still unable to move or cry for help. She could only stand there and stare at the flames. She did not feel any anger or rage, only cold, nameless horror.

Thalionmel was entirely alone, abandoned by the Twelve and humanity alike, and she knew what held her there was not a dream or a drug-induced hallucination, it was harsh reality. No dream had ever been at once so full of horror and so empty of hope as that moment. It wouldn't make sense to scream, she thought. No one would hear her—no man, no god. Why bother to pray? The Twelve were so distant, so inconceivably distant . . . and they always had been, although she had not realized it until now. The Twelve did not participate in human destiny, and a human life meant as much to them as a grain of sand in Satinav's enormous hourglass. They did not care if her parents lived or died, it didn't matter to them.

"But it matters to me," the girl suddenly freed herself. Defiantly she marched toward the wall of flames. "I will at least try to rescue them," she mumbled, "and if I die trying that's all the better, because my life is unimportant as well." Hearing a hollow, barely human cry through the raging wind and fire, she ran to the narrow space between her parents' rooms. She stood there, not knowing who to save first—her father or her mother?

Greedily the flames ate away her path. The doors of the three rooms were long burned away and behind them it only glowed in red, yellow, and white. Driven by the wind or perhaps nameless powers, the flames raced up to the ceiling, through the wood paneling, and across the floorboards, whose wax polish hissed and melted when it was licked by the flames.

Thalionmel did not feel the heat singe her eyelashes and brows, nor did she notice that the flames had become a blazing tunnel from which there would soon be no escape. She did not see the sparks dancing on her hair and clothes, and she did not hear herself scream. Stunned, she stared at the blaze around her. "If I have to die, I want to die!" she thought. Something in front of her burst into flames, fell, and gave the fire more air and fuel. The flames hissed toward her, wrapping around her feet and legs. "No, you must live!" said a voice in her head. Suddenly, she turned around and ran off.

Thalionmel ran and ran and came to her senses only as the first fat drops of rain hit her head and shoulders. She was standing in the kitchen garden, alone and far off from the tumult in the yard. Screaming and panicking, people rushed around the yard, not knowing what to do. "Like ants whose hill is destroyed," thought the girl, laughing coldly. From her vantage point she could see the action clearly. She stood far enough away to see the entire show, but close enough that she could also make out the details. "The right seat for a baroness," she thought. "The place of honor."

Fire now engulfed the roof. Bright and wild, the flames burst through the windows and doors, licking and playing with each other in a wild rampage. Each time a window burst, a beam fell, or the flames found a new opening, a triumphant fountain of sparks shot into the black night to be caught up in the wind and spun in glowing ribbons. Most of the burning areas went out quickly, but others caught fire and grew with the wind, spreading their seeds as they searched for new fuel.

The panicked chaos in the yard gave way to increasing order. Lead by a dark, familiar voice, the men and women began to form a human chain that reached from the well to the manor, as close as the hot flames allowed. Thalionmel did not understand what the Tulamidian was yelling—the storm tore the words from his mouth as soon as he said them—but it seemed that the people could hear him clearly and they followed his senseless orders.

When the girl saw the tiny buckets, pitchers, and pans passing steadily from hand to hand, a laugh crossed her soot-blackened face. How could those few drops ever be enough against the great force of the storm-driven flames? No more than the heavy single drops of rain the storm bore with it. Although there was hissing and steam when the opposed elements met, the flames thought it all to be a game and laughed as they won.

Thalionmel laughed, too. She could not stop laughing. She rocked with laughter until her sides ached, forcing her smoke-filled eyes to cry. "Well, Rondra," she called out when she finally caught her breath, "do you like this sight?" She shook her right hand angrily. "Do you like this sight?" she repeated, "Are you satisfied? Do you wish to marry Ingerimm instead of Efferd, who courts you so pitifully?" she stomped her foot. "Is that your divine decision, to kill the righteous and spare the wicked?"

A bright flash crossed the sky and briefly turned the night to day, and just as the girl's eyes grew accustomed to the glowing redness, she saw a fiery rain come down on the roof of the horse stable. Like tiny, glowing sprites the sparks rushed across the shingles looking for footing against the powerful winds. The storm fanned them on rather than running them off, and soon the first glowing sparks became hungry little flames that began to eat at the dry wood. "The horses! Save the horses!" cried Thalionmel, but no one heard her.

It was the horses who made themselves heard. Just as the girl's cry faded away, a shrill whinny cut through the whipping of the storm and fire. The screams of the horrified animals stopped the human chain. The people spread out, lead by a commanding voice. Elgor stepped forward. "He should have let them out sooner," thought Thalionmel, as he disappeared into the burning building. "Now they will trample him to death in their panic."

But that was not what happened. Only a few moments later, but enough so that half of the roof was covered with flames, the girl saw the clouds of smoke pouring out of the doors as the stable master tried to lead a wild gelding to freedom, and before Elgor was able to step clear of the smoke, the other animals forced their way past, screaming and running at a gallop. Thalionmel called each one by name as they ran from the flames: Aldare, Praios Flower, Sindar, Horoban, Nella, Windchild, Mora . . . Where is Alrik? "Alrik!" she yelled. "Dear Alrik, where are you?" But Alrik did not appear, and as the roof crashed down over the stable her senses left her.

※ ※ ※

Dawn was breaking as Thalionmel awoke. The storm had let up, but now it rained heavily. Before she opened her eyes she knew what had happened, and it took a moment for her to decide to look at what she knew awaited. Stiff and trembling from the cold, she stood up, pushed back her wet hair, and rubbed the water from her eyes. She blinked, but her eyelids did not want to open. "You must open your eyes!" she commanded herself. "You have to look."

There was not much left of the manor, although it was not burnt to the ground. The once white walls were black ruins against the gray sky, the remaining beams were also black. Even the kitchen was gone, but the servants' quarters and washhouse remained. Where the horse stable once stood was a jumble of rubble and smoking beams. Busy people rushed around the yard to extinguish the last of the fire. Thalionmel wanted to tell them not to bother, but her cries would have been just as useless, so she remained silent and shook her head. She could now hear clearly what was being said. She heard Foxfell giving commands. "What? You haven't found the baroness?" he screamed at a few distraught knaves and maids. "Then keep looking! Perhaps she is still alive and can be brought to safety!"

"They're looking for me," thought Thalionmel. "No, they can't find me. I have to live!" She crouched down, slipped between the bushes and cut across the wet grass along the ditches and hedges until she reached the field where the path lead to the safety of the forest.

The Praios corn stood taller than the girl, and she fought her way forward, protecting her face with her hands. She thought of nothing and felt nothing, plodding on mechanically. When the hard, wet leaves stopped whipping her, she knew that she had reached the path and she commanded her legs to run.

Brelak was far behind her, darkness had already fallen, and the girl kept running. "Why do I have to live?" she thought, grabbing her painful flank. "So that I can feel the pain of a side stitch? No, my life is over. I'm a homeless orphan, without a future, without joy, and I will never laugh again." She did not know if it was rain or tears that flowed from her eyes, and she did not care either way. She did not bother to wipe them off. She forced herself to keep her eyes open, despite the stinging water. When she closed them she saw images she could not bear—her beloved parents, the burning manor, and her uncle's demonic face.

"Foxfell!" cried Thalionmel loudly in the darkness until the realization hit her. That was why she had to live. To avenge her parents and kill her uncle. "Foxfell!" she cried again. "Wicked uncle! Murderer! Listen to me. I shall hunt you down and kill you!"

A Glossary of Arkanian Lore

Deities and Months

1. **Praios** – Sun God and God of Justice; corresponds to July
2. **Rondra** – Goddess of War and Storms; corresponds to August
3. **Efferd** – God of Water and Wind and Lord of Seafaring; corresponds to September
4. **Travia** – Goddess of the Hearth, Hospitality, and Marital Love; corresponds to October
5. **Boron** – Lord of Death and God of Sleep; corresponds to November
6. **Hesinde** – Goddess of Wisdom and the Arts and Mistress of Magic; corresponds to December
7. **Firun** – Lord of Winter and God of Hunting; corresponds to January
8. **Tsa** – Goddess of Life and Ressurection; corresponds to February
9. **Phex** – God of Thieves and Merchants; corresponds to March
10. **Peraine** – Goddess of Fertility and Mistress of the Healing Arts; corresponds to April
11. **Ingerimm** – God of Fire and Lord of the Trades; corresponds to May
12. **Rahja** – Goddess of Wine, Drunkenness, and Love; corresponds to June

The Twelve – the totality of the deities
The Nameless One – the adversary of the Twelve

The Four Points of the Compass

Rahja = East
Efferd = West
Praios = South
Firun = North

Measures, Weights, and Currency

1 mile = 1,000 strides
1 stride = 5 spans
1 span = 10 fingers

1 gold ducat = 10 silver crowns
1 silver crown = 10 copper bits

Characters, Places, and Terms

Achmad'sunni – a Tulamidian she-warrior
Albernia – a western coastal province of the Central Empire
Alveran – the home of the Twelve
Baltrir – one of the seven winds
Beni Novad – a Tulamidian tribe
Boltan – a popular game of dice and cards
Bosparanjer – an expensive sparkling wine
Brabak – a harbor town and capital of the Kingdom of Brabak, located at the southern end of Arkania
Camel – a popular Tulamidian strategy game
Central Empire – Arkania's largest state
Cycle of Praios – the Arkanian term for the passing of one day
Cycle of the Twelve – the Arkanian term for the passing of one year
Dabla – a small Tulamidian drum

Difar – an exceptionally nimble Arkanian demon

Duglum – an exceptionally foul-smelling Arkanian demon

Duglum Plague – a mysterious, rare illness that is believed to rob a person's life and soul

Elenviner – a breed of horse

Ethra – the primitive world on which Arkania exists; most Arkanians believe it to be flat

Gareth – the imperial capital of the Central empire

Garethi – Arkania's most widespread idiom, spoken in the old and new empires.

Golgari – Lord Boron's messenger, who appears in the form of a giant black raven. He bears the souls of the dead across the Sea of the Netherworld

Hairan – the Tulamidian title for tribal leader

Khom – a desert in south Arkania

Kor – Son of Rondra and the dragon Famerlor; God of mercenaries

Kuslikana – a courtly dance

Madamal – the Arkanian term for the moon

Medena – a harbor town in east Arkania

Mengbilla – a city state on Arkania's west coast

Mhanadistan – the region inhabited by the Tulamidians

Moha – a dark-skinned tribe that inhabits the damp woods near the Rain Mountains in southern Arkania

Muhrsape – a swamp near the western port city of Havena

Nightwind – a large, dangerous night bird

Nivesians – a nomadic tribe in northern Arkania; the Nivesians have almond-shaped eyes and are mostly red-haired

Noiona – an Arkanian patron saint and protectress of the mentally ill

Old Empire – Arkania's first empire, built by immigrants from the legendary Golden Land

Praiosdisc – the Arkanian term for the sun

Rondra's blade – a two-handed sword with a tempered blade

Satinav – a large, bright star in the eastern sky; in astrology the Satinav represents time

Seven-horned one – an Arkanian demon

Shadif – a Tulamidian breed of horses, or the steppes in the south of Kohm

Sharisad – a Tulamidian dancer

Shivone – a fast, Arkanian sailing vessel

Skull Owl – a large owl native to the forests of Northern Arkania

Sword of Swords – the highest of the Rondra priests

Thalusian – a region inhabited by the Tulamidians

Tsafest – birthday

Tulamidians – a proud race of desert nomads who reside in the Khom and neighboring regions

Twelve – short for the twelve gods

Vinsalt – the capital of the rich and fertile land of Lovely Fields in southwest Arkania

Zorgan Pox – a serious epidemic; its virus is believed to be spread by the Nameless One

Thalionmel's fame surged with each of her heroic acts, and as time went on tidings of the beautiful and courageous she-warrior traveled beyond the walls of Neetha and throughout the land. When she was eighteen, people knew her name in Methumis and Drôl. At nineteen they knew it in Vinsalt, Perricum, and Keft. Three weeks after her heroic duel they knew about her in the desert and spoke of her with repugnance. And while she stayed in Wobran with Quendan, the allies of the self-proclaimed servant of the true faith, Harain Mukkadin of Keft met in Khom.

One week later all the tribe elders gathered at the oasis. . . .

The Alliance of the Nameless One has taken notice of the brave Thalionmel and now the fate of Arkania lies in her hands. Will she prove herself worthy to her Lady, Rondra? Will the orphan be called upon to make the ultimate sacrifice?

Find out in *Realms of Arkania: The Sacrifice* (Book Two in the Saga of Brave Thalionmel), coming this summer from Prima Publishing.

And may the Twelve have mercy. . . .

Ina Kramer is a major contributor to the mythical world of *Das Schwarze Auge* (literally, "The Black Eye"), Germany's extraordinarily popular pen-and-paper role playing game. Her contributions include the game's elaborate design details, drawings to a companion dictionary that covers the historical, political, and social aspects of the realms of Arkania, and a series of novels based upon this huge roleplaying system. She lives in Germany.

Amy Katherine Kile divides her time between Munich, Germany, and San Luis Obispo, California, where she founded the international communications firm, German Akzent. Ms. Kile has also translated *Realms of Arkania: The Charlatan* and *Realms of Arkania: The Sacrifice* (forthcoming) for Prima Publishing.